FBI Code Red

a J.T. Ryan Thriller

A Novel
By

Lee Gimenez

RRP

River Ridge Press

FBI Code Red
by
Lee Gimenez

This is a work of fiction. The names, characters, places, incidents, and dialogues are products of the author's imagination and are not to be construed as real. Any resemblance to actual persons, living or dead, is entirely coincidental.

Printed in the United States of America.

Published by
River Ridge Press
P.O. Box 501173
Atlanta, Georgia 31150

First edition.

Cover photos: Copyright by PhotoMediaGroup and Netfalls Remy Musser used under license from Shutterstock, Inc.

Cover design: Judith Gimenez

ISBN-13: 978-0692924884
ISBN-10: 0692924884

Other Novels by Lee Gimenez

The Media Murders

Skyflash

Killing West

The Washington Ultimatum

Blacksnow Zero

The Sigma Conspiracy

The Nanotech Murders

Death on Zanath

Virtual Thoughtstream

Azul 7

Terralus 4

The Tomorrow Solution

Lee Gimenez

FBI Code Red

a J.T. Ryan Thriller

Lee Gimenez

Chapter 1

"Lies and more lies," Erin Welch murmured as she paced the empty conference room, waiting for the FBI Director to arrive. The more times she visited Washington, the truer those words became.

Erin stopped pacing, crossed her arms, and stared out the large window of the conference room. Dark, ominous clouds hung over the city, which reinforced her foul mood. She was an attractive, slender brunette in her late thirties dressed in a stylish Dior skirt and jacket. But her long hair was pulled back carelessly into a ponytail and the dark circles under her eyes reflected a week of fitful sleep.

Hearing the door open behind her, she turned as FBI Director Tucker entered the room.

"Director," she said.

Tucker, a solemn look on his face, closed the door behind him and sat at the conference table. He motioned her over. "Have a seat, Erin."

She remained standing. "Sir, have you reviewed the pending indictments we discussed? The Bureau has solid cases on them. We should move to impanel grand juries."

"I'm sorry, Erin. Those cases are too sensitive right now." He shrugged his shoulders. "You know how D.C. works."

Lies and more lies, she thought.

"I do know it, Director. All too well."

Director Tucker gave her a long, appraising look. "How long has it been since I put you in charge of the Bureau's Atlanta Field office?"

"Two years and seven months."

Tucker nodded. "You got the job because you're the best Special Agent I have. You loved the job at first." Obviously sensing her frustration, he added, "But lately I've noticed a change. What happened?"

Erin pulled out a chair and sat across from him. "May I be frank, Director?"

"You've never been the shy type. Go ahead."

"Sir, I took this job because I wanted to make a difference. To catch the bad guys and put them behind bars."

"That's what we do, Erin."

"With all due respect, that's absolute bullshit. I think we spend more time protecting the guilty than prosecuting them."

Tucker's cheeks flushed and his jaw clenched. "Listen, I won't have you or anyone else impugn the integrity of the Bureau!"

Erin forced herself to stay calm. "Then approve the indictments I recommended. Refer them to the Justice Department to impanel grand juries. As I said, we have very strong cases."

He leaned forward in his chair. "We can't do that."

"Why the hell not? You're an intelligent man, Director. You know these cases are a slam dunk."

Tucker slowly shook his head. "I can't do it."

"You're the FBI Director. Of course you can do it."

"It's not that easy, Erin. As I said before, the people you want to indict are .... " His words trailed off.

"Connected," she replied, finishing the sentence for him.

Director Tucker was a heavyset man with solid gray hair, tired eyes, and a haggard-looking face. He appeared much older than his age of 58, Erin thought. It was a casualty of his job.

"Forget about those cases," he stated, a hard edge to his voice. "I have something else that needs your immediate attention. Something much more important."

"What is it, sir?"

The man reached into the briefcase he had brought with him and pulled out a red file folder. The FBI logo was stamped on its cover. He slid the folder across the conference table towards her.

Leaning forward in his seat, he said, "I'm declaring an FBI Code Red alert. I'm adding a new person to the terrorist watch-list. He's been declared an enemy of the state and he's to be hunted down and brought to justice."

"Who is it, Director?"

"John Taylor Ryan."

One Month Earlier

Chapter 2

FBI Field Office
Atlanta, Georgia

"How's my favorite Assistant Director in Charge," J.T. Ryan said with a grin, as he walked into Erin Welch's corner office.

The brunette looked up from her laptop, then closed its lid. "How many ADICs do you know, Ryan?"

"Besides you?" he said as they shook hands. "None."

"Then I guess that's not much of a compliment."

Ryan smiled. "Just trying to brighten you day." He sat in one of the visitor chairs that fronted her desk.

A stern look crossed her face, then her features softened. "Do you ever stop joking around?"

"Only when someone is pointing a gun at me."

Erin suppressed a grin. "All right, smart guy. As I told you on the phone, I've got another case for you."

"Something big?"

"Probably not, J.T. We got a tip from one of our informants about a possible money-laundering operation here in Atlanta. All of my agents are slammed with active cases, so I'm giving this to you."

Ryan gave her a mock salute. "John Taylor Ryan, private investigator and FBI contractor, at your service."

Erin reached into a desk drawer, pulled out a file folder and handed it to him.

He scanned the contents, which were sparse. "Not much here."

"You've worked a lot of cases for me. You're a good investigator. If there's anything to the informant's tip, you'll find it."

Ryan nodded. "My usual fee?"

"Yes."

"Good." He stood.

"One more thing before you go," she said. "Try not to shoot someone this time."

Ryan grinned. "I only discharge my weapon in self-defense."

Erin shook her head slowly. "I know your 'Dirty Harry' tactics."

"Isn't that why you hire me?" he replied. "Because I'm not afraid to kick ass and take names?"

She folded her arms in front of her, a serious expression on her face. "I hire you because you get results."

"And here I thought you hired me because of my charm, wit, and good looks."

Erin pointed to the door. "Don't let it slam on your way out."

"Yes, ma'am," he said, turned, and left the office.

***

Ryan made his way down to the FBI building's underground lot, located his Chevy Tahoe and drove north out of Atlanta's downtown. Traffic was light and he was at his mid-town office building in twenty minutes. When he reached his office, he found a young woman standing by his closed door.

"Mr. Ryan?" she asked as he approached.

"That's right, I'm J.T. Ryan." He studied the woman, who was probably in her mid-twenties. Slender and attractive, she had shoulder-length blonde hair, gray eyes, and a pixie look to her that exuded innocence. She was also short, no more than 5 foot tall. Ryan, who was 6' 4", rugged, and powerfully built, towered over her. She was wearing a conservative knee-length black skirt, a gray jacket, and black frame eyeglasses that some attractive women wear to downplay their good looks. Her makeup was muted, except for her red lipstick.

"I'm Lisa Booth," she said. "I'm here about the job."

"The job. Of course."

They shook hands, he unlocked his door and they went into the sparsely furnished office.

"Have a seat," he said pointing to one of the folding metal chairs in front of his desk. She sat down primly as he went to a coffee maker on top of his file cabinet.

"Want a cup?" he said. "It's not good, but it's hot."

"No, thank you."

Nodding, he poured out a cup of coffee for himself, then went to his metal desk, pulled out his chair and sat down.

"I wasn't expecting a woman to answer my ad for a private investigator," said Ryan.

"Do you have a problem with women, Mr. Ryan?"

He chuckled. "No, I don't. It's just that in this profession, things get dicey at times – we get into rough situations. Sometimes we have to subdue tough characters, that kind of thing."

"I'm aware of that, sir. I'm very well qualified." She reached into her briefcase and took out several sheets of paper, which she handed to Ryan. "This is my resume. I have a Criminal Justice degree from the University of Georgia. I graduated at the top of my class. Aced my private investigators exam. I'm also proficient in judo and boxing, so I can take care of myself."

Ryan scanned her resume and was impressed. "On paper you're well-qualified. You don't have much practical experience, though."

"That's why I'm here. I want to get more experience in the field. I hope one day to open up my own PI firm."

Ryan laughed. "So already you want to be a competitor."

She frowned. "I'm sorry. That came out wrong."

He waved a hand in the air. "Just kidding. If you start working here, you'll have to get used to my lame attempts at humor."

"Yes, sir."

"You don't have to call me sir."

"Yes, Mr. Ryan."

"I'm only 38 – Mr. Ryan makes me sound like I'm 58. You can call me J.T. – everyone else does."

"Okay."

Ryan took a sip of coffee. "I'm looking for someone to help me with my case load. My client list is growing and I can't handle it all myself. Plus, I travel overseas on assignments and I need someone to man the office." He grinned. "Or is the PC word now 'person' the office?"

Lisa frowned, then must have realized he was making a joke because she smiled. "I'm not very politically correct either."

"That's good. Question for you. Do you have a carry permit?"

"Of course."

"Could I see it?"

She reached into her jacket, took out her gun permit, her PI license, and her drivers license and handed them to him.

Ryan inspected them closely, placed them on his desk and booted up his laptop computer. He spent the next ten minutes doing online background checks on the young woman. Next he made several calls to the references listed on her resume. Satisfied with her credentials, he handed back her documents.

"Everything checks out, Lisa. Are you carrying now?"

"Yes, J.T."

"May I look at it?"

Pulling aside her jacket, she removed a semi-automatic pistol from her hip holster, ejected the clip, and handed him the weapon, butt first.

Ryan took the pistol, which was a Glock model 17. He inspected the nine-millimeter weapon closely, field stripped it, and reassembled it. Glocks only have five moving parts, so the process of field stripping the weapon was very quick. To her credit he noted that the gun was well-oiled and well-maintained. "I assume you're proficient with this?"

"I practice at the range twice a month. I consistently hit the bulls-eye at ten yards."

"Good." He handed back the weapon and she put it away.

"Okay, Lisa. You appear qualified for the job. But you're young. I was hoping to find someone with more experience."

She leaned forward in her chair. "I'm a good detective, Mr. Ryan. I can do this job. I did research on your background before I came here. You have an excellent reputation in the PI industry. I'd like to be a part of that."

"All right," he said, thinking about all of the other candidates he'd already interviewed. Lisa Booth was by far the best qualified, he realized. Still, he wasn't sure.

Lisa must have sensed his uncertainty, because she glanced around the sparsely furnished and sparsely decorated office, studying it carefully.

"As I said before, sir, I'm a good detective. From the way you decorate your office, I can tell you're single or if you do have a woman in your life, she didn't help you furnish the place. By the inexpensive off-the-rack blue blazer and jeans you're wearing, you have simple tastes. You drink coffee out of a foam cup – another sign you have inexpensive tastes. Most likely you live in a sparsely furnished apartment and you don't drive a luxury car. I also noticed you have blood-shot eyes which indicates you like to drink, sometimes to excess. My guess is you're a beer drinker."

Ryan nodded. "That's good. Correct on all counts. What brand of beer do I drink?"

"I'm good, but not that good."

He smiled. "May I see your eyeglasses."

"My glasses?"

"That's right."

Frowning, she took them off and handed them to him. He looked through the lenses. "Just as I thought. These are clear glass – I assume you wear these to look older and more intelligent."

Her face turned bright red. "How did you know?"

"I'm a good detective too." He returned her glasses and she put them back on. "If I hire you, Lisa, I can't pay you a big salary at first." He mentioned a sum. "After you get more experience, I'll raise it. How does that sound?"

"It sounds fine, sir."

"Okay."

"Okay what, sir?"

"You got the job."

The young woman's face brightened with excitement. "I do?"

"Yes, you do."

"That's great, Mr. Ryan!"

He extended his hand and they shook. "But please, call me J.T."

Chapter 3

Atlanta, Georgia

It was raining outside.

J.T. Ryan listened to the drumming on the roof of his Chevy Tahoe as he viewed the nearby office building through his binoculars. He was parked in a commercial area populated with similar one-story buildings. There was no activity in the place he was watching. In fact, there hadn't been any since they had started the surveillance.

Lisa Booth, who was in the passenger seat, said, "Are you sure this is the right building?"

Ryan put down his binoculars. "This is it. According to the FBI informant, this is where he suspects the money-laundering is happening."

"We've been sitting here for two hours, J.T. We haven't seen any cars come or go into the parking lot. And no people have gone in or out of the place. Don't you think that's odd?"

Ryan nodded. "Yep. But remember, a lot of private investigation is watching and waiting. It's not all glamour like you see in the movies."

"I know."

"We'll give it another hour. If nothing turns up by then, I'll go in."

"Okay, J.T."

Ryan took a sip of his now cold coffee and settled in to wait. Outside the rain had stopped and sunlight was filtering through the gray clouds.

"Tell me about yourself, Lisa."

"It was all in the resume you read yesterday."

He glanced at his watch, then stared back at the building. "Why'd you want to become a PI in the first place? You certainly don't look the type."

Lisa frowned. "I've been told that before. At the last PI firm where I worked, they put me on the reception desk answering phones and greeting clients. I'm good with computers so every once in a while they let me do Internet searches."

Ryan turned toward her. "I bet you were the cutest girl in that office."

"You're my employer," she said as her face flushed. "You're not supposed to say things like that."

He chuckled. "I just tell it like it is. Like I said before, I'm not very PC. But don't worry. I'll never come on to you. I have rules I live by. Ryan's Rules. Rule number 6 is to always treat women with respect."

She gave him a long look, then nodded. "Okay. I'm kind of sensitive about my appearance. In my last job they referred to me as the 'cheerleader' behind my back, because I'm a cute blonde. Which really pissed me off – I think I was a better investigator than most of the men there."

"I don't doubt it, Lisa. I wouldn't have hired you if I didn't think you were qualified. But you didn't answer my question."

"What question?"

Ryan stared at the office building, which was still quiet. "Why'd you get into the PI business?"

"My dad was a cop."

"So why didn't you become a cop?"

She shook her head. "Too many procedures and regulations to follow."

"We're a lot alike in that respect. Erin at the FBI has asked me several times to become an agent. But they have way too many restrictions on what they can do."

Lisa nodded. "You do a lot of work for her, don't you?"

"I do. Erin's sharp – in fact, she's the best law enforcement officer I've ever worked with. I do security contract work for a lot of federal agencies, but many of my cases come from the FBI."

Lisa took a sip of her coffee and grimaced. "You were right about the coffee you make. It is *awful*. Specially when it's cold."

For the next hour they kept a close eye on the seemingly deserted building as they continued chatting. Eventually Ryan said, "Okay, time's up. Nothings happening, so now I make it happen."

"We're going in?"

"Correction. I'm going in. You stay in the car, Lisa."

"Why can't I go too?"

"Because."

"Because I'm a woman?"

"Because you're five foot tall, weigh a hundred pounds, and this could be a dangerous situation. Until I know what we're dealing with here, you'll stay in the car."

Her eyes flashed in anger. "I can take care of myself."

"I'm not doubting that one bit. But I just hired you yesterday. I'm not having my new employee getting shot, or stabbed, or beaten up in their first week. Don't worry. We're only a two-person PI firm. You'll see plenty of action. Trust me. And anyway, I need you here as my backup in case something goes wrong."

"Oh."

"That's right – if I need help, I'll call you on my phone."

"Okay, J.T."

"One other thing. If you hear shooting, call 911."

"All right."

Ryan pulled his .357 Magnum revolver from his hip holster, checked the load, clicked it shut, and re-holstered it. Then he zipped up his windbreaker and got out of the SUV.

As he approached the front of the building, he closely checked out the lone car in the parking lot. It was a silver Toyota Corolla and it had been parked there since they had started their stakeout.

Going to the glass-front doors, he went inside, finding a well-appointed lobby area. The reception desk was staffed by a mousy-looking woman with frizzy hair who looked to be in her fifties.

As he approached the desk, the woman said, "May I help you, sir?"

"Yes. My name's J.T. Ryan and I'd like to talk to the person in charge."

"In charge?"

"Yes, the office manager."

"Sir, we don't have an office manager."

"Okay. Is there someone else I could talk with?"

She shook her head. "There is no one else here."

Ryan frowned. "You're the only employee?"

"That's right."

He glanced around the large lobby area and he could see several corridors, lined with vacant conference rooms and offices. "This is a big place. Hard to believe you're the only one here."

The woman smiled pleasantly but didn't reply.

"What is this place, ma'am?"

"We're a satellite office for the Summit Corporation."

"I see. What does this corporation do?"

"Do?"

"Yes, ma'am. What does it sell? Or produce?"

She seemed perplexed. "I'm not sure, actually."

"How long have you worked here?"

"A year."

"And you're not sure."

"I know it seems odd."

"May I ask your name, ma'am?"

"Sure. Barbara Cooper."

"Ms. Cooper, I noticed you don't get many visitors here."

"None, actually. You're the first in a month. Occasionally someone stops by to get directions, but other than that it's very quiet."

Ryan studied the woman closely, trying to decide if she was telling the truth. He'd been a PI for years and nothing about her screamed dishonest. "Don't you find it strange that you're the only employee here and you get no visitors?"

Barbara nodded. "Very strange. I'm used to the solitude now, but when I first started, it drove me nuts. But I'm paid well, so I have no complaints."

"What do you do all day, ma'am? Do you write reports or some other type of office work?"

"No. I open up the place in the morning, sit at my desk, and surf the Internet to pass the time. At five I lock up the building and go home."

Ryan nodded, realizing the place was probably a front for some type of illegal activity. But Barbara Cooper didn't fit the profile of a criminal. "Where is the head office of the Summit Corporation?"

"I'm not sure. I was interviewed and hired here."

"Okay. I'll check them out."

For the first time since they'd met, a look of concern crossed the woman's face. "I need this job, Mr. Ryan. I don't want to lose it."

"Don't worry. I'll keep you out of it."

She gave him a nervous smile. "Thank you."

Ryan left the building and walked back to his Tahoe. Climbing in the SUV, he found Lisa still in the passenger seat, holding the binoculars. Resting on her lap was her pistol.

"You can put the gun away, Lisa. You won't be needing it."

The young woman holstered the Glock. "What'd you find?"

He recapped what had happened.

"Pretty suspicious, J.T."

"I agree. No doubt this place is a front for criminal activity."

"You think the woman is involved?"

Ryan started up his SUV. "I've put lots of criminals behind bars, so I'm familiar with their MO. She didn't seem the type. But you never know for sure."

"What do we do now?"

He pulled away from the curb and drove south. "I'll drop you back at the office. You said before you were good with computers. Here's your first assignment. Find everything you can about this Summit Corporation. And do a thorough background check on Barbara Cooper."

Lisa smiled and seemed enthused by the prospect of working on the case. "Got it, Chief."

He returned the smile. "Don't call me chief and I won't call you junior detective."

"Deal," she said. "What are you going to do?"

"I'm coming back to this place at night and continue the stakeout. If anything illegal is happening here, it'll most likely happen then."

Chapter 4

Atlanta, Georgia

J.T. Ryan glanced at his watch: it was 3 a.m.

He'd been observing the building from his SUV for over five hours, and just like in the daytime, nothing was happening.

It was a full moon tonight so visibility was fairly good. No lights shone inside the building and the parking lot was dim and empty. The only illumination in the area came from a floodlight at the structure's entrance, and floodlights at the side of the building, over a wide garage-style door.

Climbing out of the Tahoe, Ryan stretched his muscles, stiff from all of the sitting. To break the monotony, every hour or so he had stealthily approached the building and walked around it to make sure there was no activity. He began to do so again, and when he completed the circuit, he started to trek back to his vehicle. But when he reached it, he noticed approaching headlights on the street. Crouching behind some shrubbery, he observed a large cargo van drive into the parking lot and pull around to the side of the structure. The closed garage door slowly rolled upwards, the cargo van drove inside, then the door creaked closed.

A few lights came on inside the building and the PI sprinted closer to get a better look. He hid behind a hedge and waited. Fifteen minutes later a second vehicle approached the structure. This time it was a Mercedes-Benz truck and it too drove into the structure using the same garage door. Ten minutes later the Mercedes truck exited the building and sped away.

As it passed him, Ryan caught a glimpse of the truck's license plate. Although he couldn't make out the number, it was a Chinese Embassy plate. Whatever was happening, Ryan knew, was illegal. Why else would it take place at 3 a.m.? Knowing the answers were inside, he raced back to his Tahoe, fired it up, and drove it to the side of the building, where he parked right in front of the closed garage door. He had effectively blocked the escape route, should the van try to flee.

After pulling his revolver, he got out of the SUV, sprinted to the building's entrance and began knocking loudly on the door. As he expected, he heard the creaking of the garage door as it opened. Racing back there, he pressed himself against the wall and peered inside the well-lit interior. The large cargo van was there facing forward, a man at the wheel.

Ryan pointed his pistol at him as he stepped inside the garage. "Stop! Put your hands up or I'll shoot," he shouted.

The man complied.

"Get out of the vehicle," the PI said. "And keep your hands up."

The driver slowly opened his door and stepped out, then in quick succession pulled a gun and fired off three shots. The weapon was obviously suppressed because all Ryan heard were thuds.

Ryan felt one round whiz inches over his head and heard the others ricochet off the concrete wall behind him. His adrenaline pumping, he threw himself flat on the ground.

He rose to a crouch, took cover by the side of the van, and heard racing footfalls on the parking lot pavement. Peering around the van's bumper, he saw muzzle flashes and ducked as the rounds clanged into the vehicle's bodywork.

His heart racing, he pointed his weapon forward with both hands and peered around the vehicle again. This time he saw nothing.

Ryan advanced forward cautiously and searched the building's grounds, but the man was long gone.

Going back to the garage, he accessed and quickly searched the rest of the building's interior rooms. Finding no one else there, he returned to the van. After searching the front of the vehicle, he opened the back doors of the cargo van. There he found thirty large suitcases. Opening several of them, he saw what was inside.

Neatly stacked in the suitcases were bundles of $100 bills.

He did a quick count of the money and realized there was about 100 million dollars in cash.

Chapter 5

FBI Field Office
Atlanta, Georgia

After going through the security checkpoint, J.T. Ryan drove the cargo van into the FBI building's underground lot, parked in a slot, and settled in to wait. He'd called Erin Welch earlier and told her to meet him here.

A half hour later he heard the squealing of tires, then saw Erin's red Jaguar sedan pull up behind the van. He climbed out and met Erin as she got out of her Jag.

Despite the early hour, the attractive brunette was impeccably dressed as usual, wearing a Versace dress, Louboutin heels, and a lightweight Burberry jacket. By the look on her face he could tell she wasn't happy.

"Do you know what time it is, Ryan?"

He glanced at his watch. "Four thirty a.m."

She folded her arms across her chest. "This better be good."

Ryan nodded. "It is."

With a flourish he opened the van's cargo doors, unzipped several of the suitcases and flipped the lids open, revealing the stacks and stacks of bundled $100 bills.

"Holy shit," Erin said as she stared at the cash.

Chapter 6

Midtown
Atlanta, Georgia

J.T. Ryan entered his office and found Lisa Booth sitting at his desk, hard at work on her computer. She glanced up from the laptop. "How'd it go, Chief?"

"Don't call me chief," he replied.

"Sorry."

Ryan recounted what had happened at the Summit building and when he got to the part about the shootout, her eyes got wide.

"I told you we'd see action in this job, Lisa. Are you ready for that?"

"Yes, sir."

"Good." Then he told her about finding the $100 million in cash and his meeting with Erin Welch.

"Where's the money now?" Lisa said.

"I left it with Erin. She'll have her FBI techs check it out and see if they can trace it back to the source."

"Okay."

Ryan sat in one of the visitor chairs fronting the desk. "You're sitting at my desk."

Lisa nodded. "No choice. There's only one desk in your office."

"You're my first employee. Never needed another desk. I'll buy you one and put it over there," he said pointing to the left side of the room.

"Can we get better visitors chairs, J.T.? The ones we have now aren't comfortable."

He shifted in the lightly padded, metal folding chair he was sitting on. "All right. But after that I draw the line. I'm not getting new drapes or new carpeting."

She glanced around the sparsely furnished and sparsely decorated office. The walls were painted in a dull, gray color and industrial grade carpeting covered the floor. "The place could use some help," she murmured under her breath.

"I heard that," he said.

"Don't you want to grow your business, J.T.? You need to make this office more hospitable, specially since you meet clients here."

Ryan had never thought about that before. "We'll talk about that another time. Let's get back to the case. What'd you find out?"

Lisa pointed to her laptop. "I've been doing Internet searches on the Summit Corporation. Summit is a very generic name used by hundreds of companies. But it turns out this particular Summit is a shell company, registered in the Cayman Islands. Summit is owned by another holding company and that one is registered in Switzerland. I was able to trace that back to another shell company, this one in Russia. After that the trail goes cold, but it looks like there's several layers of companies after the Russia connection. It's clear the people who own Summit are trying to hide their identity."

"So we don't know what Summit really is," Ryan said.

"I'm sorry. I wish I could have found more."

He leaned forward in the uncomfortable chair. "No, you did good. Better than I could have. You found that there's an international connection, and that whoever's behind it is secretive. What about Barbara Cooper, the Summit employee? What's her story?"

"She's clean," Lisa said. "No arrests of any kind, nothing on her record, not even a parking ticket. She's 54 years old, lives alone in an inexpensive apartment in Sandy Springs. Owns a five-year-old Toyota Corolla, which she is still paying off. That's the car we saw in the parking lot. She's an Atlanta native, has worked in a variety of office jobs her whole life and been employed by Summit for a year."

Ryan nodded. "She didn't strike me as a criminal."

"I was also able to access her bank records," Lisa continued. "She has one checking and one savings account, with about $2,000 in total. If she were part of a criminal conspiracy, she'd have a lot more."

"How'd you access the bank records without a court order?"

Lisa smiled. "I told you I was good with computers."

"I guess I made the right decision hiring you."

Her smile widened. "Can I have that raise now?"

Ryan was about to protest, then realized she was joking. "What's our next move, J.T.?"

"We have two leads. One is Barbara Cooper. We'll interview her again – she may have more info."

"And the second lead?" she said.

"I told Erin about the Mercedes truck having Chinese Embassy plates. She'll follow up on that."

"Okay."

Ryan stood, went to the coffee maker on top of the filing cabinet, and filled a cup. "Want one?"

"No thanks, J.T. I've already had plenty this morning."

He took a sip of the hot, savory coffee, then said, "That's odd."

"What is?"

"This coffee. It tastes really good."

"I forgot to mention it. I threw out that generic brand you had. I bought good Colombian coffee at Whole Foods."

Ryan shook his head slowly. "Jesus. What's going on here? First you convince me to get new client chairs, and now you buy expensive coffee. What's next?"

She eyed his worn blue blazer. "You could use a new jacket, Chief."

He gave her an exasperated look. "Who's working for who here?"

"Well, you do want to grow your PI business, don't you?"

Chapter 7

FBI Field Office
Atlanta, Georgia

Erin Welch picked up the handset on her desk phone and punched in a number. A female voice answered and Erin's call was quickly routed to the office of the FBI Director in Washington.

"Erin," Director Scott Tucker said, "I'm glad you called. I've been reviewing your recommendations on the Abrams case. I think your assessment is good, but I want to table that investigation for now."

"But sir, we have clear evidence of criminal activity on that case."

"I'm not disputing that. I just want to postpone an indictment."

Erin felt a surge of bile rise up her throat. It was becoming a familiar pattern. Too familiar, she fumed. This was the second investigation this month D.C. was delaying. "Director, we should move forward on the Abrams case."

"I've made my decision and it's final. Do you understand?" Tucker replied.

"Yes, sir."

Erin took a deep breath to calm her frustration.

"Do you have anything else for me, Erin?"

"I do. I have a new case I'm working on. Suspected money-laundering. After a shootout at an Atlanta location, one of my guys found $100 million in cash."

"Did you say $100 million?"

"Yes, Director."

"That's a hell of a lot of cash. Tell me more."

"There's a company involved, although it appears to be only a front. The name of the firm is the Summit Corporation."

"The Summit Corporation?"

"That's right, sir. Do you know anything about them?"

Tucker didn't answer at first, then said, "Never heard of it."

"There's something else. Something really suspicious. The money was brought to the scene in a truck that had Chinese Embassy plates."

"What? Are you sure?"

"Absolutely. I trust the investigator on the case implicitly. If he said he saw it, it's true."

"Okay, Erin. Here's what I want you to do. Send me a copy of the complete file on this investigation. Since this has international implications, I want to be involved."

"You're a very busy man. As ADIC, I can handle this on my own."

"Send me the files," he replied curtly. "And email me progress reports on this with any new developments."

She was about to protest the micro-management when she heard a click and realized the director had hung up.

Chapter 8

Atlanta, Georgia

J.T. Ryan slowed his Tahoe and parked on the street in front of the Summit building. Yellow crime scene tape was strung from police barricades that cordoned off the area. An FBI CSI van was parked in front of the building as were two black-and-white police cruisers. He noticed several uniformed cops walking around.

"Looks like the Bureau people are here," Lisa Booth said, who was sitting in the passenger seat, "and local PD."

Ryan opened his door and stepped out of his SUV. "Let's go see what they found out."

The young woman climbed out and followed Ryan as they approached one of the men wearing a CSI vest.

Ryan held open his cred pack, which consisted of his PI license and his FBI contractor ID. "I'm J.T. Ryan and I'm working with ADIC Welch."

The man nodded. "Ms. Welch told me you'd be stopping by."

"What do you have?"

"We're still processing the scene. We found the shell casings from the shooter's gun. He must have been wearing gloves because there were no finger prints on the casings. We've dusted the whole area for prints. The only conclusive match are from a woman named Barbara Cooper."

"Yeah, she works here," Ryan said. "Is she inside?"

"No. Nobody's in the building. We've been here for two hours and nobody's shown up."

The PI looked at his watch. "It's eleven a.m. She should be here by now. By the way, did you find any files or computers in the building?"

The forensics tech shook his head. "That's the strange part. We searched every office. We found nothing at all."

"That tracks," Ryan said. "The place was a front."

Lisa faced him. "What now?"

"Now we go to her apartment. Since she's not here, she'll probably be there."

After handing the tech his business card, Ryan and Lisa left the scene and drove to Barbara Cooper's apartment building in Sandy Springs, a suburb north of Atlanta. The building was not upscale, and in fact appeared run-down. The roof needed replacing and the paint was peeling in spots. The cars in the parking lot were older models, many with dents and scrapes.

"If she was a criminal," Ryan mused as they got out of the Tahoe, "she wouldn't be living in this dump."

"There's her car," Lisa said, pointing to the parked Toyota nearby.

"Good," he said, "she's home."

They made their way into the structure and up to the third floor. As they approached the apartment door, Ryan instantly spotted a problem. The door was slightly ajar and the lock had been broken.

"We got trouble," he said in a low voice as he pulled his revolver and hugged the corridor wall to the right of the door.

Lisa likewise un-holstered her gun and took a position on the opposite side.

"I'll go in first," he whispered. "Cover me."

She nodded, racked the slide on her Glock and crouched by the door.

Holding his weapon with both hands, Ryan kicked in the door, flinging it fully open as he charged inside, sweeping the living room with the gun. Seeing no one, he searched the vacant kitchen, dining room, and bathroom, with Lisa close behind.

Then Ryan stepped into the bedroom and immediately saw Barbara Cooper.

It was a gruesome scene.

Cooper had been tied to a chair and duct tape covered her mouth. She was naked, and congealed blood splattered down her neck and nude torso. Her head sagged and rested on her shoulder, though her lifeless eyes were wide open. The sickening copper scent of blood filled the air.

Ryan crouched by her side and felt for a pulse, although it was clear the woman was dead. Standing, he quickly searched the rest of the room, the adjoining bathroom and closet, found no one else then came back to the corpse.

Lisa, her face ashen, was staring silently at the body.

"Is this your first DB?" Ryan asked her.

The young blonde woman nodded.

"It gets easier to process," he told her, "the longer you do this. But I still get a sick feeling in my gut whenever I find a corpse."

Then Ryan inspected the body closely, noticed the bruises on Cooper's face and saw two small holes at the back of the neck. He studied the bloody carpet by the chair, looking for ejected shell casings and found none. Then he touched Cooper's arm – the body was stiff and cold.

He glanced up at Lisa, saw the that the color had come back to her face. "You okay now?"

"Yes, sir. I have to be. It's part of the job."

"That's right, it is." Wanting to verify her detecting skills, he said, "Call the scene."

"Yes, sir. Ms. Cooper was overpowered, beaten, stripped, tied to the chair, and most likely interrogated. She was stripped of her clothes to make her feel more vulnerable during the questioning. Then she was shot with rounds from a small caliber weapon, probably a .22."

"Good. That's my assessment too. What else, Lisa?"

"What else? I can't think of anything else."

"The corpse is stiff and cold, which means she's been dead at least four hours, the typical time for rigor mortis to set in. And something else – there's no shell casings on the floor, which means the killer cleaned up his brass. That and the fact he used a small-caliber pistol, two shots to the back of the head means this is a professional hit. A pro did this."

"I agree, J.T. Do you think this is related to her working at the Summit Company? The money drop and the shootout you were involved in?"

"I'm sure of it. It all ties together. Whoever did this was trying to keep Cooper from talking. To tell you the truth, I don't think she knew anything. But the killer, whoever he is, didn't want to take any chances."

"What now?" Lisa said.

Ryan pulled out his cell phone. "I'll call it in and have Erin send over an FBI forensics unit to process the scene. If there's evidence, they'll find it."

"And after that?"

Ryan glanced at Barbara Cooper's beaten and bloody corpse, the sick feeling in his gut returning. "Then we find the bastards who did this."

Chapter 9

Beijing, China

Amber Holt noticed one the buttons on her phone console blinking and instantly knew who the caller was. Reaching across her desk, she picked up the handset. "Yes?"

"We've had a setback," the male voice on the other end said.

"What kind of setback?"

"A serious one," the man said.

"Is this call encrypted?"

"Of course."

Amber, a beautiful redhead, picked up her glass of merlot and took a sip to calm her nerves. "Tell me."

"The last money transfer, the one in Atlanta, didn't go as planned."

She gritted her teeth as she tried to control her anger. "Damn it. You know how important this is."

"Yes, ma'am. I know."

"Give me the details," she stated in a steely voice.

"There was a shooting at the Summit building. Thankfully our man was able to get away."

"And the money?"

"That's the worst part, Amber. We lost the money."

"How much?"

"All of it. All of the $100 million."

"Fuck!" she screeched, literally shrieking into the phone. "What do you mean you lost all the money? Where the hell is it?"

"We're still trying to sort that out. But we think the FBI has it now."

The redhead rubbed her forehead as she processed the implications. She drained her glass of merlot, refilled it from the wine bottle on the desk and gulped it down.

"Are you still there, ma'am?"

"Of course I'm still here, you idiot."

"What do you want me to do now, Amber?"

"Do nothing. Do absolutely nothing until I get there."

"You're flying over?"

"Of course, you fucking moron. You just lost $100 million of *my* fucking money. What did you expect I'd do."

"Yes, ma'am."

The redhead slammed down the phone, then pressed another button on the console.

A moment later there was a muted tap at her door. The door opened and a petite Asian woman dressed in an ornate, embroidered kimono dress stepped inside Amber's office.

The Asian woman bowed slightly and said in Mandarin Chinese, "How may I be of service?"

"Get my jet fueled and ready to go. I want to leave in an hour," the redhead replied in Chinese. Although she was American, she had lived in China for years and her Mandarin was flawless.

"Of course, Miss Amber. To what destination shall I tell the pilot?"

"Washington, D.C."

Chapter 10

*FBI Field Office
Atlanta, Georgia*

Erin Welch was starting to get a bad feeling about all of the Washington stonewalling. FBI Director Tucker was slow-walking her investigations, refusing to proceed with what she thought were slam-dunk indictments.

She continued pacing her corner office as she mulled over the situation. Big-money donors and influence peddling had always been a problem in Washington politics, but in recent years, she felt, the problem had gotten much worse, influencing decision-making even at premier law-enforcement agencies like the FBI. It was the main reason Erin had decided to leave her position as head of the Bureau's Joint Terrorism Task Force after only a short time. That job was based in D.C. and she had felt the politics involved were too corrosive.

Erin stopped pacing and stared out the wall-to-ceiling windows of her office, which overlooked the downtown skyline. It was an impressive view, a view that came with the status of being in charge of the Bureau's Atlanta Field Office. An empty title, she was beginning to suspect, since Director Tucker was micro-managing her every move.

This latest case, the one involving the $100 million in cash, was a good example. Tucker was calling her on a daily basis, wanting status reports on the case. The odd thing was, she sensed he didn't want to solve the case, but rather to 'contain' the situation, whatever the hell that meant.

But now that a woman had been murdered, Erin was going to get to the bottom of the whole thing. She folded her arms in front of her as she continued to gaze out the windows, sorting through her options. She could assign a larger team of her agents to work on the case. The problem with that was, deep down, she didn't trust some of her guys. Half of them had worked in D.C. previously, and their allegiance was more to Tucker.

Her second option was to have Ryan continue working the case. He used Rambo tactics and got himself in trouble sometimes. But he was honest and he got results. And as an FBI contractor, he was able to do things her own 'Special' agents couldn't or wouldn't do.

Finally coming to a conclusion, she turned and left her office.

Chapter 11

Midtown
Atlanta, Georgia

Erin Welch parked her Jaguar sedan in the building's lot and made her way up to J.T. Ryan's office on the seventh floor. Entering the office, she found a young woman sitting behind one of the desks in the room.

"May I help you?" the young woman asked in a cheerful tone.

"I'm Erin Welch, FBI. You must be Lisa Booth." She extended her hand, they shook, and Erin sat in front of the desk. "Ryan told me he'd hired you recently." She studied Lisa closely. She was short, slender, blonde and cute, with an aura of innocence that made her appear younger than her age.

"You don't look 25," Erin said.

"I get that a lot, ma'am."

"I'm sure you do." Erin noticed the black frame eyeglasses Lisa was wearing. "I'll give you a piece of advice. You can drop the fake glasses thing – it's not fooling anyone."

Lisa frowned, then took off the eyeglasses and dropped them into the waste basket that was next to her desk.

"Where's Ryan?" the FBI woman said.

"I don't know, ma'am."

"It's noon. I thought he'd be here."

Lisa glanced at her watch. "I know. He always here by 8 a.m. I called his cell several times and left messages, but I haven't been able to get a hold of him. Actually, Ms. Welch, I'm getting worried something's happened to him."

"Like being shot or kidnapped, that kind of thing?"

Lisa nodded, a look of concern on her face.

"I guess that's possible," Erin replied. "You're in a dangerous business. But before you call 9-1-1, I'd go check his apartment first. He may be there."

"Okay."

"How long have you worked for him, Lisa?"

"Two weeks."

"That's not that long, so you may not be aware of some of his issues."

"Issues?"

"Actually, it's only one. He was in a long-term relationship, but the woman broke up with him. He's been taking it very hard. My guess is you'll find him at home, passed out from too much booze."

Lisa frowned. "Really? I had a feeling he drank, but I didn't think it affected his work."

Erin leaned forward. "It hasn't up to now. But as much as I like him and appreciate how good he is as a PI, I can't tolerate a boozer conducting FBI investigations."

"I understand, Ms. Welch."

Erin glanced around the office. "You like working here?"

"Very much. I'm actually doing investigative work now, which is what I always wanted."

"In that case, here's what you need to do. Find Ryan, get him cleaned up, and get his head back in the game. Otherwise my FBI contracts with him are going to go away. As are, I'm sure, all of his other government security work."

"Yes, Ms. Welch. I'll take care of it."

Erin studied the young woman again. She appeared resourceful and very determined. "I think you will."

Erin looked at her watch, then back at Lisa. "Okay, enough about that. Let's get to why I came here in the first place."

Lisa picked up a pen and held it poised over a yellow legal pad. "Yes, ma'am."

"It has to do with one of the cases you're working on for me. The one involving the large amount of cash."

"Of course, Ms. Welch. I'm very familiar with that investigation."

"After Ryan did the initial work on it, I had planned to turn it over to my internal team of agents. But ...."

"Yes?"

"I've changed my mind. I've run into some roadblocks at the Bureau."

"What kind of roadblocks?"

"That's not your concern. What's important is that I want your firm to continue working on it."

"That's great!" Lisa said enthusiastically. "I know we'll do a very good job for you!"

Erin gave her an amused look. "You are the eager one. You may be exactly what this office needs." She reached inside her leather briefcase, took out a file folder, and handed it to Lisa. "In there is additional information about the case. The ME's report on the dead woman and several other reports. I want you and Ryan to follow up on them."

Lisa jotted notes on her legal pad for the next several minutes as the FBI woman gave her more instructions.

Then Erin picked up her briefcase and rose. "Any questions?"

"No, ma'am."

"Since we're going to be working together, you can call me Erin from now on."

"Yes, Ms. Welch," she replied earnestly.

Erin slowly shook her head, smiled, and left the office.

Chapter 12

Washington, D.C.

The man in the perfectly-tailored gray suit and matching gray tie picked up the handset on his phone desk and punched in a number. As he waited for the other side to pick up, he gazed out his office window at the skyline. He could see the Capitol building in the distance.

When the call was answered, he said, "My boss is on her way here."

"To D.C.?"

"That's right – and she's not pleased."

"What do you want me to do?"

"Try to clean up this mess before she gets here."

"What are the rules of engagement?"

The man in the gray suit thought about this a moment. "The stakes are too big. We can't afford another screw up. Do whatever it takes."

"So there are no rules of engagement?"

"That's correct. You know what has to be done. Do it."

Chapter 13

Midtown
Atlanta, Georgia

Lisa Booth watched Erin Welch leave the office and pondered their conversation. It was clear she had to take action. And soon. Otherwise Ryan's FBI contracts would go up in smoke, along with her own promising career as an investigator.

Standing, she went to J.T.'s desk and rummaged through the top drawer. She remembered him telling her that he'd left a spare set of keys to his apartment there, in case of an emergency. Finding the keys, she pocketed them, then went back to her own desk, removed her Glock, holstered it, put on her jacket, and made her way down to the parking lot. Locating her black Mustang, she climbed inside and drove to Ryan's apartment. She had never been there before, but the address was easy to find. The man lived in a high-rise in Atlanta's midtown area not far from his office and she was there in fifteen minutes.

When she reached the apartment she knocked on the door several times but there was no answer. Next she banged on the door with her fist and again there was no response. Not sure what she'd find inside, her pulse quickened as she inserted the key in the lock, her other hand resting on the butt of her pistol.

She entered the place, quickly scanned the dim interior, and closed the door behind her.

"Mr. Ryan, are you here?"

There was no one in the sparsely furnished living room. "J.T? Are you home?" she called out as she flicked on the lights.

She noticed an empty pizza box and several empty beer cans on the floor by the well-worn sofa. Then she spotted more beer cans on the sofa itself, turned on their side. There was also an empty bottle of Jack Daniels whiskey on the coffee table. Shaking her head slowly, she realized Erin Welch had been right.

After searching the vacant kitchen and dining room, she went into the dimly-lit bedroom. Lisa turned on the lights and saw J.T. right away, snoring, his nude body sprawled on the bed. She blushed, averted her eyes, and walked towards him. Picking up a crumpled sheet from the floor, she covered his mid-section with it. Then she leaned down and checked his pulse, which was fine. She had always seen him fully clothed before and when she glanced at his broad chest, heavily-muscled shoulders, and his overall rugged physique, she blushed again. Pushing away inappropriate employee-employer thoughts, she tapped his shoulder to wake him up. But J.T. continued to snore.

"Wake up, Mr. Ryan," she said loudly, but there was no response.

She noticed more empty beer cans littering the floor and an empty bottle of vodka on the nightstand. Also on the nightstand was a framed photo of a very pretty woman, smiling at the camera. No doubt that was the woman Erin had mentioned.

After several more unsuccessful attempts to wake him, she went to the kitchen to make a strong pot of coffee.

It was going to be a long day.

***

J.T. Ryan, his head pounding from a massive headache, took a sip from his steaming cup of coffee. He was wearing a bathrobe, although he didn't remember putting it on – hell, he didn't remember anything after he'd climbed into bed.

He was sitting at the kitchen table looking on as Lisa Booth bustled around the room, breaking eggs and adding them to the frying pan, then inserting bread into the toaster.

"Good coffee," Ryan said groggily.

Lisa stopped what she was doing and glared at him. "Keep drinking it. You need it." She went back to her cooking, as he unsteadily got up from the chair, shuffled to one of the cabinets, took out a bottle of Excedrin, shook out five tablets and swallowed them dry. Then he eased himself back onto the dinette chair, closed his eyes, and tried to will away his massive headache.

Sometime later he smelled the savory aroma of scrambled eggs, bacon, and hash browns. He opened his eyes and found a heaping plate of food in front of him.

Lisa, who was wearing an apron over her prim jacket and skirt, sat down across from him and drank from her cup of coffee.

"You're not eating?" he asked. The Excedrin had kicked-in and the cloud of pain in his head had lifted somewhat.

"I'm not hungry," she stated as she placed her cup down. "We need to have a talk. A serious talk."

Ryan rubbed his forehead with a hand. "Now?"

"Yes, now."

Ryan picked up a fork and dug into the heaping plate of food, which was hot and delicious. A hell of lot better than his own cooking, he mused. "It'll have to wait. I'm busy eating."

"I'll talk, you listen."

Irritated by her tone, he said, "You may have forgotten, but you work for me, remember?"

"I haven't forgotten, *sir*. But we still need to have a serious talk."

He ate some bacon, chewed on the buttered toast, and took a long swallow of coffee. "Go ahead, then."

"This shit has to stop, Ryan."

Ryan almost choked on his coffee hearing this. "What?"

"You heard me, sir."

His headache came back full force and he massaged his forehead again.

"I'm sorry to be so blunt, Mr. Ryan, but you've got to get this problem under control."

"What problem?"

"Your drinking problem."

"You're out of your mind! I don't have a problem."

Lisa said nothing, stood, went to the trash container in the kitchen, and pulled it across the room so that it was next to him. Then she opened the lid: inside he counted at least 15 empty beer cans and a couple of empty liquor bottles.

She closed the lid on the trash bin and sat back down again.

"Okay, young lady, you've made your point. But it's still none of your business."

She pointed an index finger at him. "But it is my business. If you lose your government contracts, I'll be out of a job."

He waved a hand in the air. "That's not going to happen."

"Erin Welch came to our office today."

"She did?"

"She did," Lisa said, her tone hard. "And she told me in no uncertain terms. If you don't get your act together, it's adios amigos."

"Shit."

"That's right, sir."

Ryan took a long pull from his coffee and drained the cup.

"Tell me about her," Lisa said, her voice softer now.

"Tell you about who?"

"The woman who broke up with you. I assume that's her in the photo in your bedroom."

Ryan's anger flared and he was about to tell Lisa to go fuck herself for prying into his business. Then he realized she was only trying to help. After taking in a long breath, he said, "Her name is Lauren Chase and I loved her very much."

"Looks to me like you're still in love with her. How long has it been?"

"Since she left me?"

"Yes."

"A year. I've tried a million times to get her back, but she won't have it."

"A year. That's a long time, J.T."

"It is. It's been tough. I try to mask it with humor and the drinking helps me get through it."

"I'm sure it does – for a little while. Then after the hangover is gone, the pain from thinking about her comes back, doesn't it?"

Ryan eyed the young woman. "You're pretty wise for someone who looks like they just graduated from high school." He let out a long breath. "What's the best way for me to get out of this mess?"

"Quit cold turkey. Don't drink another drop. It's the only way."

"What makes you so certain?"

Lisa nodded. "Remember me telling you my dad was a cop? Well, my uncle was one too. After all the years on the force, all the double shifts, and dealing with all the crap beat cops deal with every day, they both became alcoholics. My dad was lucky. One day he got tired of the drinking and the hangovers and missing work, so he quit cold turkey. Stopped drinking and never went back to it."

"And your uncle?"

A sad look crossed her face. "His story didn't have a happy ending. One day, after he got drunk, he ate his gun. He put his service pistol in his mouth, pulled the trigger, and blew his brains out."

Lisa got up from her chair and said quietly, "Something for you to think about, J.T." Then she turned and left the apartment.

Ryan sat there for the next half hour, processing what she'd said.

Afterward he rose, pulled out a garbage bag from one of the kitchen cabinets and opened the refrigerator. There were three six-packs of unopened beer inside which he took out and placed in the garbage bag. Next he opened the pantry, removed several bottles of Jack Daniels he'd stored there, and likewise put them into the bag.

That done, he went into his bedroom and stared at the framed photo of Lauren on the nightstand. Picking up the picture, he traced his finger slowly over the woman's face and felt the pang of heartache. A heartache he'd felt for over a year.

"It's time, Lauren. It's time I let you go."

He carried the framed photo to his bedroom closet and rummaged around until he found what he was looking for. A cardboard box filled with old mementos from years gone by. After taking another long look at the picture, he placed it in the box and closed the lid. He put the box back where he found it, on the top shelf.

Then he left the closet, closed the door shut, and pushed the thoughts of Lauren out of his mind.

It was one of the most difficult things he had ever done in his life.

Chapter 14

Ministry of National Defense
Central Military Commission Building
Beijing, China

General Xi Chang stared out the window of his expansive office, which overlooked the vast acreage of Tiananmen Square. Further away he could make out the ornate, ancient architecture of the Forbidden City.

The general was worried. More than worried, actually. The American woman had told him she would resolve any issues, but he was having second thoughts about the whole project. The prize was great, but the cost if the plan didn't work, would be greater. Problems had crept into their operation, problems that could jeopardize his standing as a key member of the Communist Party Politburo and his position as a four-star general in the People's Army.

General Chang glanced at his watch. He had a staff meeting to conduct. He'd deal with the American woman another time. Turning away from the window, he smoothed-down his uniform jacket and left his office.

Chapter 15

Washington, D.C.

The man wearing the perfectly-tailored gray suit and matching gray tie waited anxiously in his office for his boss to arrive. The woman's jet had touched down at Dulles an hour ago and she would be arriving any moment. He dreaded meeting her now when things were not going well. But it was unavoidable. She was a headstrong woman and never took no for an answer.

Just then there was a knock at his office door, the door opened, and his assistant showed in Amber Holt. His assistant left and closed the door behind him.

Amber, a stony expression on her sculpted good looks, marched to one of the couches in the large office and sat down.

The man in the gray suit got up quickly from his desk, approached her and extended his hand. "Amber, it's so good to see you."

The redheaded woman ignored his outstretched hand and said, "You can drop the bullshit act. The last thing you wanted was for me to show up in the middle of your fuckup."

"Amber, please ...."

She pointed to the credenza in a corner of the office. "Do you have any wine in there?"

"Yes."

"Good. Get me some."

"Of course." He strode to the credenza and removed the bottle of cabernet he always kept there for her visits. After filling a glass, he handed her the wine and sat down opposite her on another couch. He watched the beautiful redhead as she sipped from her glass. Today she was wearing a sleek burgundy dress, outrageously expensive he assumed. The dress enhanced her hourglass shape and its color complemented her long red tresses, which extended past her shoulders. A long time ago, when she'd first hired him, he had entertained thoughts of a sexual relationship. But he soon realized the woman was cold as ice and focused entirely on business. He still secretly lusted for her, but was now content that she had made him a very wealthy man.

Amber drained her glass of wine and set it down on the coffee table in front of her.

"How was your trip from Beijing?" he asked, hoping to delay talking about their current operation.

"Long. 13 hours long. I hate that flight – even on my own plane."

"You didn't have to come, Amber. I told you that. I can handle the problem on my own."

Her eyes narrowed. "Could you, Gray Man? I'm not so sure."

"Please don't call me that. I have a name."

She smiled, but the smile had no warmth in it. "I prefer calling you Gray Man. Fits you perfectly, don't you think? Always the gray suits and gray ties, which matches your gray hair and gray mustache. And always the same dour expression. You're the most non-descript man I know."

"I'm good at my job," he said defensively.

She gave him a long look. "You have been. You've run the foundation well. Until now."

"I said I'd take care of the problem."

Amber ran a hand through her long hair. "I'm sure you would, eventually. But I don't have the luxury of time. We're too close now. And I'm worried about the general. He suspects something's wrong."

Gray Man's gut wrenched. "How could the general know?"

"He's a smart man. Even though you bribed the Embassy people to keep it quiet, I'm sure he'll eventually find out that the money was seized. Where's the money now?"

"The $100 million?" he replied.

"Of course the 100 million, you fucking idiot."

"The FBI has it. According to my sources, it's at their field office in Atlanta. I assume its locked up in the evidence room there."

Amber shook her head. "This is bad. Very bad. We'll never get that money back. And it's not like I can ask the general for another $100 million."

Gray Man had already realized this days ago and said, "We can still fund the project. We can tap several foundation bank accounts. We can cover the loss and also have plenty left over."

Amber's face reddened. "I know that, damn it." She pointed to herself. "But the foundation's money is *my* money."

"I'm sorry. I didn't mean to imply anything else. I'm just trying to find a solution."

She picked up her empty glass and held it out to him. "More wine."

"Yes, of course." He took the glass, refilled it and handed it back to her.

Amber drained it in one long pull, then said, "Fine. Tap the other foundation accounts. I need this operation to succeed. Our relationship with the general is too important. I've become rich with the Chinese connection. After we get this deal done, they'll be plenty more."

"Yes, I'll take care of it." He paused a moment, unsure if he wanted to bring up the next topic. Knowing it was unavoidable, he said, "What about the other pending operations. Should I proceed with those?"

"The Russian and Iranian ones?"

"Yes."

"Put a hold on those for now, Gray Man."

"Of course."

Amber rubbed her temple as if she had a headache. "What about your man in Atlanta? What's his status?"

"He's monitoring the situation closely."

"He knows what to do?"

"I gave him specific instructions, Amber."

"Good."

"Will you be heading back to China soon?"

She gave him a stony look. "No. I have something else to take care of while I'm in D.C."

"I see. I'll be glad to help you with it in any way I can."

"No, Gray Man, this is something I have to take care of personally."

Chapter 16

Midtown
Atlanta, Georgia

"You're looking a lot better, Chief," Lisa Booth said when J.T. Ryan came into the office.

"I feel a hell of lot better," Ryan replied. "I slept for two days solid – all the booze is out of my system." He grinned. "And don't call me chief."

Lisa returned the smile, but it was tentative. "Are you really okay now?"

He perched on the corner of the desk she was sitting behind. "Yeah."

"You think you have your problem under control?"

"I haven't had a drop since you left my apartment. And I put Lauren's photo away. I realized I had to move on with my life."

Lisa nodded. "I'm glad."

"By the way, I wanted to thank you."

She looked puzzled. "For what?"

"For letting me know what happened to your uncle. That's what convinced me to sober up."

Ryan glanced around the office, noticing something was different, but not sure what. "The office looks better. I must be hallucinating."

She gave him a mischievous smile. "You're not. I painted the office while you were gone."

"You what?"

"Do you like the color? I picked blue. I figure all men like blue, so I thought you'd be okay with it."

Ryan shook his head slowly. "Lisa ...."

"You don't like the blue?"

"The color's fine. It's the fact you did it without asking first. It is *my* office, after all."

"Actually, boss, it's technically our office. I'm part of the team. Anyway, I bought the paint for a good price at Home Depot and I did all of the painting myself. I told you I was handy." She waved a hand in the air. "Don't you think the place looks better now? More professional?"

Ryan was about to object again, then simply shrugged. "Okay. It does look better. But we've got bigger things to work on now."

He stood. "Get your coat. We're going for a ride."

Lisa rose, grabbed her jacket from the back of her chair and put it on. Then she reached in a desk drawer, took out her Glock and slipped it in her hip holster. "Where we going?"

"The Chinese Embassy in downtown," he said. "Time to get some answers."

Chapter 17

Midtown
Atlanta, Georgia

Ryan and Lisa rode the elevator down to building's underground parking lot and stepped out. It was ten a.m. and the area, which was a hive of activity early in the morning and at five p.m. when employees came to work and left, was now deserted.

But the lot was full of parked cars and he'd left his Tahoe in a slot at the far end. He headed there now, with Lisa at his side.

Out of the corner of his eye he sensed movement in the shadows by a pickup truck nearby. Instinctively he pulled his revolver and grabbed Lisa's arm, quickly pulling her to the ground.

At the same instant he saw muzzle flashes and heard three loud thuds, two of the incoming rounds shattering a nearby windshield, the third one ricocheting off the concrete floor. His heart racing, he fired off two rounds at the moving shadow. He spotted a man dressed in all black, sprinting away from them. Ryan aimed carefully and fired again, and this time the shot found its mark. The fleeing man collapsed.

He was about to race over and make sure the assassin was no longer a threat when he glanced down.

His heart stopped.

Lisa was sprawled flat on her back on the concrete floor, blood seeping from her forehead.

Chapter 18

Bethesda, Maryland

Amber Holt went into the exclusive restaurant and walked toward the maitre-d' station. She liked the upscale bistro when meeting her other D.C. contact, not because of its sophisticated decor or sumptuous food, but because of its discreet location far away from the power corridors of Washington.

The maitre-d' recognized her immediately and escorted her to their usual booth at the back of the restaurant. Her contact, Robert, was already there, and seeing her, he stood up from the table and smiled. "Amber, you look beautiful as always."

She gave him a light kiss on his cheek and sat opposite him.

Robert motioned the waiter, who brought her a glass and filled it from the wine bottle on the table. Then the waiter moved away and they had complete privacy, since there were no other occupied tables nearby.

"Hope you're well, Robert."

"I can't complain. Washington is a cesspool, but you know that already."

Amber gave him a radiant smile. "Actually, that's the reason I love D.C. so much. That it is a cesspool. It makes my job so much easier." She studied the tall, lean man in his late fifties. He was handsome, she had always thought, and he carried himself with an imposing bearing, something that helped him rise up the ranks of Washington power-brokers.

"I'm sure it does," he said.

She took a sip of the merlot. "I wired your offshore account this morning. In addition to your monthly retainer, I added a 50% bonus. The total amount was $1.5 million."

The man's eyebrows shot up. "Very generous of you. Thank you. You must want something special."

Amber reached across the table and covered one of his hands with hers. "I do. I've run into a serious complication with one of my ... operations ...."

"I see."

"You remember the Chinese deal I was working on, Robert?"

"You never told me the details, but I have a sense of what's going on."

She took another sip of wine. "Well, something went wrong. A large amount of money was seized by the FBI."

A frown crossed his face. "If you're suggesting I get the money released, that's impossible. I couldn't do that. It would raise all sorts of red flags and be way too dangerous for me to do."

She patted his hand. "I know that. I'm asking for something much simpler. The case is being investigated by the Bureau's Atlanta office. I need you to have the case transferred to someone ... who can keep it under wraps."

"You want it to go sideways?" he asked, using law-enforcement jargon for an investigation that won't be pursued.

"That's right, Robert. Slow-walk it. Give it to your man in D.C. You have him on a short leash."

"That's true. I do. But he's already suspicious about my interference on some of our other projects."

Amber squeezed his hand. "This is important to me. If my operation is revealed, it could be linked to my foundation. If that happens, those monthly retainer fees ...." Her voice trailed off and she didn't finish the sentence.

He blinked rapidly and he gulped down some wine.

"But that's not going to happen, my dear Robert. We're partners, you and I. Have been for quite a while. You help me and I help you. Isn't that right?"

"I'll take care of it."

"Excellent! I knew I could count on you." Her eyes bore into his and she began to gently rub the back of his hand, her fingers sensually tracing his skin. After a moment of this she sensed he was sexually aroused.

Their relationship had always been a business one, but several times before she had teased him like she was doing now, hinting that their partnership could evolve into a sexual one. She did this not because she wanted him, but because she was cunning and knew her looks as much as her intelligence had been a reason for her success. She had learned from an early age that men were weak when it came to sex. Even the promise of sex with a beautiful woman was something many men couldn't resist.

With her eyes still locked on his, Amber continued to sensually rub the back of his hand. Then she said, "I'm thinking of having the Dover sole. What do you think, dear? Is that a good choice?"

Chapter 19

Grady Memorial Hospital
Atlanta, Georgia

"How is Lisa doing?" Erin Welch asked, as she stepped into the Intensive Care waiting room and sat next to J.T. Ryan.

Ryan glanced at Erin. "The bullet grazed her forehead. The doctor says she suffered a concussion and that she's lost a lot of blood. They're going to keep her in Intensive Care for a couple of days for observation, but they expect a full recovery and no lasting side effects."

Erin nodded, relieved at the news. "That's good." She looked around the waiting room and realized they were the only ones there, which was unusual. Grady Memorial was the city's go-to-place for gunshot wounds and trauma cases, which made it Atlanta's busiest hospital.

Ryan shook his head slowly. "I feel like crap about this."

"The fact Lisa got shot?"

"That's right," he said glumly.

"I read the police report – the guy ambushed you. You're lucky to be alive, as is Lisa. If you hadn't killed him you'd both be at the Fulton County morgue right now."

He shook his head again. "I never should have put her in danger in the first place. She's just a kid."

Erin placed a hand on his shoulder. "Lisa Booth is 25 years old. She's an adult who took the job knowing the risks involved. Her father was a cop, for Christ's sakes. Don't beat yourself up."

Ryan stared at her and she could see the worry etched on his handsome face.

Finally he nodded and said, "You're right."

She smiled. "Of course I'm right. I'm always right."

Ryan's glumness appeared to lift with her attempt at humor.

"Now who's the wise guy," he said. "Who was the man I killed?"

"No ID on him. We're running his prints and DNA through NCIC," she said, referring to the FBI's National Crime Information Center database. "When something pops I'll let you know. He's probably the same guy who took a shot at you at the Summit building. He was carrying a suppressed Heckler & Koch 9 mil semi-auto. Same caliber of shell casings we found at Summit. We're trying to trace the pistol back to its purchase point."

"Heckler & Koch – that's a sophisticated weapon, Erin – it confirms he was a contract killer."

"He was a pro, all right – a hired gun. Question is, who hired him."

"You want me to continue working the case?"

She stared long and hard at him and studied his eyes closely to make sure they weren't blood-shot. "You got the drinking under control?"

"I'm done with that," he stated forcefully.

Erin extended her hand and they shook. "Good. I'm glad you're back. I need you on this investigation."

"Before Lisa got shot," he said, "she told me you were getting push-back from D.C. on this case. What's going on?"

"I don't know for sure, but it's not good."

"Well, you can count on me, Erin."

"That's what I wanted to hear."

Ryan stood and said, "I'll get started right away."

"Where you going?"

"To the place I was headed before we got ambushed. The Chinese Embassy."

Chapter 20

*Downtown
Atlanta, Georgia*

The Chinese Embassy is located downtown, alongside many other foreign government buildings in an area known by locals as Embassy row. Atlanta, a world-wide hub for commerce, is home to 68 foreign Embassies. Technically the Chinese Embassy in Atlanta is actually a Consulate. The official Chinese Embassy in the U.S. is located on Wisconsin Avenue in Washington D.C., with the satellite offices, called Consulates, situated in large American cities.

Ryan had never been there before, and after parking his Tahoe SUV in the building's lot, he made his way through the security checkpoints and was shown into the office of Mr. Jiang , the foreign affairs officer at the Embassy.

After inspecting the PI's cred pack, the balding Asian man said, "How may I help you, Mr. Ryan?"

"I'm investigating a case," Ryan said. "There was a shooting in Atlanta recently. Right before the shootout, I saw a Mercedes-Benz truck with Chinese Embassy plates enter the building where it all happened."

Jiang's eyebrows arched. "You found it?"

"Found what?"

"The Mercedes truck, of course. We reported it stolen."

Ryan shook his head. "No, it hasn't been located. Atlanta PD and the FBI have an APB out, but so far it hasn't turned up."

"I am sorry to hear that. That is an expensive vehicle."

"We did find something else, Mr. Jiang. A very large amount of cash. Do you know anything about that?"

The Asian man's face was inscrutable. He didn't reply for a long moment, then calmly said, "No, I do not. Is there anything else I may help you with?"

Ryan rubbed his jaw, felt the stubble there. He'd been at Grady's ER and then Intensive Care for twenty-four hours and hadn't had a chance to shave. "Since I'm here, I'd like to interview the employee who normally drives the truck. I may be able to get a lead from him."

Jiang placed his hands flat on the desk in front of him and a chilly smile formed on his lips. "I am sorry, but that is impossible. You are in a Chinese Consulate. By international law, this is considered part of the Chinese mainland. You, nor any other U.S. authority, have jurisdiction here."

Ryan already knew this, but wanted to get the man's reaction to his request. "I see."

"My secretary will show you out," Jiang said.

***

Ryan left the building and when he was back in his SUV, he pulled out his cell phone and punched in a number.

"I'm just leaving the Embassy," he said to Erin when she picked up.

"What'd you find out?"

"About the case, nothing. But I did learn one thing."

"What's that, J.T.?"

"The Chinese official I met with. I can't prove it and it's only a gut feeling. But he's lying through his teeth."

Chapter 21

Atlanta, Georgia

Gray Man had taken the seven a.m. Delta flight from Reagan National in D.C. to Atlanta's Hartsfield. When he landed, he rented a car and drove to an area south of Marietta, an Atlanta suburb. Long ago the area had been a thriving community, but because of crime, drugs, homelessness, and urban poverty, it had deteriorated. The fashionable shopping plazas had been replaced by semi-abandoned box-stores and run-down strip malls, populated with massage parlors, tattoo places, run-down bars, and pawn shops.

Gray Man was there now, in the back office of one of those seedy pawn shops. As usual he was wearing an impeccably tailored gray suit. Sitting across from him was the portly, cigar-chomping owner. A gun display case hung on the wall of the office, filled with an assortment of handguns, most likely stolen, Gray Man suspected. The small office reeked of cigar smoke, and he knew he'd have to dry clean his suit as soon as he got home.

The fat man took a puff from his cigar and blew out a cloud of foul-smelling smoke, then tapped the ashes on an overflowing ashtray.

Gray Man coughed, and said, "Your man is dead?"

"That's right," the portly man replied. "Happens sometimes in this business."

"What happened? All I know is I stopped getting progress reports from him."

The obese guy took another puff from his cigar. "From what I can piece together, he was trying to take down the two people investigating the case. A man and a woman. My guy got shot instead. He was D.O.A."

"I'll need a replacement," Gray Man said.

"Already working on it. It'll be more expensive than last time, though."

"Why?"

The fat man tapped his cigar on the ashtray, then coughed a wad of phlegm into a trashcan. "Dead bodies have a way of attracting attention. Cops, Feds, you know what I mean. I only hire experienced pros. And pros have ears."

Gray Man mulled this over. His options were limited. Amber didn't know about this latest setback and he planned for her to remain in the dark. "All right. How much?"

The man mentioned a sum and then took another puff from his foul-smelling stogie.

Gray Man opened his briefcase, took out a large envelope, counted out the cash, and slid it across the desk.

Taking the money, the fat man did a quick count and put the cash in a desk drawer. "Pleasure doing business with you," he said with a grin, which exposed his crooked, nicotine-stained teeth.

***

Gray Man, glad to be away from the foul-smelling pawn shop, climbed into his rented Cadillac CTS sedan and drove east. Reaching I-75 a while later, he headed south. He had one more stop to make before going back to D.C.

Chapter 22

Buckhead, Georgia

Often referred to as the Beverly Hills of the South, Buckhead is one of the wealthiest communities in the Atlanta metro area. A busy financial center, it's also a world-class shopping, dining, and entertainment district. Multi-million dollar mansions and luxury condo towers are the norm, not the exception. Gray Man was there now, having just driven past Phipps Plaza and Lenox Square mall, which was close to his destination.

Soon after he reached the business district, he pulled into the parking lot of an ultra-modern, three-story office building. Constructed of high-end glass-and-steel, the edifice was an imposing structure, its mirrored windows reflecting the bright mid-day sun. The building's only signage was a small chrome plaque by the entrance, which read, *Veritas Foundation*.

After greeting the receptionist in the lobby, he went to his office on the third floor, unlocked the door, and went inside. Spacious and luxurious, the office was furnished with an expensive teak desk and matching teak cabinets. At the center of the room was a large sitting area with gray suede-leather couches. Lush gray carpet covered the floors and the floor-to-ceiling window shades were platinum in color. Although Gray Man spent half his time here, he preferred his office in D.C., and lived in the suburbs of Washington.

Taking off his suit jacket, he draped it on the back of his executive chair and pressed the intercom on his desk.

"Steve," he said, "come to my office. And bring the book with you."

He sat at his desk and a moment later a tall man with close-cropped sandy hair and ruddy features came into the room. The man was wearing a dark blue three-piece suit and was carrying a large three-ring binder under one arm. His name was Steve Nichols and his official title was President of the foundation. Nichols placed the binder on the desk and sat in one of the wingback chairs fronting it.

Gray Man picked up the binder and quickly leafed through the contents. "Revenues are down for the month."

"Yes," Nichols replied. "We've seen a drop off in donations, particularly from small donors."

"What's causing the drop?"

"We're getting increased competition from the big charities – the Red Cross and Salvation Army for disaster relief."

Gray Man closed the cover of the three-ring binder. "Amber won't be happy."

"I know."

"Why is this happening, Steve?"

"Those other organizations are real charities – the money they collect goes to those in need. They have a long-standing reputation for doing good."

"And we don't, damn it?" Gray Man groused, slamming a fist on the desk.

"Well, sir ...." Nichols didn't finish the sentence.

Gray Man thought about this a minute, then said, "Here's what you need to do. Increase our advertising budget. Get the marketing agency working on some new TV ads – our current stuff is looking tired. I want to see new television ads showing desperate, destitute mothers holding crying, malnourished babies in places like Haiti and Africa – you know what I mean."

"Yes, sir."

Gray Man steepled his hands on the desk. "Okay, enough about that. Let's talk about the other projects."

"The Russian deal?"

"No. Amber put a hold on that. She wants us to focus on the other operation."

"Yes, sir."

"Let's run through the latest numbers." Gray Man pointed to a large chalk board that hung on the wall by the desk. The board looked out of place in the otherwise sumptuously appointed office. But it was a necessity, since Amber and Gray Man both wanted as little documentation as possible for this part of the foundation's business.

Nichols stood, picked up a piece of chalk and started writing. By the time he was done a few minutes later, most of the board was covered with words, numbers, names, and diagrams.

Gray Man leaned forward in his chair as he studied the information. "So, where are we exactly?"

"The United States," Nichols began, "produces over 3,300,000 pounds of uranium a year. A majority of that comes from uranium mines in Utah, Wyoming, Texas, and Nebraska, with lesser amounts from mines in Arizona, Colorado, and South Dakota." He pointed to one of the diagrams. "Through our holding companies, we've been able to purchase most of the corporations that own the mining rights and the mines themselves."

"What per cent of the total production do we own now?"

"As of this week, 83%."

"That's excellent. Amber will be pleased."

"Yes, sir."

"What about the rest of it?"

"As you know, uranium is used primarily to fuel the U.S.A.'s nuclear power plants. So it's considered a strategic ore and its sales are regulated by the Congress, the Department of State, and the Department of Energy." Nichols paused and pointed to a list of names written on the board. "There's a lot of people involved."

Gray Man nodded. "How successful have you been on that end?"

"Fairly successful. But there's still some holdouts. And for that we need more cash."

"We've had a serious setback recently," Gray Man said, letting out a long breath.

"Yes, the money I was expecting didn't come in. What happened?"

"You don't need to know, Steve."

"Sir, we still need to convince two senators, three congressmen, and a key person at the State Department to give us approval to purchase the balance of the mining companies."

"How much will that take?"

Nichols stated a very large sum of money.

"All right. Amber has approved tapping into several of our foundation's bank accounts. We'll go over the details later today."

"Yes, sir."

Gray Man leaned back in his chair. "Once we have the money in cash, how long will the process take?"

"I estimate two months."

"Unacceptable, damn it. Amber wants this to happen quicker than that."

"Yes, sir."

"I'll take over the disbursement of the cash personally. I need to monitor the situation more closely."

"Of course, sir."

"That will be all for now. But erase the board before you go, Steve."

Chapter 23

Midtown
Atlanta, Georgia

"What the hell are you doing here?" J.T. Ryan asked, seeing Lisa Booth come into their office.

She grinned, put the laptop she was carrying on her desk and sat in the desk chair. There was a large bandage on her temple. "I'm back at work. I figured you'd appreciate an employee with a good work ethic."

Ryan shook his head slowly. "You're supposed to be at home. Resting from your concussion. Doctor's orders, remember?"

"Oh, yeah." She grinned again. "I guess I forgot about that. Must be because of the concussion."

"You're getting to be a real smart-aleck."

She pointed at him. "I learned from a master."

Ryan stood, walked over to her desk and perched on the edge of it. "I was really worried about you. Still am," he said in a somber voice. "I felt ... feel ... responsible for putting you in a dangerous situation."

"I *love* this job, Chief. It's what I want to do. You didn't put me in danger. I put myself there." She gingerly touched the bandage on her forehead. "Anyway, I'm fine now. This'll heal in a couple of days."

Ryan studied the young woman, appreciating her spunk. "All right. You can stay and work in the office. But no field trips for you."

Lisa smiled. "Thanks, Chief."

"And don't call me chief."

"Okay, J.T. So what's happening on the case?"

"Good news and bad news. The good is that Erin's turned it over to us. Which means you don't have to worry about your paychecks bouncing."

"And the bad?"

"We're at a dead end. The only promising lead was the Chinese Embassy connection. But they're stonewalling me."

Lisa opened the lid on her laptop. "I got bored watching TV at home, so I was surfing the Internet."

"Hopefully you weren't trolling porn sites," he deadpanned.

Her face blushed and she covered her mouth with a hand. "Oh, my God! Of course not!"

Ryan grinned. "I know. Got you didn't I?"

"Oh ... yeah, you did."

He folded his arms in front of him. "So what'd you find out about the case?"

"Remember I told you I was good with computers?"

He rolled his eyes. "More than once."

"Okay. Anyway, it bugged me that I hadn't been able to trace back the ownership of the Summit Corporation. So I kept at it while I was home."

"And?"

Her expression brightened. "I found it. Summit is owned by multiple layers of shell companies, foreign affiliates, and offshore dummy corporations, set up with the sole purpose of disguising the true owner."

"I'm with you so far. So who owns Summit?"

"A non-profit organization. A charity."

"Really? That's incredible. What's the name of the charity?"

"The Veritas Charities Foundation," Lisa replied.

Chapter 24

Midtown
Atlanta, Georgia

Ryan rubbed his jaw. "Veritas? For some reason, that name sounds familiar."

Lisa closed the lid on her computer and looked up at him. "It should. You probably saw some of their TV ads. They run them on the cable channels, asking for donations."

He snapped his fingers. "Of course. That's one of the charities that does relief work after natural disasters."

"I did research on Veritas," she continued, "and found they've only been in business about ten years. Their official name is the Veritas Charities Foundation, but they're referred to mostly as the Veritas Foundation. Their reputation is spotty, from what I could tell. They're not rated very high by the charity ratings agencies. From what I found online, they're not in the same league as the excellent non-profits like the American Red Cross, Salvation Army, the USO, Catholic Relief Services, United Way, or the other big ones."

"Good work, Lisa. So if this Veritas Foundation owns Summit Corp., they must be involved with a money-laundering scheme."

She nodded. "And I found out something else about Veritas."

"What?"

"Although the foundation is based here in Atlanta, in the layers of shell companies I detected several connections to China."

Chapter 25

FBI Field Office
Atlanta, Georgia

"Good news," J.T. Ryan said, as he walked into Erin Welch's office. "We got a lead on the money-laundering case."

Erin looked up from the stack of reports strewn on her desk. "We could use it. Grab a chair."

He sat across from her. "Summit Corporation, through layers of shell companies, is owned by a non-profit outfit named Veritas Foundation. Their official name in the corporate records is the Veritas Charities Foundation, but mostly they go by the name of Veritas."

"Good work, J.T."

"I can't take credit for it. Lisa found the connection on her own."

Erin nodded. "She's a sharp girl. You're lucky to have her."

"I am."

She beamed. "Imagine that. It took a woman to get the break on the case."

Ryan was about to protest, then simply smiled back.

"What else did she find out about this foundation?" Erin said.

"They're based here in the Atlanta area – in Buckhead. The president of Veritas is listed as a Steve Nichols. And there's something else, something that seems to tie it all together."

"What's that?"

"Veritas has a connection with China. It's unclear how exactly, but Lisa was able to trace it back to there."

Erin's phone desk rang and she glanced at the caller ID. "It's Director Tucker from D.C.," she said. "I'll put it on speaker so we can tell him the lead you just got on the case." Erin pressed a button on the console and said, "Director."

"Erin," the FBI director said, his authoritative voice filling the room. "I need to go over something regarding one of your cases."

"Of course, sir. Which one?"

"The money-laundering investigation."

"Yes, Director."

"Erin, I'm transferring that case to our headquarters office here, effective immediately."

Erin's jaw dropped. "But why, Director? We're making good progress on that."

"That's not your concern."

Ryan was about to speak up, but Erin put a finger to her lips.

"Sir, I deserve an explanation."

"Actually you don't," Tucker replied tersely. "Pack up all your files on this investigation and send them to me. And that's a direct order."

"But, Director –"

There was a click on the line and both Erin and Ryan realized the FBI director had hung up.

"What the hell was that about?" Ryan said.

Erin, a stunned expression on her face, shook her head. "I told you things were getting bad. But I didn't realize how bad until just now."

Crestfallen, the PI let out a long breath. "What happens now?"

"You heard the director."

"We can't let this go, Erin. I can't let this go. One person was killed. Barbara Cooper – an innocent woman. And Lisa and I were almost murdered."

"I'm aware of that, damn it. What the hell do you expect me to do?"

Ryan thought about this for a long moment. "Technically, I don't work for the FBI. I'm an independent contractor."

"What's your point?"

"What I do on my own time is my business."

Erin's face showed a range of emotions as his words sank in – surprise at first, then concern. "I could lose my job over this."

"I'll pursue this on my own, Erin. When I have answers, I'll let you know. In the meantime, you're out of the loop."

She didn't reply for several minutes, obviously weighing what they had discussed. Eventually she said, "All right, J.T."

Ryan stood. Then he gave her a half-salute, turned, and left the office.

Chapter 26

Atlanta, Georgia

After leaving the FBI building, Ryan went to his apartment and changed out of his customary blue blazer and casual slacks and into one of his few suits. Next he donned a tie and checked his appearance in the mirror. He looked the part, he thought.

Making his way out of his apartment, he got back in his Tahoe and drove towards Buckhead. Soon after he found the address Lisa had given him for the Veritas Foundation, which turned out to be an upscale glass-and-steel building in the business district.

Parking his SUV, he went inside and approached the reception desk. Pulling out a business card which read *John T. Ryan, Financial Investments*, he handed it to the young woman at the desk.

"I'd like to see Mr. Steve Nichols," Ryan said with a broad smile. "I'd like to make a large donation to the foundation."

The receptionist returned his smile and said, "Of course. Let me call him." The woman spoke into the phone, then rose and said, "I'll take you to his office."

Ryan followed her toward the elevator banks. Exiting at the third floor, she led him into a large office. She quietly left and closed the door behind her as a well-dressed man with sandy hair and ruddy features came around his mahogany desk and extended his hand.

"Mr. Ryan. Great to meet you. I'm Steve Nichols, President of Veritas."

Ryan shook his hand and they sat across from each other on the red leather couches at the center of the room.

"My secretary tells me you'd like to make a donation," Nichols said. "That's excellent news. We do a lot of good work here at Veritas, as I'm sure you're aware."

"Actually, I'm not here to donate money."

A puzzled expression crossed the other man's face. "But you told her ...."

"I lied."

"I don't understand, Mr. Ryan. What is this about?"

"I'm investigating your foundation for money-laundering and racketeering."

Nichols's ruddy complexion blanched white. "You can't be serious."

"I'm dead serious." Ryan unbuttoned his suit jacket, letting the man see the holstered pistol on his hip. "I know about the $100 million in cash and your foundation's connection to the Summit Corporation."

Nichols jaw dropped.

"An employee of Summit was killed in cold blood," Ryan continued. "Which means you're an accessory to murder, in addition to racketeering. If you talk to me and tell me who else is involved, I can help you get a deal with the DA when he files charges."

Nichols tugged at his necktie as perspiration beaded on his forehead. "I don't know ... what ... you're ... talking about ...." he stammered.

"Cut the crap, Nichols, and start talking."

Suddenly the foundation president bolted off the couch and raced back to his desk. He pressed a button on the phone console. "Get security in here now!" he yelled into the speaker. Then he cowered behind his desk as Ryan stood and approached him.

A moment later two beefy men wearing security guard uniforms burst into the office, their hands resting on the butt of their holstered pistols.

Ryan assessed the situation and calmly said to the guards, "All right, guys. There's no reason for gunplay. I was just leaving."

"Get him out of here!" Nichols shrieked.

The PI, his palms up in the air, slowly walked toward the exit. When he was close, he punched one of the guards solidly on the solar plexus, quickly spun around and elbowed the other one on the face. The first guard staggered back as the second, his nose bleeding, yelled in pain and went to one knee.

Ryan kicked the first guy in the balls and the man howled as he clutched his groin. Then the PI delivered a powerful side-kick to the other, sending him sprawling to the floor, his bright red blood staining the lush white carpet.

A piercing alarm went off in the building, echoing loudly in the room, and Ryan knew he had no time to interrogate Nichols.

He faced the foundation president and pointed an index finger his way. "This isn't over, friend. Not by a long shot."

Then he turned and raced out of the office.

Chapter 27

Beijing, China

Amber Holt was in her office poring over financial spreadsheets when her desk phone buzzed. She picked up the handset immediately.

"What is it, Gray Man?" she said.

"We have a problem," the man answered. "A big problem."

Fuck, she thought. "What?"

"I just got a call from Steve Nichols in Atlanta. A man came to the foundation building asking questions. Nichols didn't answer any of his questions and told the guy to leave, but not before the man beat up two of our security guards."

"What kind of questions, damn it?"

"About Summit and the murder of Barbara Cooper and the 100 million in cash and the connection between Summit and Veritas ..."

A sinking feeling settled in the pit of Amber's stomach. "How's that possible?"

"I have no idea, Amber."

"Who was this guy?"

"John Ryan – the FBI investigator who killed the hit man I hired."

Fuming, the redhead ground her teeth in anger. She had explicitly told Robert to call off the FBI investigation. *What the hell was happening?*

"What should I do?" Gray Man asked.

"Tell Nichols to beef up his security staff. Double it – no, triple it. I don't want this Ryan anywhere near our building again. And if anybody else shows up there, have Nichols lawyer up. He's to answer no questions."

"Yes, ma'am. Anything else?"

"No," she replied. "I'll handle the rest from my end." She hung up the phone, picked up her glass of merlot, and drained it in one long gulp to steady her nerves. Refilling the glass from the wine bottle on the desk, she drank that down as well.

Amber picked up the handset and tapped in a telephone number in D.C. she'd memorized long ago. "I need to talk to Robert," she said when the line was answered by a female voice.

"Of course, Ms. Holt," the other woman replied. "He's in a meeting right now. I'll have him call you as soon as he's done."

"I have to talk to Robert right *now*. Get him out of the fucking meeting!"

"Ah ... well ...."

"Do it, you stupid bitch, or I'll have your job!"

"Yes, Ms. Holt. I'll do that right away."

Exactly three minutes later, Amber heard Robert's voice on the line. "This is highly irregular, Amber. I was in an important meeting."

"Listen, you fucking idiot, you screwed up! You need to fix this mess."

"Amber, please, don't use that kind of language."

She took in a couple of deep breaths to calm down. After a moment she said, "You're right. I'm sorry. It's just that everything I've worked for is now in serious jeopardy."

"Tell me what's happening."

"An FBI investigator is asking questions at the foundation."

"That's impossible. I made arrangements. I had that case pulled from the Atlanta office."

"Obviously your effort failed, Robert. This just happened. Fix this and fix this now, or that cushy monthly retainer could vanish overnight."

"Please don't say that. I need that money."

Amber knew that to be a fact. Robert and his wife had become accustomed to a lavish lifestyle. "I'm not threatening you, dear. But if my deal goes south, if my foundation is exposed, I stand to lose everything. Do I need to say more?"

"I understand, Amber. I'll take care of it. Who was the FBI investigator?"

"His name is John Ryan."

"Ryan? From what my man at the FBI told me, he's a contractor – he's not actually a Bureau agent. That's probably how this got away from us."

The redhead gripped the phone tightly. "I need to have this Ryan destroyed. Discredited. Eliminated. I don't care what you do, but you need to fucking get rid of him. Now!"

There was a long pause, then Robert said, "I'll take care of it. And I know exactly how to do it."

Chapter 28

Hoover Building, FBI Headquarters
Washington, D.C.

"Lies and more lies," Erin Welch murmured as she paced the empty conference room, waiting for the FBI Director to arrive. The more times she visited Washington, the truer those words became.

Erin stopped pacing, crossed her arms, and stared out the large window of the conference room. Dark, ominous clouds hung over the city, which reinforced her foul mood. She was an attractive, slender brunette in her late thirties dressed in a stylish Dior skirt and jacket. But her long hair was pulled back carelessly into a ponytail and the dark circles under her eyes reflected a week of fitful sleep.

Hearing the door open behind her, she turned as FBI Director Tucker entered the room.

"Director," she said.

Tucker, a solemn look on his face, closed the door behind him and sat at the conference table. He motioned her over. "Have a seat, Erin."

She remained standing. "Sir, have you reviewed the pending indictments we discussed? The Bureau has solid cases on them. We should move to impanel grand juries."

"I'm sorry, Erin. Those cases are too sensitive right now." He shrugged his shoulders. "You know how D.C. works."

Lies and more lies, she thought.

"I do know it, Director. All too well."

Director Tucker gave her a long, appraising look. "How long has it been since I put you in charge of the Bureau's Atlanta Field office?"

"Two years and seven months."

Tucker nodded. "You got the job because you're the best Special Agent I have. You loved the job at first." Obviously sensing her frustration, he added, "But lately I've noticed a change. What happened?"

Erin pulled out a chair and sat across from him. "May I be frank, Director?"

"You've never been the shy type. Go ahead."

"Sir, I took this job because I wanted to make a difference. To catch the bad guys and put them behind bars."

"That's what we do, Erin."

"With all due respect, that's absolute bullshit. I think we spend more time protecting the guilty than prosecuting them."

Tucker's cheeks flushed and his jaw clenched. "Listen, I won't have you or anyone else impugn the integrity of the Bureau!"

Erin forced herself to stay calm. "Then approve the indictments I recommended. Refer them to the Justice Department to impanel grand juries. As I said, we have very strong cases."

He leaned forward in his chair. "We can't do that."

"Why the hell not? You're an intelligent man, Director. You know these cases are a slam dunk."

Tucker slowly shook his head. "I can't do it."

"You're the FBI Director. Of course you can do it."

"It's not that easy, Erin. As I said before, the people you want to indict are .... " His words trailed off.

"Connected," she replied, finishing the sentence for him.

Director Tucker was a heavyset man with solid gray hair, tired eyes, and a haggard-looking face. He appeared much older than his age of 58, Erin thought. It was a casualty of his job.

"Forget about those cases," he stated, a hard edge to his voice. "I have something else that needs your immediate attention. Something much more important."

"What is it, sir?"

The man reached into the briefcase he had brought with him and pulled out a red file folder. The FBI logo was stamped on its cover. He slid the folder across the conference table towards her.

Leaning forward in his seat, he said, "I'm declaring an FBI Code Red alert. I'm adding a new person to the terrorist watch-list. He's been declared an enemy of the state and he's to be hunted down and brought to justice."

"Who is it, Director?"

"John Taylor Ryan."

Chapter 29

Special Operations Division, CIA Annex Building
Langley, Virginia

CIA operative Rachel West was in the building's underground shooting range, firing her Glock 43. Fifteen yards in front of her the exact center of the paper target was literally shredded.

Rachel was the only person in the range today and the handgun's boom echoed in the empty concrete room. The sulfuric scent of gunpowder hung in the air. Quickly empting the six-round clip, she deftly ejected the magazine and slammed a fresh one in its place. Then once again she assumed a shooter's two-handed stance and aimed at a different part of the target. She began firing, the 9 mm rounds tracing a tight pattern on an area above the target's center, which was represented by a silhouette of a person's head.

Rachel was a tall and curvaceous woman in her mid-thirties. Her striking good looks made her seem more like a model than a covert agent, which was at times useful in her line of work. Today the leggy, blue-eyed blonde was dressed casually in jeans and a black polo shirt, which didn't disguise her drop-dead good looks. As usual her long hair was pulled into a ponytail and over her hair she wore sound-deadening earmuffs.

After emptying the clip in her pistol, she pressed the controls in the firing range booth and the paper target slid back on the overhead rail to a position in front of her. She studied her firing pattern. Satisfied with the excellent marksmanship, she replaced the target with a new one and inserted a fresh clip in her Glock.

Just then she sensed someone behind her, quickly turned, and saw her boss Alex Miller standing there.

Putting down her weapon, she took off her earmuffs.

"Read this," Miller said, handing her a sheet of paper. "I was reviewing the new National Intelligence Report this morning and came across this. I knew you'd want to know."

"What is it?" Rachel asked.

Her boss, always a man of few words, said, "Read it." He was a balding, dour-looking man in his sixties. Without another word, he turned and went toward the exit door.

Rachel scanned the sheet and paused at the section that had been highlighted by a yellow marker. It was a bulletin issued by the FBI. They had a added a new person to the terrorist watch-list. When she saw the name by the Code Red alert, her heart sank.

"That's impossible," she murmured. "It can't be."

Hoping it would be a different John Taylor Ryan, she read further and saw it was all there: J.T. Ryan, private investigator and U.S. government security contractor. His Atlanta home and office addresses were listed, as well as other personal details she knew were correct. Her heart pounded and a sick feeling settled in the pit of her stomach. She and Ryan had history together – he had saved her life on a covert mission. But there was more than that – they had become lovers, if only for a brief time. It was something she had instigated.

"Damn," she said loudly, the sound reverberating in the concrete-walled room. Her thoughts raced furiously, trying to sort through her next steps.

Quickly pulling out her cell phone from a pocket, she scrolled through the stored numbers. Pressing a key, she waited anxiously for the other end to pick up, praying the call wouldn't go to voice mail.

After the fourth ring, she heard a familiar male voice say, "Hello?"

"J.T., it's Rachel," she said.

"Hey! My favorite CIA agent," Ryan said, humor in his voice.

She could visualize his rugged good looks, his face lit up in a smile.

"This is no time for jokes, J.T. Listen and listen carefully. You're in trouble. Big trouble."

"Don't tell me," he said with a chuckle. "You're pregnant. But we only did it that one time."

"Cut the shit, Ryan. I'm serious like a heart attack. You're in big fucking trouble."

That must have sunk in because his tone was all business when he said, "All right. I hear you loud and clear. What is it?"

"I just read the National Intelligence briefing report from this morning. The FBI has issued a Code Red alert for you. You've been placed on the terrorist watch-list."

"What? That's crazy, Rachel. I do a lot of work for the Bureau. In fact, I'm working on a case right now."

"I know it's crazy. I know you too well – you wouldn't go to the other side."

There was a long pause, then Ryan said, "Must be a mistake."

She gripped the phone tightly. "It's no mistake. The FBI doesn't issue a Code Red by mistake."

"All right. I'm on a stakeout just north of Atlanta. I'll drive to the Bureau office downtown and talk to Erin. She'll straighten this out."

"Don't! Don't do it!"

"Why? I've worked with Erin Welch for years. I'm sure she can fix this."

"I'm telling you, J.T. Don't do it. A Code Red can only be issued by the FBI Director himself. This is above Erin's pay grade."

"Jesus Christ," he murmured. "What the hell do I do?"

"Listen very carefully. You only have one option. You have to go dark. You have to completely go off the grid. Entirely. The Bureau probably has a dragnet out for you already. The only way to evade them is to not use your credit cards, or your phone. Throw away the cell phone you're holding. Buy burners and pay in cash. That's the most important thing – use only cash from now on. And the car you drive – leave it parked where it is. Do not use it again. And don't go to your apartment or office until you clear your name. Got it, J.T.?"

It was a lot for him to absorb, she knew. But he was a bright guy, and a former Green Beret and Delta Force soldier who handled himself well in emergency situations.

"Okay," he said, "I got it. But I can't go off the grid forever. I have to clear my name."

"Maybe I can help," Rachel said. "But first we have to figure out how you got on the terrorist watch-list to begin with."

"Somebody must have set me up."

"I agree, J.T. Someone wants to destroy you, get you arrested and throw away the key. Can you think of who that could be? You said you were working on a case for the FBI now. Tell me about that."

Ryan spent the next five minutes giving her the details of a money-laundering investigation involving a shady foundation.

"Okay, I got the picture," she said. "I may be able to help you with the Chinese connection. I was scheduled to go on assignment to Shanghai in two weeks. I'll talk to Alex – get him to move that up."

"Thanks, Rachel."

"No thanks needed. You and I .... " her voice trailed off she recalled their time together and their lovemaking a while back. "We have history, you and I."

"That we do."

Then Rachel remembered something and said, "You and Lauren – when we were in Spain, you two had broken up by then. Did you and her ever ... get back together?"

"No, we never did," he said, and she heard the sadness in his voice. "That part of my life is over now."

Relieved by this news, she said, "Okay. Do you know what you have to do right now?"

"Yes, Rachel. Throw away my phone. Walk away from my car. Don't go to my office or apartment. Don't use my credit cards. Use only cash."

"Good. We should probably hang up now."

"I guess we should. Will I ever see you again?"

Rachel thought about this question for a long moment, knowing it was doubtful. Pushing away that depressing thought, she said, "Of course you will."

Then she hung up the phone.

After packing her pistol and ammunition into her gun case, she strode out of shooting range. Not wanting to waste time locking up her case in the building's armory, she went directly to Alex Miller's office.

The man was there, sitting behind his desk working at his laptop.

She rested the gun case on the floor and sat in one of the visitors chairs. "Sir, I have vacation time accrued. If it's okay with you, I'd like to take that time now."

Miller closed the lid on his computer and gave her an annoyed look. "This wouldn't have anything to do with John Ryan, would it?"

"Of course not," she lied.

The man drummed his fingers on the desk. "It's a felony to aid and abet a known terrorist," he said, a hard edge to his voice.

"I'm aware of that. But my vacation has nothing to do with J.T. Since I'm scheduled to go to China on assignment in two weeks, I want to go early and catch some of the sights. You know I've been there before. It's a beautiful country. It's time I play tourist."

Miller said nothing, simply stared at her.

It was clear to Rachel that he wasn't buying her story. But she hoped her exemplary record at the CIA would allow her some slack.

"I'm your best agent," she said with a grin. "That should count for something."

"You're *one* of my best agents, young lady," he corrected, no jesting in his voice. She knew the man had no sense of humor. "But since you do have accrued vacation time, you may take it now."

"Thank you." She picked up her case and rose.

"But remember this, Rachel. I've been the Director of Special Operations for a long time. And I know when someone's lying to me."

Chapter 30

Atlanta, Georgia

It had taken J.T. Ryan over three hours to walk from the stakeout location to where he was now, a branch bank in midtown. On the way he had stopped at a Wal-Mart and bought three prepaid cell phones and a backpack.

Going into the bank, he avoided the teller stations and the ATM, knowing that cashing a check or withdrawing cash would be traceable. Instead he went to where the safe-deposit boxes were located.

After signing in and showing his ID to the bank clerk, he got his box and took it into the privacy room, closing the door behind him. Flipping open the lid, he rummaged around and found what he was looking for – a large envelope. The packet contained three sets of fake IDs – driver's licenses, passports, and several other items. Also in the envelope were bundles of cash. He had stored these items years ago, hoping to never have to use them. But his motto had always been to hope for the best but prepare for the worst. In his line of unpredictable work, the worst sometimes hit you like a ton of bricks.

Taking off his back pack, he stuffed it with the items he'd removed from his safe-deposit box. Then he removed an ankle-holster containing a snub-nose revolver and strapped it to his lower leg. That done, he put the box back in its place and left the bank.

Several blocks away he found a wooded park with very few people around. Hiding among the vegetation, he pulled out one of the burner phones, knowing that what he was doing was probably a mistake. Still, he had no choice. He had to be certain that what Rachel had told him was true.

Ryan tapped in a number and the line was picked up right away.

"It's Ryan," he said, keeping his voice low.

"J.T.," Erin replied, "what the hell is going on?"

"You tell me. I was informed I'm on the terrorist watch-list."

"It's true. I just got back from D.C. Director Tucker issued a Code Red. There's a BOLO out for your immediate arrest. You've got to turn yourself in. What have you got yourself mixed up with, Ryan?"

"Nothing! I'm being set up!"

The telephone line went quiet and he said, "Are you still there?"

"Yes, I'm still here," she said, her voice sounding stressed. "We've worked together for years and I know you're a standup guy. But I still have a job to do. Turn yourself in, maybe I can straighten this out."

"If I come in, what happens then?"

"Tucker will have you shipped to D.C. He'll be handling this out of headquarters now, along with several of my other cases."

"That makes no sense, Erin."

"I know it doesn't. But it's out of my control."

Damn, he thought. *Rachel's right. This is way over Erin's pay grade.*

"Please turn yourself in, Ryan. There's a nationwide alert on you. The FBI, NSA, and Homeland Security are all on the lookout for you. And it's not just the Feds – the local authorities across the country all have you in their databases now. It's just a matter of time before you're caught. Since you're on the terrorist watch-list, they'll assume you're armed and dangerous. They may shoot first and ask questions later."

His thoughts racing, Ryan made a split-second decision. He had to go off the grid completely and he had to do it now.

Turning off the burner phone, he threw it to the ground and smashed with his boot.

Then he raced away from the area.

Chapter 31

Midtown
Atlanta, Georgia

Erin Welch crouched among the SWAT team in the corridor as they hugged the wall. Like the rest of her FBI squad, she was outfitted with a black uniform, a Kevlar vest, a Kevlar helmet, a Heckler & Koch MP5 sub-machine gun, tactical boots, and other security gear.

Erin's heart pounded, not knowing what they would find in J.T. Ryan's apartment.

Was he there now? she wondered. *Will there be a shootout? Had he booby-trapped the place?*

The point man on the SWAT team, the one carrying the battering ram, turned towards her, waiting on her signal. Erin nodded and he and the rest of the squad shuffled forward, taking positions right outside the closed door. Although they tried to be extremely quiet, their boots squeaked on the linoleum floor. Since it was 2 a.m., she prayed none of the building's residents would hear them and come out of their apartments. Luckily none did and Erin breathed a sigh of relief.

The point man glanced her way again. She gave him a thumbs-up and gripped her MP5. Instantly the man slammed the door with the heavy battering ram: once, then twice, and the wooden door cracked and gave way, splinters flying in all directions.

Two SWAT team guys, their assault rifles trained forward, rushed inside, quickly followed by Erin and two other men.

As the team spread out through the apartment they yelled, "FBI! FBI! Hands up!"

Their helmet flashlights illuminated the dark rooms in a crisscross pattern and their boots thudded loudly.

Erin heard the lead guys call out "Clear!" as they finished searching the rooms, signaling no one was there. She flicked on the lights in the vacant living room, kitchen, and dining room, then went into the bedroom and did the same. Clearly Ryan had fled.

"You need to see this, Ms. Welch," one of her agents called out from another room.

Erin entered the room, which was empty except for a row of boxes stacked along one wall. Her SWAT team guys crouched next to several open boxes, inspecting the contents.

She approached as one of her agents let out a low whistle. "There must over twenty pounds of C-4 in here," he said.

Erin took a closer look inside the box, confirming what the man had said. The boxes were packed with bricks of C-4, a military-grade form of plastic explosive. The use of this explosive was highly restricted and required a Federal government license to purchase. C-4, she knew, was one of the most lethal types of bombs, utilizing a chemical named RDX nitroamine, a type of nitroglycerine. The explosive is stable and safe to handle, and requires blasting caps in order to detonate. A putty-like material, C-4 is used primarily by armed forces of the U.S. and many other countries around the world. It's also favored by terrorist groups because of its high destructive capability.

Erin's heart sank as she realized Director Tucker had been correct in issuing the Code Red.

The FBI agents continued inspecting the boxes and found other types of explosive devices, including blasting caps, grenades, and Semtex.

"Jesus Christ," one of the SWAT team guys muttered when he opened another box. "Take a look at this, Ms. Welch."

The ADIC approached the man as he pulled out a thick stack of 8"x10" photographs and riffled through them. He handed some of the photos to her and she studied the images closely, shocked at what she saw. They were pictures of the Freedom Tower, the skyscraper in New York City. This was the building that had replaced the Twin Towers, which were destroyed by terrorists on September 11, 2001. Among the pictures were also photos of the White House and the Capitol Building in Washington D.C. There were also close-up photos of the President and the Vice-President of the United States.

Erin shook her head slowly as her stomach churned with revulsion. "What the hell have you gotten yourself into, Ryan?"

Chapter 32

Ministry of National Defense
Central Military Commission Building
Beijing, China

Amber Holt had always found General Chang to be a repulsive man.

She was thinking that now, as she waited for the general to arrive. She liked being in the company of attractive people, like her dear Robert, or her assortment of male and female Chinese friends.

General Chang, on the other hand, was just the opposite. Unlike most Chinese people who are lean, the general was portly, with a thick neck and thick fingers stained yellow by nicotine. He was also short, which further emphasized his squat appearance, and which was made worse by his military uniforms which fit him too tightly. In addition, his fleshy face was deeply scarred by what she assumed were wounds suffered in some long-ago combat.

But it was his smell which bothered her the most. The man must not have bathed frequently, because an unsavory body odor always enveloped him, exacerbated by the stink of his chain-smoking.

As the redhead glanced out of his office window, which overlooked the vast open area of Tiananmen Square, she mused that putting up with the repulsive man was definitely worth it. His funding of many of the foundation's projects had made her an incredibly rich woman. As head of the Ministry of National Defense, the general had control of a large chunk of the Chinese military budget. He had used part of that money to buy U.S. military secrets – detailed Pentagon plans for advanced weapons systems such as the F-35 fighter jet, the Trident-class nuclear-powered submarine, and anti-ballistic missile technology that she had been able to obtain through her black-market D.C. contacts.

Money has a way of opening doors, she thought, a smile settling on her face. *And big money opens lots of doors.*

Just then the office door was opened by Captain Zhou, who was General Chang's aide and the general stepped inside. Amber rose from her chair as the aide left and closed the door behind him.

"General," she said sweetly in Chinese, "it's so good to see you again."

She extended her hand and he held it in his fleshy paw and gave it a squeeze. His hand felt clammy from perspiration and the stench of the man enveloped her. She forced a wide smile on her face as she fought the urge to retch.

"Amber," he replied, nodding slightly as he let go of her hand. He proceeded around his desk and sat behind it. She sat back down, the fake smile still plastered on her face. His custom-designed executive chair made him appear taller than he was. Although Amber was a good foot taller than he, the chair allowed him to gaze down at her.

General Chang lit up a cigarette and slowly exhaled the smoke.

"You wanted to meet, General?" she said, still smiling sweetly. She had dreaded this meeting, guessing the general had learned of the recent complications, but had determined it was best to put on a brave front.

He tapped the cigarette ashes into an ashtray. "Yes. I understand we had a problem with the money I gave you."

"Problem?"

"I talked to my Embassy people in Atlanta," he said. "They, reluctantly I may add, admitted the transfer of cash had gone badly." He arched his bushy brows. "If I did not know better, I would say they were bribed to keep it quiet."

She forced another grin. "We had a small setback, nothing more."

The general gave her a hard look. "I do not think 100 million in U.S. dollars is a small setback."

"Please, don't worry about it. I've already handled the situation."

He had small black eyes, but they were fiercely intense, and they bored into hers. "How, *exactly*, have you handled it? I gave you the money expecting specific results." He pointed a fat index finger at her. "I cannot give you more until I get those results."

"I've replaced the lost money with my own."

Chang nodded. "Good. That must have been painful."

"It was – but it will be worth it. We've worked together for a long time, General. I want our relationship to grow and prosper."

The general took a long puff from his cigarette and exhaled slowly, the acrid smoke blending with his foul body odor. Once again she fought the urge to vomit.

"About that," Chang said, "I've been having second thoughts about our latest operation. I think it is becoming too risky." He waved a fleshy hand around the large office. "I have a lot to lose if it goes bad. If the Politburo finds out, the consequences for me would be severe."

He gave her a cold, tight grin. "The People's Republic of China is not like the United States, where if a general fucks up he is demoted or at worst sentenced to prison. Here the trial would be quick and the sentence pre-determined, death by firing squad."

Alarmed by the prospect of the man canceling their operation, Amber blurted out, "But we're very close to our goal now."

His eyebrows arched again. "How close?"

"We're at 83% ownership. And the balance will be ours soon."

"How soon, Amber?"

The redhead hated giving false promises, but by his tone she knew Chang was ready to pull the plug. "Weeks, General. It's just a matter of weeks."

Chang said nothing for a long moment, deep in thought as he continued puffing on his cigarette. Finally he said, "All right. Let's continue. But do not disappoint me, Amber." He ran a finger across his throat. "Remember, if they send me to face a firing squad, I will not be going alone."

Chapter 33

Ministry of National Defense
Central Military Commission Building
Beijing, China

As Amber Holt was being escorted out of the military headquarters building, she turned toward Captain Zhou, the general's aide. Unlike Chang, the aide was tall, slender, and handsome, and he cut a dashing figure in his pressed military uniform.

"Captain," she said in a low voice, "I'd like to be kept in the loop as things progress."

The two people were walking down a long corridor and the man stopped in his tracks and looked at her quizzically. "What do you mean, Miss Holt?"

She pointed to a nearby alcove which was out of the coverage area of the security cameras. After they strode to it, Amber lightly touched the man's arm. "I know you're aware of every meeting the general attends and that you discuss many issues with him, Captain. I know he trusts you. I'd consider it a personal favor if you would let me know in advance what the general was planning regarding my current project."

Zhou's eyebrows arched. "That would be highly irregular."

She rubbed her hand slowly along his arm. "Please," she purred. "I would make it worth your while. Monetarily. And in other ways ...."

The captain gave her a salacious look, obviously taking in the redhead's many assets. It was clear that he had always considered her off-limits before.

As the meaning of her words sank in, he grinned. "I am sure we can work something out, Miss Holt."

"Please," she replied, returning his smile, "call me Amber."

Chapter 34

FBI Field Office
Atlanta, Georgia

"Do you know why you're here?" Erin Welch asked in a terse voice as she looked down at Lisa Booth.

Lisa was seated at the table in the interrogation room, a worried expression on her face. "Am I in trouble?" she replied.

Erin, who was standing, folded her arms across her chest. "Hell yes, you're in trouble."

"Why? What did I do?"

"Depending on your involvement, you may be charged with terrorist acts against the United States."

The color drained from Lisa's face. Her mouth opened and she tried to say something but no words came out.

Erin leaned down, her eyes locked on the other woman's. "Where's Ryan?"

"I ... don't know."

"Why the hell not? You work for him."

"I haven't seen him or heard from him for two days," Lisa said, her voice trembling. "I tried calling him but all I get is voicemail."

The FBI woman studied Lisa, looking for 'tells', the subtle clues people give off when lying, but so far she hadn't detected any. Deep down she didn't think the young woman was involved in a crime, but as a Bureau ADIC she needed to verify.

"Bullshit, Lisa. You're lying."

"I'm not! Tell me what's going on, please! Is J.T. in trouble?"

"An FBI Code Red alert has been issued for Ryan. He's been put on the terrorist watch-list."

Lisa's eyes went wide. "That's crazy, Erin. And absurd. J.T. may have had an issue with drinking, but he's no terrorist. He's a decorated war hero. He's about the most pro-American man I know. You've known him a long time – you *know* it can't be true."

Erin let out a long breath, then pulled out a chair and sat across from the other woman. "I have known him a long time. And you're right, the whole situation sounds absurd. At least it did until we raided his apartment last night."

"What did you find?"

Erin said, "Plenty. And all of it incriminating." She gave Lisa a long, hard stare. "Are you conspiring with Ryan to commit terrorism?"

Lisa shook her head forcefully. "Of course not! And J.T. isn't either. He wouldn't do that!"

"Do you want a lawyer? By law you're entitled to one."

The young woman shook her head again. "Hell, no. I don't need an attorney. I'm not guilty of anything." The worried look on her face had been replaced by defiance. "And neither is J.T."

Erin liked the woman's spunk and realized she wasn't involved in any criminal conspiracy. "All right. I'm not going to charge you with anything. For now. You're free to go."

"What? You have to tell me what's happening. Please, Erin. I want to help."

The ADIC mulled this over a long moment. "Okay. But what I'm going to tell you is confidential." She pointed an index finger at her. "Clear?"

"Yes, ma'am."

"All right. We found over twenty pounds of C-4 plastic explosive at Ryan's place. We also found grenades, Semtex, and bomb-making materials. Those items are highly restricted and illegal for citizens to possess. And we found something else, something equally disturbing."

"What?"

"We found photos and architectural diagrams of the Freedom Tower in New York City, the White House, and the Capitol Building in D.C. There were lots of photos, taken from a multitude of angles. And the diagrams showed floor plans and entry points for each building. We also found pictures of the U.S. President and Vice-President."

Lisa's face blanched white. "Oh, my God ...."

"That's what I said too, when I saw all this."

Lisa said, "He's being framed. No way he's a terrorist ...."

"As an FBI agent, I'm paid to assess the facts. And all of the facts point to one conclusion."

"Fuck the facts!" Lisa blurted out. Then she must have realized she cursed because she covered her mouth with a hand. "Sorry about that – I never talk like that. What I meant to say is, the facts are wrong. Ryan is not a criminal and he's not a terrorist."

Erin let out a long breath, desperately wishing the other woman was correct. "I hope you're right ... I really hope you're right. But until I can prove he's innocent, I have a job to do. And that job is to arrest him."

Chapter 35

Atlanta, Georgia

J.T. Ryan glanced at his watch. It was 2:15 a.m. He'd been doing surveillance on the apartment building for over three hours and hadn't noticed any unusual activity. No parked vans nearby, no unmarked FBI cars or police cruisers. The vehicles parked on the street all looked like civilian cars – it was clear the authorities weren't watching the place. And in fact, the activity into and out of the building had been minimal after midnight. He wouldn't have expected anything different, Ryan thought. The apartment complex was exactly the kind of quiet place a no-nonsense type of girl like Lisa would reside.

The area was lit by street lamps and he took another look in every direction, then stepped out from behind the cluster of trees in the adjacent park and crossed the street.

Going into the building, he climbed the stairs and quietly strode down the corridor, stopping at 301, the apartment number he remembered from Lisa Booth's resume. Ryan tapped lightly on the door and waited.

A few minutes later he heard footfalls from the other side of the door and sensed he was being observed from the spy-hole.

The door chain rattled, a deadbolt clicked, and the door swung open. Lisa stood there, wearing pajamas and holding a pistol at her side. She said, "Get inside, quick."

Ryan entered the apartment and she closed the door behind her.

"You're in a world of trouble, J.T."

"I know. They put me on the terrorist watch-list. How'd you find out?"

"Erin interrogated me. She told me about the explosives in your apartment."

"What explosives?" he said, confused.

"They found C-4 and a bunch of other bombs, and pictures of the Freedom Tower, the White House, and the President. They think you're planning to blow them up."

"That's ridiculous!"

"I want to believe you, J.T. But the evidence ...."

"No way! I'm being set up!"

She said nothing, then simply nodded. "I think you're being set up too. But I'm not the one you have to convince."

He pointed to her handgun. "Since you believe me, can you put that away?"

Lisa rested the pistol on the living room coffee table as he studied her attire. She was wearing yellow pajamas which had tiny pink flowers printed on them.

"I like your outfit," he said with a grin. "It suits your innocent, Girl Scout look."

She glanced down at herself and blushed. "Yikes! I wasn't expecting company." She pointed toward the kitchen. "Go in there. I'll be back in a moment."

Ryan went to the kitchen, flicked on the lights and took off his backpack and set it on the floor. Then he sat at the dinette table. He glanced around the small room and was amazed how everything was tidy and neatly organized. Even the cute animal magnets stuck on the refrigerator door were perfectly aligned in a row.

Lisa came in a moment later, now wearing a white terry-cloth robe over her yellow PJs. She began making a pot of coffee, then went to the fridge and took out a plate of cinnamon rolls. "You hungry?" she asked.

He grinned. "I'm always hungry."

She set the plate in front of him and went back to making the coffee.

Ryan hadn't eaten anything in eight hours and was famished. By the time Lisa set a steaming mug of coffee in front of him, he'd devoured all of the cinnamon rolls.

"I guess you were hungry," she said. "Can I get you anything else?"

"What do you have?"

Opening the fridge again, she said, "Spaghetti and meatballs. I'll heat it up for you."

"Don't bother, I'll eat it cold."

She shook her head slowly. "Suit yourself." She took the bowl of pasta out of the refrigerator, and after getting cutlery from a drawer, set it on the table. Then she poured a cup of coffee for herself and sat down across from him.

Ryan plowed into the spaghetti and meatballs, which were savory and excellent, even cold. When he finished, he drank down the cup of coffee.

Lisa took a sip of her coffee and looked at him over the rim of her cup. "What do we do now, J.T.?"

He shook his head. "We don't do anything. I'm the one who has to fix this. I just wanted to talk to you and let you know I'm not guilty of anything."

"I want to help."

"I'm sorry, Lisa. I don't want you getting in trouble. I'm radioactive. Anyone associated with me will be suspected of terrorism."

She set the cup down. "That's not fair. I'm your partner, remember?"

He grinned, in spite of the seriousness of the situation. "Technically, we're not partners. You're an employee."

Lisa shrugged. "No difference. Anyway, I want to help. What can I do?"

"I don't know."

She placed her hands flat on the table. "What are you going to do? Erin told me all of the federal agencies are on the lookout for you."

"True. They are."

A worried expression was on her face. "So I ask again. What are you going to do?"

"I've gone off the grid. I'll stay off until I can find out who set me up."

"Okay."

Ryan reached into his backpack and took out one of the burner phones he'd bought at Wal-Mart. Handing it to her, he said, "I won't be seeing you again until I clear my name. It may be a long time. Maybe never. If you need to contact me use this cell phone. Stored in it is the phone number to another burner I have." He looked into her eyes. "Try not to call me, except in an emergency. The FBI and NSA are really good at their job. They can track almost everything everyone does."

Ryan studied the young woman, saw the sadness on her face.

Then he stood, picked up his backpack, and put it on.

"Goodbye, Lisa."

Chapter 36

Shanghai, China

CIA operative Rachel West strode along the Bund, the bustling promenade that overlooked the Huangpu River. As usual the area was crowded with locals and tourists, since the Bund was Shanghai's cultural center. Across the river she could make out the futuristic skyline of the Pudong district with its soaring skyscrapers of every shape and size. But a heavy blanket of smog hung over the whole area, making visibility difficult. China's air-pollution problem was substantial and Rachel noticed many of the locals wearing cloth masks covering their nose and mouth.

As she walked she scanned the crowds for her contact, Edward Smith, an informant she had utilized before on previous assignments in China. Not spotting him, she continued along the wide sidewalk, passing the tall bronze statue of Chen Yi, the first mayor of Shanghai, a statue most people assumed was of Chairman Mao.

The crowds had thinned in this area and she saw Smith sitting at a stone bench nearby.

As she approached, the thin man rose, took off his bowler hat and gave her a nod and a smile. The informant was wearing a three-piece brown tweed suit, which seemed out of place considering the heat and the humidity of the city.

"It's good to see you, Rachel," he said in his clipped British accent.

"Likewise," she replied, taking a quick look around to make sure she hadn't been followed. Then they sat next to each other on the bench, their gaze on the wide river and the skyscrapers beyond.

Smith donned his bowler hat and said, "What brings you to Shanghai?"

"Officially I'm on vacation."

A small smile played on his lips. "On the phone you said you needed information. I'm assuming this isn't CIA business then."

"Your assumption is correct."

He gave her a long look, taking in the leggy blonde's curvaceous figure, piercing blue eyes and long hair. As usual, she was dressed in baggy jeans and a loose casual shirt to downplay her good looks. She also wore no makeup and had pulled her hair into a ponytail, over which she wore a baseball cap.

"Since you're off the clock, then," he said with a slight leer, "maybe I'll supply you with whatever information you need and you don't need to pay me with cash, as you normally do." The leer grew. "Maybe you can compensate me in other ways."

Rachel grinned. "How generous of you."

She took one of his hands with both of hers and caressed it slowly. Then she grabbed his middle finger and pulled if back forcefully. The leer on his face vanished and his eyes watered form the pain.

He tried yanking his hand away but she held it tight, continuing to pull his finger at a nearly 90 degree angle, close to the breaking point.

"Ow! That hurts!" he yelped. "Please, Rachel ... please let go ...."

She released his hand, an icy grin on her face. "Pull that shit again and I'll break it next time."

Smith shook his hand to alleviate the pain and he slid further away from her on the bench. "I'm sorry ... I meant no disrespect."

"Yeah. I'm sure. Now let's get down to business, all right?"

Smith nodded. "Of course."

"I'm looking for a Chinese connection to an Atlanta based charity named the Veritas Foundation. Ever heard of it?"

The informant shook his head. "No. Does the Chinese person you're looking for live here in Shanghai?"

"I don't know. They could be anywhere."

Smith waved a hand in the air as if to encompass the vast metropolis around them. "Shanghai has a population of 27 million. The country of China has a population of over 1.3 billion. Finding one person out of that many won't be easy."

"I'm aware of that, Smith. But you've lived in China your whole life. You have a lot of contacts."

He gave her a perplexed look. "You're a CIA agent. You have a lot of resources in China. Yet you're not using them. Why is that?"

The last thing Rachel wanted was to involve her local Agency people. Specially since Ryan was on the terrorist watch-list. "This is a personal matter," she said.

"I see. This will be expensive."

"How much, Smith?"

He mentioned a high sum. Luckily, as a field agent, Rachel had access to discretionary funds that she could use as she saw fit. She reached into her jeans pocket and took out a wad of Chinese Yuans and counted out part of the money. Handing him the cash, she said, "Here's a deposit. Find out useful info and I'll pay you the rest."

Smith riffled through the Chinese currency and pocketed the money. "Pleasure doing business with you. How can I reach you?"

"It's better if I call you at your regular number."

"That's fine, Rachel."

The man stood, touched the brim of his bowler and said, "Till we meet again." He turned and walked away and she lost sight of him as he merged with the others on the promenade.

Rachel gazed across the river toward the Pudong district, the skyscrapers almost invisible now as the blanket of smog settled lower over the area. She breathed in the slightly acrid air and coughed, wondering if she was doing the right thing. She was treading on thin ice. If the Agency found out what she was pursuing, her whole career at the CIA would come to a screeching halt. She might even be prosecuted for helping a criminal. Then her thoughts turned to Ryan, and she remembered their time together. It had been brief, but it was one of the few times in her life she had felt really connected to someone.

Pushing aside the conflicting thoughts, Rachel stood and walked away.

Chapter 37

Buckhead
Atlanta, Georgia

J.T. Ryan watched as the Infinity sedan pulled up to the front of the mansion and stopped. Two beefy men in ill-fitting suits climbed out, then a third man, Steve Nichols, came out of the sedan. The trio went in the home and a moment later lights flicked on inside.

Ryan was in the nearby woods that bordered the lushly landscaped mansion. He glanced at his watch: 10:35 p.m. Too early for him to slip inside, he thought. Better to wait two hours and give Nichols, the president of Veritas Foundation, time to go to bed and for his security people to let their guard down.

Ryan took off his backpack and sat on the ground, his eyes scanning the quiet, affluent residential area. The house was set well back from the road and sat on a very large lot, typical for Buckhead residences.

Earlier in the day the PI had used his burner phone to find Nichol's address on the Internet. He turned on the phone again and while he waited he tried to collect additional information about the man and his shady charity.

Two hours later Ryan stood and scanned the home, which was now completely dark inside. After donning his backpack, he quietly made his way through the woods, and approached the house through the backyard, a large area that contained a swimming pool, a tennis court, and a flagstone patio.

He sprinted across the patio and hugged the back wall. Ignoring the French doors, he instead focused on the large glass slider and looked inside the dim interior. No lights were on inside the home, save for a tiny pinprick of red, which Ryan suspected was the control pad for the alarm system.

From a pocket he pulled out his Swiss Army knife and his magnet set. Crouching, he placed the magnets on the slider track and switched on the device. Then, holding his breath, he pried the lock on the slider door, slid it open, and slipped inside. The alarm didn't go off and he breathed a little easier. The high-tech magnet device had worked.

Putting away his knife, he pulled out his revolver and scanned the dim room, which was a spacious, opulently furnished den. Listening closely, he heard nothing except the hum of the ventilation system.

Crouching, he slowly made his way through the mansion, passing several vacant rooms, until he came to a wide, marble staircase. He figured the bedrooms were upstairs so he climbed the steps, his weapon trained forward.

At the top of the landing, he looked both ways of the second floor corridor. Spotting a double door at one end of the hallway, he assumed that to be the master bedroom. Silently treading over the plush carpet, he stopped at the closed double door and pressed his ear against the surface. It was quiet inside and Ryan slowly turned the knob and stepped inside, quietly closing and locking the door behind him. He studied the dimly-lit massive bedroom and saw one prone figure on the king-size bed – a snoring Steve Nichols dressed in sleepwear.

Ryan crept forward and crouched by the bed. He clutched Nichols's throat with one hand and pressed the muzzle of his gun to the man's forehead.

Nichols woke up abruptly, his eyes wide.

"Yell," Ryan whispered, "and you're a dead man."

The man struggled and tried to pull away but the PI, who was much stronger, squeezed the man's throat tighter until his face turned red and his eyes bulged in their sockets.

"All ... right ...," Nichols gasped, "I'll ... be quiet ...."

"That's better," the PI whispered as he let go of the man's throat. "You and I are going to have a long talk, my friend." He continued pressing his weapon against Nichols's forehead as the man massaged his now bruised neck.

Just then Ryan heard the sound of cars approaching the house. Sprinting to the windows, he glanced outside and saw three FBI SUVs pull up to the front of the mansion, their roof light-bars flashing blue.

How the hell did they find me so quickly? Ryan's mind churned. The Internet searches, he realized suddenly. The Bureau had been tracking searches and put two and two together.

"You're fucked now!" Nichols yelled, a wicked grin on his face.

Knowing the man was right, Ryan raced out of the bedroom and down the corridor just as one of the bodyguards came out of his room. The PI body slammed him and the man dropped to the floor, as Ryan sprinted down the stairs.

Hearing the loud banging on the front door, he raced toward the back and once he got to the den, went outside, just as a couple of men wearing SWAT gear were approaching the back entrance.

"Stop!" one of the SWAT guys yelled. "FBI! Stop or we'll shoot!"

His heart thudding in his chest, Ryan made a snap decision. Hoping the federal agents wouldn't fire until they could be certain it was him and not the homeowner, the PI sprinted through the patio, zigzagging past the pool area, and into the nearby woods.

Chapter 38

Atlanta, Georgia

Lisa Booth could hear the pounding of the music even while sitting inside her car. She was in the strip club's parking lot, screwing up her courage to go inside. After eyeing the seedy exterior of the building one more time, she got out of her Mustang and strode nervously to the front entrance and paid the cover charge.

Once inside the strip joint, the ear-splitting rock music assaulted her ears, while the flashing strobe lights momentarily blinded her. The lights bathed the stage where a group of female strippers danced and gyrated on poles. Lisa blushed, then found an empty table far from the stage. The club was crowded, the patrons mostly men wearing worn jeans and work shirts, although she spotted a few couples in the audience, one of them getting a lap dance by a stripper.

The whole place stank of cigarettes and stale beer and the air was thick with smoke.

An almost nude waitress strolled over and said, "What do you want to drink?"

"I'm looking for Candy," Lisa said.

The waitress nodded and moved away and a minute later a tall, statuesque brunette wearing only pasties, a tiny G-string, and high-heels sashayed to her table. The waitress had tired eyes, a heavily pockmarked face, and a haggard look as if she'd had a very long day.

"I'm Candy," the woman said. "Do I know you?"

Lisa averted her eyes from the woman's huge double D's, her nipples barely covered by the pasties.

"I'm a private investigator," Lisa said. "I work for J.T. Ryan."

Candy gave her a long up-and-down look, sighed, and gave her a tired smile. "You sure you're a PI, honey? I should card you, make sure you're old enough to drink."

Lisa frowned. "I'm old enough."

"What do you have, sweetie?" Candy said.

"Have?"

"What do you want to drink?"

"Actually nothing. I just want information."

"That's not how it works. First, you have to buy a drink. Then maybe we can talk. Beers are 20 bucks."

"Do you have 7-UP?"

Candy rolled her eyes. "Yeah. But it's still 20 bucks."

Lisa pulled out a twenty dollar bill from her pocket and placed it on the tray the waitress was carrying. The woman moved away and came back a moment later and placed a filled glass on the small table. Lisa eyed the chipped and somewhat dirty tumbler and frowned. Then she looked back up at the statuesque Candy and blushed at the sight of the woman's huge breasts and the rest of her almost nude body.

Candy gave her a tired smile. "You've never been to a strip club before, have you?"

"What makes you say that?"

"I can always tell the newbies. So, where's J.T.?"

"He's ... traveling right now."

"Okay. You really work for him?"

Lisa pulled out her business card and handed it to the other woman. "I started about a month ago."

The waitress nodded. "You're looking for info?"

"Yes. J.T. told me you were a reliable informant – that if I ever needed to learn about the seamier side of what happens in Atlanta, you were a good source."

Candy tucked the business card in her G-string. "That would be me, honey. But just so you're clear, I don't give lap dances. All I do is provide info."

Lisa's cheeks reddened. "Oh ... I ...."

Candy smiled. "Just joshing with you, girl. I can tell you're the wholesome type." Her smile vanished. "But I only talk if you have cold, hard cash. No plastic."

The PI reached into her pocket and half-way pulled out a wad of cash so the other woman could see it.

"Okay," Candy said. "I get a break in fifteen minutes. We can talk in the parking lot. What kind of car you got?"

"A black Mustang."

"I'll find it."

The waitress turned and went to serve another table as Lisa quickly stood and left the club, glad to get away from the smoke-filled, sleazy place.

Fifteen minutes later Lisa spotted Candy exit the club and walk toward her car. The woman was now wearing leggings, flats, and a loose sweater. She climbed in the Mustang and said, "I need $500 up front."

Lisa frowned. "But you haven't told me anything yet."

"Those are the rules, honey. Money up front."

The PI folded her arms across her chest. "That's bull. I'm young but I'm not stupid. I'm not paying anything until I have a pretty good idea you'll deliver."

Candy gave her a hard look but eventually a smile settled on her face. "Just testing you, honey. I know how the game's played. What's you looking for?"

"We're investigating a shady operation based in Atlanta by the name of the Veritas Foundation. We believe they're laundering money. And they're connected to a recent murder in the area." Lisa continued telling her more details about the case, then said, "I'm looking for anything you can find out about this foundation and their president, Steve Nichols."

Candy nodded. "Okay – I get the picture. I'll find out any dirt they got. I know a lot of the shit that goes on in this town. But I'll need a deposit. $250, up-front."

"$200," Lisa said.

"All right." She extended her hand and Lisa shook it. Then the PI reached in her pocket, took out the wad of cash, counted out the money, and handed it over.

"My phone number is on my card, Candy. Call me as soon as you have anything."

"Will do, sweetie. By the way, I was going to tell you, you're a lucky girl working for J.T. He's a class guy – a real gentleman. I've been his informant for years and he's never asked me for a lap dance, a blow job, or a quick roll in the back seat. Considering the riff-raff I deal with every day at that dump ...." Candy pointed toward the strip club. "Ryan is a prince."

Lisa nodded. "You seem like a smart woman. Why do you work there?"

A sad look settled on her features. "I got a ten year old daughter. Kids are expensive to raise on your own. I make real good money on tips. A hell of a lot more than I would being a clerk at an insurance company or some other low-paying bullshit job." She glanced at her watch. "Got to go, honey. My break's over. I'll call you."

Candy climbed out of the car and strode toward the building.

Chapter 39

Washington, D.C.

The three people were in Gray Man's office, sitting on the couches at the center of the large room.

"I thought we should meet in person," Amber Holt said, opening the meeting. She turned to the man in the perfectly-tailored gray suit and tie. "What's the status of the operation?"

"Things are going according to plan," Gray Man replied.

Amber tucked her long auburn hair behind her ears and glared at him. Today the redhead was wearing a sleek blue dress that Gray Man assumed cost thousands.

"I didn't travel all the way from Beijing," she said icily, "to get generalities." She fixed her gaze on the third person in the room, the man with the ruddy complexion. "Fill me in, Nichols."

"Of course," Steve Nichols replied. "To date we've purchased the assets of 89% of the uranium companies in the U.S."

Amber nodded. "That's an improvement. What about the rest?"

"We're working on that, Amber."

"Well, work faster. The general is getting anxious. Which means I'm getting anxious."

"Yes, ma'am," Nichols said.

Amber turned towards Gray Man. "Bring me some wine."

Gray Man rose. "Of course." He went to the credenza in the corner of the office and poured her a glass of cabernet. Then he handed her the glass.

Amber downed it and said, "Another."

"Yes, ma'am."

After refilling the glass and giving it back to her, Gray Man sat down. "Amber, we need to tell you about something that happened recently."

She gave him an icy stare. "By your tone it's not good."

"I'm afraid so, ma'am. The private investigator who was working the case broke into Nichols's house and tried to interrogate him."

"What?" she blurted out, almost spilling her glass of wine. "What happened? Did you give up any information?"

"Luckily not," Nichols interjected. "The FBI arrived at my house right after the man broke in."

"Did they arrest him?" the woman said.

"No, he got away."

"Damn!" Amber rubbed her temple as if she sipped the wine. "At least the FBI prevented him from finding out anything. So the precautions I took are working. Thank God, Robert was able to help us."

"You're right," Gray Man said. "Now that Ryan is on the terrorist watch-list, he won't be able to evade the police for long."

Chapter 40

Fayetteville, North Carolina

J.T. Ryan stood at the window of the motel room, pulled aside the tattered shade, and peered outside at the nighttime scene. The parking lot was dim and quiet, the lone flood-lamp flickering over the trash-littered lot. An overflowing dumpster stood at the far end. There were a few parked cars and pickup trucks, all older models, all showing lots of rust, and dents, and scratches.

Ryan had picked the no-tell motel on purpose. It was one of those cash-only places, renting rooms by the hour, to accommodate the clientele of hookers and johns. The motel had peeling paint, a sagging roof, threadbare carpets, and cheap furniture. The perfect place for him to hide out. Hopefully the last place the Feds would go looking for him.

He methodically studied the parking area, looking for any sign he had been followed. Spotting no late-model SUVs or government-issue sedans, he breathed a sigh of relief and holstered the handgun he was holding.

Ryan had been on the run for over a week. He had almost been captured several times since his near-arrest at Nichols's mansion in Atlanta. Although he was using only cash and burner phones, the FBI and the cops seemed to be everywhere.

After fleeing Atlanta, he'd bought a used clunker and driven north into Tennessee and then into Virginia, only to have the local police somehow track him down. Finally he'd ditched the car and continued on foot, making his way to the rural central part of North Carolina, where he was now. He knew the area well, since he'd been stationed at Fort Bragg, a nearby Army post that serves as the headquarters for Delta Force and the Green Berets. Realizing that being in heavily-populated centers was dangerous, his latest plan was to roam the rural and mountainous areas of the Carolinas until he could figure out his next step.

Satisfied things appeared safe, he left the window, took off his backpack, and fully-clothed, stretched out on the lumpy, heavily-stained bed. The motel room stank of urine, mildew, and cleaning solvent, and the room's heater growled loudly, but Ryan was so exhausted from running that after staring at the cracks in the ceiling for a few moments he fell into a fitful sleep.

He woke minutes or hours later, he wasn't sure which, and turned on his side as the bed springs groaned in protest.

Just then a light flashed into his window and he jumped off the bed, pulled his gun, and crept to the window to peer outside.

He spotted it immediately – a late-model black SUV, driving slowly around the lot, obviously checking out the parked cars. The large SUV had all the tell-tale signs of an undercover government vehicle, further confirmed when it came to a stop and six men in dark suits and ear wigs climbed out of it. Drawing their pistols, the men fanned out across the parking lot.

Ryan's adrenaline raced as he racked his brain, trying to figure out how the hell they'd tracked him down.

Doesn't matter! his brain screamed. *It doesn't matter how. Run. Run now!*

Grabbing his backpack off the floor, he sprinted to the room's dilapidated bathroom and stared at the window. It was small, probably too small to fit his big frame, but it was the only way out.

His pulse pounding, he unlocked the window and slid up the glass pane, but realized he'd never fit through the lower part that was now open. He knew the sound of breaking glass would alert the Feds but he also knew he had no choice.

Using his gun like a hammer, he struck the glass, shattering it. Then he cleared the remaining jagged pieces of glass from the frame and using the toilet seat to step up, he contorted his body through the small window as shards of glass cut into his skin. He landed with a thud on the ground outside.

He heard the door of his room being kicked in, followed by shouting, as he sprinted away from the motel and into the dark, heavily-wooded area behind it.

Glancing back, he noticed flashlight beams scanning the woods. Then thin red beams of light crisscrossed the area. He knew the laser lights were coming from powerful weapons, being pointed by well-trained marksmen.

Keeping his head low, he raced deeper into the woods, trampling over the low-lying vegetation and thrusting aside the branches of the pine forest. In the distance he heard voices and also the thumping of a helicopter overhead.

Ryan didn't stop for the next two hours until he reached a desolate mountainous region. Finding a rocky outcropping, he dropped down to hide behind it.

Glancing at his watch he saw it was 3:17 a.m. Exhausted, he took off his backpack and set it on the ground. He took in lungfuls of air and listened closely for unusual sounds. Thankfully he heard no voices, or chopper sounds, only the rustling of branches and the night calls of birds.

Ryan felt safe.

For now.

Chapter 41

Spring Creek, North Carolina

Ryan had trekked on foot for days, up and down the desolate mountainous region, staying well away from populated areas.

But he realized he couldn't keep it up forever. The Feds had been very adept at tracking him and would find him eventually.

He had one option left.

It wasn't a good one. But it was all he had.

The PI was on the outskirts of Spring Creek, a small town near the Great Smoky Mountains. It was dangerous to be this close to a populated area, but he had to make a phone call. The lack of cell service in the mountains left him no choice.

He was hiding behind a shuttered factory, a clothing mill of some type, its business probably lost to newer, faster, cheaper manufacturing plants in a foreign country.

Crouching by a wall, he pulled out a burner phone and punched in a number. It rang several times, then a familiar female voice answered.

"It's me," Ryan said. "Listen closely. Don't mention my name or yours. Okay?"

"Got it," the woman said.

"I'm in trouble."

"I already knew that."

"Where I am now won't work. I need to get out."

"Okay," the woman said.

"I need to come to you."

There was a long silence from the other end and a minute later the woman said, "All right."

"Where are you now?"

The woman told him.

"I'll meet you there," Ryan said and quickly hung up.

Chapter 42

Shanghai, China

After landing in Shanghai's Pudong International Airport, J.T. Ryan had taken a cab to the Four Seasons, a luxury hotel in the JingAn district of the city. He'd been lucky to get out of the U.S. without being arrested, due in no small part to the quality of his forged passport under an assumed name.

Ryan entered the lobby of the Four Seasons and was about to head up to the woman's room when he remembered she was an avid swimmer. After checking the hotel's floor plan he went to the elevator banks and punched the button for the top floor. Once there he strode past the fitness center and into the large indoor swimming pool area. The far wall of the vast room was completely made of glass, giving him a spectacular view of the city's skyline. It was nighttime and the soaring skyscrapers blazed in a kaleidoscope of neon light.

There were only a few people in the room and Ryan spotted Rachel West right away, doing laps in the Olympic-size pool. He went to the edge of the pool and called her name.

Rachel swam towards him and effortlessly pulled herself out of the pool, water dripping from her sleek and curvaceous body. She was wearing a red bikini and the sight of her took his breath away.

"J.T.," Rachel said, flashing a brilliant smile. "You found me."

Ryan gave her a long up-and-down look, taking in her sculpted good looks, long blonde hair, and vivid blue eyes.

"Since you're CIA," he said, "you must be working undercover." He returned her smile. "But by the looks of it, there's not much under cover ...."

Rachel laughed, picked up a large towel from a chaise lounge, and wrapped it around herself. "It's good to see you, J.T. Any problems getting in the country? The Chinese government keeps a tight lid on in-coming foreigners."

He shook his head. "No. My passport and visa looked real enough. I had bigger problems getting out of the U.S."

"I've been reading the Intelligence reports. You're still on the terrorist watch-list."

The PI nodded. "I had to get out of the country. I went off the grid, just like you told me. But somehow they kept tracking me down."

"Figures," Rachel said. "Once you're on the FBI Code Red, everybody on the federal and local level is on the lookout, including the NSA. The NSA is the scariest agency of them all. They've got all the tools: satellite tracking, phone call monitoring, security camera linkups, computer Internet searches. Every computer keystroke Americans make can be monitored. People don't realize how much they're being watched on a daily basis."

Ryan let out a long breath, knowing how true her words were.

She picked up her tote bag and said, "Let's go to my room. I want to change into dry clothes."

He followed her out of the swimming pool area back to the elevators and to her hotel room. Like the top floor, her room overlooked the city skyline with its riot of neon lights.

"Beautiful city," he said, gazing outside.

"It is," she replied. "Ever been here before?"

"No. I was in Beijing once, but no other part of the country. You?"

Rachel nodded. "I've had a lot of assignments in China. Probably because I'm fluent in Mandarin, the main dialect they speak here."

He waved a hand in the air, encompassing the luxury hotel suite, which included a sumptuous sitting area and dining room. "How'd you score all this?"

She smiled. "I'm always on the road traveling all over the world. I've got a lot of frequent-flyer points. Plus, I'm usually doing undercover work and appearing rich sometimes comes in handy." She pointed toward the dining/kitchen area. "Grab yourself a drink or whatever you want to eat. I want to shower and throw on some clothes."

Rachel turned and left the room while Ryan got himself a Pepsi from the large fridge. He sat down on one of the leather couches and brooded about his situation.

He heard the shower running, followed soon by the sound of a hair blower and a few minutes later Rachel returned wearing a casual polo shirt and blue jeans, her long hair cascading past her shoulders.

She sat across from him in a leather couch. "The fact you're here," she said, "means Erin Welch couldn't help you."

Ryan nodded. "That's right. Her hands are tied. She may want to help, but she still has a job to do. I really can't blame her. The evidence against me is devastating."

"Any idea who set you up?"

He shook his head. "Not specifically. But I'm sure it's connected to the case I was working regarding the foundation." He took a sip of soda. "Any progress on your end?"

"I've got a couple of informants here working on it. I should hear something over the next couple of days. And now that you're here we can tackle this together." She went quiet and studied him for a long moment.

"I'm glad you're here," she said eventually. "For personal reasons. You remember what happened last time we saw each other, J.T.?"

Ryan reflected on that covert mission. "A lot happened then. What part in particular?"

"You saved my life, remember?"

He nodded.

A small grin settled on her face. "But I'm not talking about that. I'm referring to the personal part."

"I acted unprofessional," he replied. "It never should have happened."

"I was the one who came on to you, remember?"

Ryan recalled their torrid lovemaking that one and only time. "We were on assignment ... we're both professionals ... it shouldn't have happened."

Rachel smiled. "You're *such* a Boy Scout. Tell me with a straight face you regret what we did."

Their time together had been very special. "No. I don't regret it one bit."

She nodded, a satisfied expression on her face. "I was hoping you'd say that." She leaned forward on the couch and said in a low voice, "I've missed you ...."

"And I you, Rachel."

"You told me on the phone that you and Lauren aren't together anymore?"

He shrugged. "I tried getting back together with her a million times, but ...."

"I remember why she broke up with you. She wanted kids and a husband with a regular 9-to-5 job and a house with a white picket fence, the whole nine yards."

Ryan gave her a glum look. "I kick down doors and shoot people for a living. Selling insurance or doing office work would drive me crazy."

"You're an adrenaline junkie. Just like me." She stared at the glass he was holding. "What are you drinking?"

"Pepsi."

Rachel stood. "You need something stronger than that. We both do. I'll go get us some vodka."

"I don't drink anymore."

She looked puzzled. "Since when?"

"Since it became a problem for me."

"I hate drinking alone, J.T. C'mon, just *one* drink. Please?" She gave him a radiant smile and her vivid blue eyes sparkled.

"You're a dangerous woman, Rachel West."

She laughed. "I am. It's one of the reasons we click together so well."

He knew she was right. Finally he said, "All right. But just one drink."

"That's more like it." She turned and left the room and a moment later came back with a bottle of Absolut and two shot glasses.

"I remember now," he said, "you like vodka shooters."

"Nothing better to pass the time." She poured the Absolut into the shot glasses, handed him one and held hers in the air.

"Gan bei!" she said.

"What does that mean?"

"It means 'cheers' in Chinese. Now drink up." She gulped her glass and poured herself another.

"Gan bei," he said, taking a sip of his vodka. The drink felt strong and good as it burned down his throat.

"That's better," she said, downing her second glass quickly. "You want something to eat? The fridge is fully stocked and I can have room service cook up anything you want."

"No, I'm good. I had food on the flight over."

"Long flight, isn't it?"

"Brutal. Fourteen hours. And I'm 6'4" – it's hard to stretch out in those damn tiny seats in coach."

"Next time go business class."

"Can't – I have to conserve my cash. Don't know when I'll be able to access my bank accounts – if ever." The foreboding thoughts of his predicament weighed heavily on him and he hunched his shoulders to relieve the tension.

Rachel must have sensed his mood because she came over and sat next to him. She placed a hand on his shoulder. "We'll figure it out, J.T. We'll clear your name."

"Damn, I hope so."

She picked up the bottle of Absolut, topped off his glass and said, "Have a drink, you'll feel better."

Ryan didn't sip it this time, but rather downed it in one gulp.

"That's more like it," she said as she refilled his shot glass.

He drank it and the effect of the vodka started to kick in. He hadn't had a drop of liquor in a month and the mellow rush made him a little lightheaded.

He glanced at her. "You trying to get me drunk?"

"Maybe I am," she said with a sly grin. Then her hand slid from his shoulder to his face. She caressed his skin and her touch felt electric. As he stared at the gorgeous blonde sitting next to him his breathing became labored.

"I want you," she whispered, her hand moving from his face to his chest. She unbuttoned the top buttons of his shirt and slipped her hand inside and began caressing his chest.

"Don't fight it, J.T.," Rachel said softly. "You know you want this as much as I do."

Thoughts of Lauren Chase, his longtime love, flooded his mind but he knew that chapter of his life was over. He had to move on.

"Wo ai ni," she whispered, using Chinese words he didn't understand.

"What does that mean?" he said.

"You'll have to look it up."

She pulled her hand out of his shirt and slid it lower until it rested on his belt buckle. With her vivid blue eyes sparkling, she grinned.

"Forget Lauren," Rachel whispered in his ear as she continued to caress him. "That's the past. I'm here now. I want you. Do you want me?"

His heart racing with desire, Ryan stared at the beautiful, desirable woman.

Then he pulled her head close to his and kissed her fiercely on the mouth.

They tumbled to the floor as they ripped each other's clothes off.

Chapter 43

Atlanta, Georgia

Lisa Booth had just unlocked her car and was about to get in it when she heard footsteps behind her.

Recalling the training Ryan had given her, she pulled her gun, whirled around and dropped to one knee. Her heart racing, she pointed the pistol forward and gripped it both hands. She relaxed when she saw who it was. "Oh, it's you."

"Don't shoot!" Candy said, holding her hands in the air.

Lisa holstered her pistol. "What are you doing here?"

"We need to talk, honey."

"Okay. Get in the car," she said, climbing in to the driver's side of her Mustang as the strip club waitress went around and got in the passenger seat. The vehicle was parked in the lot of Lisa's apartment building. She noticed what Candy was wearing with amusement – a fake-fur jacket in a leopard-skin design and striped black and gold slacks.

Candy pointed a finger at her. "You lied to me!"

"What do you mean?"

"The Feds are looking for J.T.! He's a wanted fugitive!"

Lisa nodded her head slowly. "Yeah. About that. Ryan is on the terrorist watch-list. But he's innocent. Someone framed him."

"J.T.'s a sweetie. I know he couldn't be a terrorist," the woman said in an indignant tone, "but you should have told me up-front."

"I know. I'm sorry about that. But I figured you wouldn't help me if you knew he was a wanted man."

"That's where you're wrong, missy. J.T.'s pulled my ass out of the fire lots of times. I owe him a lot."

"Okay, Candy. I won't make that mistake again."

A Ford sedan drove into the slot next to them and both women watched and waited silently until a man got out of the car and walked away.

"I got information for you," Candy said.

"That's great," Lisa said, her enthusiasm surging. "What did you find out?"

"Money first."

"I'm good for it."

"That's crap, sugar. You know the old saying – money talks and bullshit walks."

"All right." She pulled out her wallet and counted how much she had. "I've got $120 on me. I have more at the office."

"That'll do, honey."

Lisa took out the cash and the waitress grabbed it, unzipped the top of her faux-fur jacket, and tucked the money between her cleavage.

"So talk," Lisa said.

"I learned some interesting things about Steve Nichols, the president of that Veritas outfit."

"Such as?"

"He's into prostitutes. Likes one in particular."

"What's her name?"

Candy gave her a sly smile. "Nichols bats for the other team."

"What the hell does that mean?"

"Another old saying, sweetie. It means Nichols is gay – the prostitute he likes is a man not a woman."

"Oh. What did you find out?"

"Apparently this Nichols likes to talk – pillow-talk you might say. And he's always cursing about his boss who's a woman."

"What's her name?" Lisa said.

"Don't know. But she's a redhead and a real looker."

"Okay, that's helpful. What else did you learn?"

"That this woman is hell on wheels. A real bitch."

Lisa nodded, glad for the info but disappointed Candy didn't know the woman's identity. "Anything else you found out?"

Candy scrunched her face in concentration. "Oh, yeah. There is one thing. This redhead doesn't live in the U.S."

"Where does she live?"

"China."

Chapter 44

Lafayette Square
Washington, D.C.

Gray Man strode into the tranquil, wooded park and sat on one of the benches to wait. From his vantage point he could easily see the various entrances to the historic square. At the center of the park stood a statue of President Andrew Jackson seated on a horse. At each of the square's four corners stood statues of men who had helped the U.S. in the Revolutionary War: the park's namesake French general Marquis de Lafayette, along with three other less well-known people: Baron Von Steuben, Jean-Baptiste Donatien, and Thaddeus Kosciuszko.

Gray Man, who as usual was wearing a gray suit and matching gray tie, glanced around looking for his contact. The man was obviously running late.

Gray Man's mission today was one of his job's most unpleasant tasks, but one that couldn't be delegated, since so much money was at stake. He had brought with him a very large and heavy briefcase full of cash.

Cash is king, he thought for the thousand time. Unlike wire transfers which could be traced back to the foundation, cash was every bag man's choice of currency. Likewise it was the preferred method of payment for the person being bribed as well, for the same reason.

Gray Man spotted him ten minutes later: a tall man wearing a suit, walking into Lafayette Square and heading towards him. The man, an aide to a prominent senator, sat next to him on the bench.

"You're late," Gray Man said in a low voice.

"Couldn't be helped," the aide replied. "The senator and I were in conference."

"All right." Gray Man slid the large briefcase toward the other man.

"It's all there?" the aide said.

"Yes. The same as last time."

"Good. The senator will be happy."

"We aim to please," Gray Man said with a trace of irony. "Can we can count on the senator's vote in the upcoming hearing?"

"You can."

"Excellent."

The aide grabbed the briefcase's handle, stood, and saying nothing else, quickly walked away.

After waiting a few minutes, Gray Man rose from the bench and strode out of the park. His morning errand complete, his thoughts turned to his afternoon assignment, which involved another briefcase full of cash, destined for a prominent government official in the State Department.

Chapter 45

FBI Field Office
Atlanta, Georgia

Erin Welch was walking back to her office when her assistant flagged her down in the corridor.

"You've got a visitor," he said, pointing toward the glass-walled conference room. "I put her in there."

Erin nodded and glanced into the room, recognizing the woman. She went inside and sat across from her at the conference table. "Surprised to see you here again," Erin said as she eyed the young woman. "Since I almost arrested you last time."

Lisa Booth gave her a defiant look. "But you didn't, because I'm not guilty of anything. And neither is Ryan."

"That remains to be seen." Erin leaned forward. "Have you seen or heard from J.T. since we talked?"

A flicker of uncertainty crossed Lisa's face, as if weighing the question. She crossed her arms in front of her and said, "No."

"I could still arrest you for obstructing an FBI investigation."

"But you won't, Ms. Welch."

"You seem pretty sure of yourself."

Lisa tucked her hair behind her ears. "I know J.T. is innocent and deep down you know that too. Isn't that right?"

Erin briefly glanced away as she thought about this. *Lisa's right. But I still have a job to do.* She faced the young woman again. "As ADIC of this office I have to judge a case based on the facts, not on my personal feelings."

"With all due respect, Ms. Welch, did anybody ever tell you you're a cold-hearted bitch?"

Erin's hands formed into fists as she rose from the chair. "Get the hell out of here or I will arrest you."

"I'm sorry I cursed at you, Ms. Welch. But I had to get your attention."

Erin leaned forward and placed her hands flat on the conference table. "Why are you here? What do you want? I'm a busy woman. I don't have time to waste."

"I'd like for us to work together to clear J.T."

"My job is simple: find him and arrest him."

"Please. Give me a minute of your time. You owe J.T. that much."

Erin studied the young, innocent-faced blonde, once again admiring her persistence. She sat back down and glanced at her watch. "You have exactly one minute."

"I've been working on the case on my own and I found valuable information."

"I'm listening."

"My source told me that Nichols's boss at the Veritas Foundation is a woman who lives in China. I'm sure you'll remember that at the Summit building shootout Ryan saw a truck with Chinese Embassy plates. It all ties in."

"That's a good lead," Erin replied. "Who's your source?"

"That's confidential. I have to protect my sources."

Erin stabbed her index finger at the other woman. "Tell me or this conversation is over."

"Her name is Candy."

Erin nodded. "The waitress at the strip club. Yeah, I know her. Ryan introduced me to her a while back. She's a good informant. What else did you find out?"

Lisa grinned. "I'll tell you but only if you promise to work with me to clear J.T."

Erin thought about this. As an FBI agent she had a job to do: to lock up Ryan. Still, it was clear that her boss in D.C. was lying to her and could be involved in a cover-up. This whole case smelled like week-old dead fish.

"You're pretty cocky for a twenty-five year old PI," said Erin. "Why should an Assistant Director of the Bureau collaborate with someone who looks like they just graduated from high school?"

Lisa's grin widened. "Because you need me. I work the case and find out what the hell is going on and your hands stay clean."

Erin shook her head slowly. "Now you're starting to sound like J.T."

"I'll take that as a compliment."

"Don't let it go to your head, young lady. I can still arrest you if you screw up."

Lisa frowned. "Really?"

"I'm not going to arrest you." said Erin. "I want to help Ryan get out of this mess too. Now tell me what else you found out."

"Okay. Like I said before, Nichols's boss is a woman who lives in China. She's a redhead and apparently a real tough boss."

"What's her name?"

Lisa shook her head. "Candy didn't know."

"All right. I might be able to track down this Chinese woman on my end. Anything else you want to tell me?"

"No, ma'am. That's all I have."

Erin was quiet for a long moment, then said, "You lied to me earlier."

"I did?"

"You did. I don't like it when people lie to me."

Lisa grimaced. "Am I in trouble again?"

"The first question I asked you today was if you had seen or heard from J.T. You said no. That wasn't true, was it?"

Lisa lowered her eyes and stared at the conference table.

"If we're going to be working together," said Erin, "you need to be straight with me."

Lisa looked up. "Yes, ma'am. I did lie. J.T. came to my apartment, told me he was innocent and said he was going on the run. Then he left and I haven't heard from him since."

Erin could tell that this time Lisa was telling the truth. "Okay. That's better. He is on the run. We almost arrested him a couple of times, but he's elusive and got away."

"I'm worried about him, Ms. Welch."

"So am I. There's a lot of law-enforcement people looking for him. Federal and local. I just hope ...."

"Hope that what?"

"That he gets arrested," Erin said in a sad voice. "I know him pretty well. He's tough and tenacious and doesn't like to give up. If there's a shootout, he may not give himself up. He may end up dead."

Chapter 46

Washington, D.C.

Money *makes everything possible.* That had been Gray Man's motto his whole adult life. Throw enough money at something and the obstacles in your path fade away. But the deeper he became involved in the foundation's current project, the more he realized that some things, and some people, couldn't be bought.

Sometimes you had to resort to other measures.

Gray Man stared out his office window and considered his options. Pulling out his cell phone, he tapped in a number.

When the call was answered, he said, "Where are you now?"

"Watching his building. I've been following him for a week, just like you told me to," the man on the other end replied.

"Is he there now?"

"Yes, he went in this morning."

"Good," Gray Man said. "He's being unreasonable – wouldn't take my latest offer."

"What do you want me to do?"

Gray Man picked off a piece of lint from the lapel of his thousand-dollar gray suit. "Take care of the problem."

Chapter 47

Las Vegas, Nevada

The man pocketed his cell phone, picked up his binoculars and gazed at the mining company's office building. The structure was situated in an industrial area, miles away from the city's gaudy strip of flashy casinos and glitzy hotels.

He checked his watch. It was seven p.m. and his target had left his office at about this time every day for the last week.

Fifteen minutes later he spotted his target exit the building, cross the parking lot, and get in his Lincoln Continental. The man fired up his rented cargo van and began tailing the Lincoln as it made its way out of the industrial district and past the casinos on Las Vegas Boulevard, continuing into an upscale residential area.

The Lincoln pulled into the driveway of one of the large homes, the garage door opened, and the car slipped inside. If his target stayed true to form, he wouldn't go out again until the following morning at six a.m.

The man in the cargo van eased the vehicle onto the driveway of the home and stopped. He was dressed in a brown uniform and brown jacket, similar to those used by a prominent parcel delivery company. He'd bought the clothes earlier in the week, hoping he'd get the opportunity to use them, since he always made more money killing than in doing surveillance. Donning a brown cap, he pulled it low over his eyes. Then he picked up a cardboard box from the passenger seat and, leaving the van running, climbed out and strode to the home's front door.

Pressing the buzzer, he waited a moment until the door was answered by a portly, middle-aged woman with frizzy hair.

The man held up the package. "I have a delivery for Mr. Morelli."

"Oh, I'll take it," the woman said.

"I'm sorry, ma'am. He has to sign for it."

"All right. I'll go get him."

The man in the brown uniform unzipped his jacket and gripped the butt of his suppressed Sig Sauer P220 pistol, which was tucked in his waistband.

Moments later an overweight bald man appeared at the door. "You have a package for me?"

Although the assassin was almost certain this was his target, it never hurt to ask. "Are you Mr. Morelli?"

"Yes."

"Good." Deftly pulling out his Sig Sauer, he pointed it at the man's forehead and quickly pulled the trigger three times.

Morelli staggered back and instantly dropped to the floor.

The killer turned, sprinted back to his van, and drove away.

Chapter 48

Xian, China

Amber Holt stood in a corner of the cavernous, dimly-lit building that housed the massive excavations of China's famed Terracotta Army. She half-listened as General Chang, standing behind a podium, addressed a group of reporters. As head of the country's Ministry of National Defense, one of his ceremonial duties was to commemorate the beginning of a new dig. The building they were in now, named Pit 1, housed over 6,000 of the life-size pottery statues. Pit 1 contained an army of infantry soldiers arrayed in battle formation. The figures were sculpted by skilled artists using terracotta and were all carved with individual facial expressions. The intricacy of the carvings was astonishing, Amber had always thought. They included individual hairstyles, clothing, and shoe details. They had been originally painted in vivid colors and had carried weapons, including swords and spears. But the paint had faded long ago, and the figures now were just different shades of brown. Modeled from yellow clay, the realistic-looking statues were constructed over 2,200 years ago with the intent of guarding the Tomb of Qin Shi Huangdi, the Emperor who had unified China 22 centuries ago. The tomb had been discovered in 1974 by peasants digging a well, and the Terracotta Army had become one of the country's most visited attractions.

Due to the commemoration ceremony today, the massive building had been closed to tourists. The only people allowed in were a group of reporters and a few select guests, including Amber. As a result, the general's amplified voice echoed throughout the mostly deserted, cavernous room.

Amber listened as General Chang droned on, gathering her thoughts for the upcoming meeting. Thankfully a few minutes later he made his concluding remarks and, after answering a few questions from the press, ended his speech.

The TV camera lights dimmed and the reporters and guests began to file toward the exit.

A moment later, Captain Zhou, the general's aide walked over to Amber and said, "The general will see you now."

Amber beamed at the tall, handsome captain, who cut a dashing figure in his pressed military uniform. Lightly touching his arm, she locked eyes with him. "You are so kind."

He returned her smile. "It is always a pleasure seeing you, Amber."

Zhou led her to where the general was standing and moved away.

General Chang lit a cigarette and slowly exhaled the smoke, a grim expression on his fleshy face. As usual he was wearing his tight-fitting uniform, which only served to emphasize his obesity. A very short man, he was forced to look up at Amber, which no doubt aggravated him. Normally they met in his office and his custom-designed executive chair made him appear much taller.

"General," Amber said sweetly in Chinese, "thank you for seeing me." She extended her hand and he held it in his clammy paw and squeezed it. His body odor was overwhelming and she had to force herself not to vomit from the stench.

He let go of her hand. "You told Zhou you had something important to discuss?"

She forced a smile on her face. "I do. We've had recent developments on our project."

"Good ones, I hope."

"Of course, General. My man in D.C. has cleared several of the obstacles."

"Excellent. How far are you along?"

She smiled brightly. "89 %."

He puffed on his cigarette and exhaled, for which she was grateful. The smell from his cheap cigarettes was bad, but it masked the even worse stench of his body odor. "Very good. I am glad you are making progress. I was beginning to have doubts about our joint venture."

She nodded. "I know. That's why I wanted to see you. To alleviate your concerns."

The short, portly man gazed up at her. "How soon before completion? I want to inform the Politburo of my success."

Amber's thoughts raced, trying to select an appropriate response. She knew the clock was ticking on the general's end, but she also realized the remaining hurdles she faced on the project. Finally she said, "Soon."

He glared at her. "That is not an answer."

"Next time we meet, General, I'll have a definite timetable."

"You had better. I am not a patient man. You need to deliver." He glared at her for a long moment, took a puff from his cigarette, dropped it to the floor, and ground it out with his boot.

Without another word, he turned and stalked toward the exit, leaving Amber all alone in the dimly-lit, cavernous room. She suddenly realized why the general had wanted to meet in this out of the way place, far from Beijing.

The room was a tomb, and nearby were the remains of a long-forgotten Chinese emperor.

And staring at her were the lifeless eyes of over 6,000 statues. An entire army of life-size clay soldiers. All of them seeming to glare at her.

A chill went down her spine.

Chapter 49

Shanghai, China

J.T. Ryan was on the balcony of Rachel West's hotel suite, drinking coffee, when he felt his cell vibrate. Slipping it out of a pocket, he took the call.

"It's me," the female caller said.

He recognized the voice instantly. "Are you using a burner?" he said.

"I am."

"It's good to hear your voice. But make it quick. Safer that way."

"Okay," she replied. "The group you're looking for is run by a woman. A redhead who lives in China. Don't know her name."

"That's useful. Anything else?"

"I'm working on some other leads. I'll call if I get any other info."

"Thanks." Ryan hung up and put the phone in his pants pocket.

Just then the glass slider opened and Rachel stepped out on the terrace. She was barefoot and was wearing a white terry-cloth robe. Her long blonde hair was damp from the shower she'd just taken and she was carrying a mug of steaming hot coffee.

"Who was that on the phone?" she said, sitting across from him at the ornate, wrought-iron table.

"Lisa Booth," Ryan said. "She works for me. She found out some useful information about the head of the Veritas Foundation. Happens to be a redhead who lives somewhere in China."

Rachel nodded. "Good. Got a name?"

"No ID yet, but she's working on it from her end."

Rachel looked pensive as she took a sip of coffee. "Most Chinese, men and women, have black hair, so this mystery redhead is probably not Asian."

"Or she dyed her hair red."

"There is that," she said.

It was a gray day in Shanghai with a heavy blanket of smog hanging over the city. Visibility, even from their upper-story balcony was limited. Ryan could barely see past the first row of skyscrapers that faced the hotel. A gust of wind blew, sending a wave of smog swirling into the terrace.

"Let's go inside," Rachel said, rising from the table.

Ryan followed her, and after closing the slider behind him, he said, "I couldn't bring a gun over. Can you get me one?"

She nodded. "Yeah. I've got a spare. You still favor a .357?"

"I do."

Rachel smiled. "You're so old school. Anybody tell you people carry automatics now?"

He returned the grin. "Everybody tells me that."

"I bet. Well, you're out of luck. I don't have any revolvers – but I have something you may like just as well."

"Okay."

Rachel left the living room and went to the bedroom. She returned a moment later carrying a metal briefcase. Placing it on the coffee table, she opened the case. Inside were three semi-automatic pistols. A compact Glock 43, a Sig Sauer P210 in a silver finish, and a black Heckler & Koch Mark 23.

"I use the Glock most of the time," she said, "but you're welcome to one of the other two."

"Nice armament," he said. Picking up the H&K, he admired the craftsmanship of the German made .45 caliber weapon with its 12 shot magazine. "I'll take this one."

"Thought you might," Rachel said. "That's the pistol some Special Ops units use."

"Yeah. I carried one just like it when I was in Delta."

Ryan set the gun on the table as she closed the case and set it on the floor.

"So what's next?" he said.

"I'll call my CI and give him the info on the woman in China – it may help us track her down." She grabbed her cell phone from the table and made a call.

After talking to the man and putting away the phone, she said, "Done. He'll need a day or so."

"All right. What do we do in the meantime?"

She came toward him and stood very close, her vivid blue eyes gleaming as she looked up at him. She smelled of scented soap from her recent shower. "I can think of a couple of things," she whispered.

Ryan caressed her face, once again sensing her raw sexuality. He grinned. "My mother warned me about women like you."

She unfastened the sash of her white terry-cloth robe. "Your mother was right."

He traced her cheek and lips with his fingers, then slid his hand down her neck and shoulder. It lingered there a moment before he fully opened her robe and cupped one of her breasts. He caressed it slowly, gently rubbing his thumb across her nipple.

She closed her eyes and moaned.

With his other hand Ryan pressed her body tight against him and kissed her passionately on the mouth.

Putting her arms around him, she kissed him back hungrily.

Chapter 50

Washington, D.C.

Gray Man's desk phone rang, and noting the caller ID on the info screen, picked up immediately.

"Hello, Amber," he said.

"My call is encrypted on my end," she replied. "Is it on yours?"

"Yes."

"I'll make this quick, Gray Man. I had a very unpleasant meeting with the general. We need to move up our completion date."

Gray Man swallowed hard. They were already on an extremely aggressive schedule. "But–"

"Don't interrupt me. You need to get this done."

"Amber, please ... we're already taking unnecessary risks. I've had to ...." He didn't finish the sentence. Even though the call was encrypted, he didn't want to allude to his recent actions.

"I don't care, damn it!"

"But–"

"Listen to me," she stated, acid dripping from every word, "I'm not taking no for an answer. Do whatever you have to do, payoff or kill whoever gets in our way. Do you *fucking* understand me?"

Gray Man loosened his tie and undid the top button of his shirt. "Yes, I understand. I'll take care of it."

"That's better," Amber said in a softer tone. "I know I can be a bitch sometimes, but it's only because I want to succeed. I want both of us to succeed. You do see that, don't you dear?"

Amber had never called him by a term of endearment before and his first reaction was shock. His second reaction was a surge of excitement.

But deep down he knew Amber was extremely manipulative – he knew she used sex to get her way. *Is this another one of her ploys?* With her it was impossible to tell.

"I do see that, Amber. I know we're in this together. You can count on me – I'll get it done."

"That's what I love about you," she purred, her voice as sweet as honey. "You're always there for me, always resolving our problems. I won't forget this, dear. You'll see, next time I come to the U.S."

As he visualized the image of the stunning redhead, naked, he felt himself grow hard. It was a fantasy he'd often had, but never thought would come true. His breathing labored, he said, "When will you be flying over?"

"Soon," she whispered. "But first you need to take care of our problems."

"Of course."

"I've got to go now. Talk to you soon, dear."

Gray Man replaced the handset on the phone console and took in a few deep breaths to collect his thoughts. Reluctantly pushing away images of scorching lovemaking, he focused on what had to be done.

He glanced out his office window. It was a dark, cloudy night in D.C. According to his watch it was 10:15 p.m., which meant it was 7:15 on the west coast.

Pulling out his cell phone, he pressed one of the numbers he had on speed-dial.

A man's voice answered after one ring. "Yes?"

"The congressman is not being cooperative," Gray Man said.

"I see. How do you want me to do it?"

"That's your area of expertise. But this guy is very high profile. It has to look like an accident."

"My usual fee?"

"Yes," Gray Man responded. "But do it quick. We have no time to waste." Then he disconnected the call.

Chapter 51

San Francisco, California

Congressman Rodriguez lived in the Pacific Heights neighborhood of the city, an exclusive area filled with palatial houses and very high-end town-homes. The predominant architecture of the area was elaborate Victorian and many of the homes, such as the one the congressman owned, had been declared historic landmarks.

The man wearing a gas company uniform was sitting in a white cargo van, doing surveillance on the town-home on Webster Street. He had seen Rodriguez go into his house a half-hour earlier and had not seen him leave. Since it was already nine p.m. local time, it was clear the congressman was in for the night.

The man donned his gas company cap, picked up his tool kit from the floorboard, and climbed out of the van. Like his uniform and cap, the van had the appropriate logos for the gas company that serviced San Francisco. The assassin was good at his profession and it had only taken him a day to prepare the faux logos and ID badge. Normally the killer wouldn't have gone through the trouble of creating such an elaborate ruse, but Rodriguez, a well-known congressman, would be wary of letting anyone enter his home.

The assassin crossed Webster Street, strode up the steps to the home's entrance and rang the bell.

The porch light came on and the Victorian wooden door was opened partway by a middle-aged Hispanic man with graying hair. The man looked exactly like the photos published in numerous newspaper articles.

The assassin held up the ID badge that hung on a lanyard around his neck. "Sorry to bother you, sir. But there's been reports of gas leaks in this area. We're checking each house to make sure everything is okay."

The congressman studied the ID card closely, then opened the door fully. With a worried expression on his face, he said, "Could there be an explosion?"

"Yes, sir. If we don't catch the problem in time. I need to check the gas lines connected to your furnace."

Rodriguez nodded. "Of course. My furnace is in the basement." He turned and the killer followed him through the foyer and down a staircase to a basement. In one corner of the room sat a large furnace.

While the congressman watched, the assassin took out a gas detection meter from his toolkit. He set the meter on the floor and turned on the device. Then he began inspecting the gas pipes leading into and out of the furnace. While doing this he covertly attached a magnetized metal device to the back of the furnace.

After inspecting the piping for another minute, he picked up the gas meter from the floor, and after glancing at the display screen, said, "All right, sir. You're clear. There's no sign of leaks."

"Thank God," the congressman said. "That's good news."

The killer smiled. "Yes, it is. Most of these things turn out to be false alarms, but it always pays to be sure."

"That's the truth."

"I'll be on my way then, sir. I've got more houses to check. You have a good evening."

Congressman Rodriguez escorted him back up the stairs and out of the home. After appearing to write notes in a clipboard, the faux gas company man crossed the street and climbed back in the van. Starting it up, he drove away slowly. He went north on Webster Street, took a right on Washington until he came to Gough Street. Pulling to the curb, he turned off the van. He was six blocks away from the congressman's home, a distance he deemed safe.

Pulling out his cell phone, he punched in a number and waited to hear a familiar click as the device he'd left at the home was activated. He counted off the seconds in his head, knowing it wouldn't be long.

Then he heard it.

An ear-splitting blast as the spark-igniter burst, setting off a deadly explosion in the home's furnace and gas lines. A minute later he heard the secondary blasts as the adjacent houses also blew up. It was unfortunate to have so much collateral damage, the assassin mused, but sometimes it was unavoidable.

As he drove away the echoes of the massive explosions could be heard throughout the Pacific Heights area.

Chapter 52

Atlanta, Georgia

Lisa Booth stared at the computer screen, reading Steve Nichols's emails. After several days of unsuccessful attempts, earlier today she had finally been able to break into the Veritas Foundation computer server in Buckhead.

Lisa had come to her office at the crack of dawn, determined to hack into their email system. Eventually, after what seemed like a gallon of coffee, she'd broken through. Elated at her success, she'd jumped up from the chair in excitement, pumping her fists in the air.

"I did it! I did it!" she had squealed, then glanced around the empty office, feeling silly. *Act your age*, she thought. *I'm supposed to be an ace detective, not a schoolgirl.*

For the last three hours Lisa had been poring over the Veritas emails. The more she read, though, the less enthusiastic she became. Instead of a gold mine, what she found was more tin and copper. That was because most of the emails were encrypted and undecipherable. And the ones that could be read clearly used euphemisms and indirect language to disguise their intent.

But after another hour of reading the material, one thing became evident: Steve Nichols made frequent trips to Washington, D.C. Although it was unclear who he met with, it was obvious he was meeting another man.

She continued poring over the emails, taking frequent notes of things she thought were pertinent. After several more hours, her eyes glassy from staring at the screen, she got up, stretched her arms, and got herself another cup of coffee.

When she sat back down in front of the laptop a few minutes later, she instantly noticed something was wrong. The email list was gone, replaced by her familiar Windows welcome screen.

Typing furiously, Lisa tried to hack back into the Veritas server, using the procedure she had been successful with previously. But this time it didn't work.

Apparently someone from Veritas had detected the intrusion and set up a new, stronger firewall.

Using her knowledge of computer software, she spent the next two hours trying to hack back into the system again, without success.

Chapter 53

Shanghai, China

Built in 1930, the Fairmont Peace Hotel was by far the most distinctive building in the Bund, the historic district of Shanghai. Its elegant marble-floor lobby, with its vaulted ceilings and arched doorways had a century-old charm that far surpassed in ambiance the glitz of the city's ultra-modern, glass-and-chrome hotels.

One of the best features of the Fairmont was the top-floor restaurant, with its warm mahogany decor and understated charm. The restaurant overlooked Zhongshan East Road, the Bund's main street, and the Huangpu River. It was one of Rachel West's favorite restaurants, the reason she'd picked it for today's meeting.

After taking a sip of her mineral water, she glanced at J.T. Ryan, who was sitting across from her at the table.

"Think he'll show?" Ryan asked.

"Don't worry," she said. "According to my informant, Shao Shan is very reliable."

As if on cue, a handsome Asian man with salt-and-pepper hair approached their table. He was wearing a navy blue suit, a crisp white shirt, with a red tie and red pocket square. The Asian man nodded toward Rachel, and said in slightly accented English, "I am Shao Shan. You must be Ms. West?"

"I am." She extended her hand. "Please have a seat."

Shao Shan shook it and sat down.

"This is J.T. Ryan," she said, "he's an associate of mine."

Shao nodded to him, then fixed his gaze back on Rachel. "I have been talking to our mutual friend, Edward Smith. He has told me you are looking for an auburn haired woman associated with an organization called Veritas."

Rachel took a drink of water and set the glass down. "You have a name for me?"

Shao shook his head. "Unfortunately not. I have been in the 'information' business a long time, but China is a very large country with over a billion people. And here it is not like in the U.S. Many people here are not connected to the Internet– it is easy to hide your identity."

"I'm aware of that," Rachel said, disappointed at what Shao had just told her. Edward Smith and Shao Shan had been her best hope of learning the redhead's identity.

"You believe this woman," Shao said, "is involved in criminal activity?"

"Without a doubt."

Shao Shan nodded. "Then there is one person who can help you."

Rachel felt a glimmer of hope. "Who?"

The Chinese man rubbed his thumb and index finger. "Information is not free."

"I don't mind paying. But the info has to be good."

Shao placed his hands flat on the table. "It is. You have my personal guarantee. If you learn nothing of value, I will return your money."

She studied the Asian man, recalling what Edward Smith had told her about him: *One of my best contacts. Extremely reliable.* "All right. I'll pay."

Reaching into her jacket, she took out an envelope full of Yuans. After a moment of negotiating the amount, she handed him the Chinese cash.

"Excellent," Shao said. "The man you need to see is named Guowang, which translated into English means 'king'. He runs a large criminal gang." He wrinkled his nose. "Guowang is an unsavory character. A real brute. But I have dealt with him before and know he is very well connected. He knows about all types of criminal and corrupt activity in our country. He will know who the redhead is."

"Okay," Rachel replied.

"Be very careful when you meet with Guowang. He is dangerous and lethal. He has been known to torture people he does not like."

"Sounds like a charmer," Ryan interjected.

Shao turned toward him, a serious expression on his face. "Do not take him lightly, Mr. Ryan. Go in well armed. And be prepared for anything – he is unpredictable."

"Where do I find him?" Rachel asked.

Shao looked at her and said, "Chongqing."

Rachel grimaced, knowing the city he mentioned. She had been there before. The largest of China's mega-cities, it had a population of over thirty million. It was a heavily-industrialized, smog-choked and filthy area, teeming with desperately poor people. It was her least favorite place in all of China. Unlike most of the country, which was beautiful in many respects, Chongqing was a literal cesspool.

"That's too bad," Rachel said, already dreading the trip to the crime-infested city.

Chapter 54

Washington, D.C.

"The senator will see you now," the woman said, "this way please."

Gray Man stood and followed the senator's aide down the hall toward the back office. They were in the Russell Senate Office Building, the structure reserved for the most influential members of the Senate. The woman ushered him into the lushly appointed office, turned and left the room, closing the door behind her.

"Ah, Senator," Gray Man said to the man behind the desk. "Thank you for seeing me."

The senator, a thin man in his seventies with a large, hooked nose, didn't get up to greet his guest. His face was set in a stony expression.

"You'll have to make this short," Senator Palmer replied tersely. "I only have a few minutes before my staff meeting."

Since he hadn't been offered a seat, Gray Man remained standing in front of the desk. He didn't smile at the senator, knowing it would be a useless gesture. Palmer had rebuffed all of his previous attempts to influence him, including his most recent, a cash payment of two million dollars.

"Of course, Senator. I'll be brief. I know your time is extremely valuable."

"We've had these discussions before. I've said no. I'm not sure what I can add today."

Gray Man adjusted his silk tie, a nervous habit on his part. "I'm willing to increase my offer. Three million."

"The answer is *still* no."

"I need your vote, Senator, regarding the mining deal we've discussed."

Palmer's dark eyes flashed anger, like lightning on a black sky. "I know what you need, you son-of-a-bitch." He jabbed his index finger toward the other man. "The answer is no!"

Gray Man hoped it wouldn't come to this, but saw no option. He had to lay his cards on the table. "Senator, I'd like you to reconsider. I had a similar situation come up recently. A man of considerable influence who also refused my generous offer."

Palmer glared at Gray Man. Then he checked his watch. "You're out of time."

"No, Senator, you have it wrong. It's you who's out of time. I've tried to be reasonable. I've tried being patient. But my patience has run out."

"What the *hell* do you mean by that? Are you threatening me?"

Gray Man leaned forward and placed his hands flat on the desk. "Senator, I'm sure you'll remember Congressman Rodriguez."

Palmer stared icily at him. "Of course. He was a good man. A well-respected congressman. We were all saddened by the tragic accident."

"It was no accident."

A perplexed look settled on the senator's face. "What do you mean?"

"Just what I said. The gas explosion that blew up his home in San Francisco was no accident. It was a well-planned assassination."

Palmer frowned. "That's preposterous. And anyway, how could you possibly know something like that?"

"Because I ordered the hit, Senator."

Palmer gasped and his mouth stayed open. He tried to speak, but no words came out.

"The congressman refused my generous offer. Just like you've refused my generous offer, Senator."

Gray Man took his hands off the desk and stood ramrod-straight, waiting for the other man to process the information.

After a long moment, Palmer's shoulders slumped. He pointed to one of the wingback chairs fronting his desk. "Please have a seat. Let's talk about this. How much was that last offer you made?"

Gray Man suppressed a smile as he sat down.

Chapter 55

Chongqing, China

J.T. Ryan, with Rachel West close behind, pushed past the throng of raggedly-dressed people that milled by the Yangtze River.

As they made their way to the nearby dock area, Ryan realized that the CIA operative had been accurate in her assessment of Chongqing. After their train trip from Shanghai, they'd walked through scores of squalid tenements, and had almost been robbed twice.

Reaching the dilapidated dock moments later, he scanned the area for a water taxi. Spotting one, he flagged it down and turned to Rachel who instructed the driver in Mandarin on their destination.

The man, who was wearing a torn, dirty T-shirt and frayed cut-off jeans, nodded and waited for them to climb into the rickety, wooden motor boat. Then he turned the throttle and the small engine coughed a few times before it rumbled to life. The small boat surged through the filthy, dark-gray water, pushing past the flotsam and raw sewage. The air stank of garbage, motor fuel, and excrement, and Ryan covered his nose with a hand to filter the smell.

"I told you this place was a hell hole," Rachel said.

Ryan nodded and continued scanning the scene as the motor boat sped east along the winding Yangtze. He noticed men fishing on the river banks, while women washed clothes. Young children frolicked on the soot-covered banks, their hands and faces covered with mud. All of the people seemed oblivious to the filth and pollution that choked the river.

The Yangtze widened and they came to a heavily-industrialized area bordering the waterway. They passed one, and then several, massive factories, their tall smokestacks spewing columns of black smoke. The sound coming from the buildings was deafening. The noise, Ryan guessed, was created by metal cutting, drilling, and stamping for large manufactured items like home appliances, cars, and trucks. There was no doubt that the filth and flotsam that choked the river was a by-product of these factories.

As the boat made its way past the seemingly endless row of industrial buildings, Ryan realized why China was known as the world's factory.

After another five miles the factories became less frequent, replaced by warehouses. The driver slowed the water taxi and steered it to a nearby dock and stopped.

Rachel pointed downriver as she spoke in Chinese to the driver. Although Ryan didn't speak the language, he understood enough of it to know she was telling the man they weren't there yet.

The motor boat driver shook his head forcefully. "Bu shi. Dui bu qi, " the man said. *No. I am sorry.*

Rachel turned toward Ryan. "He won't go any further. I'm guessing he doesn't want to get involved. Guowang is a pretty infamous criminal in these parts. We'll have to walk the rest of the way."

She reached into her jeans pocket, took out Chinese Yuans and handed it to the water taxi driver.

"Xiexie," the man said.

"Bu ke xie," Rachel replied as she climbed out of the rickety boat, followed by the PI.

The motor boat sped away as they strode down the dock toward a two-lane road that bordered the river.

Rachel scanned the street numbers on the buildings and pointed. "It's that way. Probably about a mile."

He nodded and they walked along the road by the water's edge, passing a long string of warehouses. The buildings thinned out and eventually they came to a warehouse complex ringed by a tall, chain-link fence which was topped with razor-wire.

"That must be it," Ryan said.

"It is," she replied, as she read the street number.

They were about a block away from the ominous-looking buildings. Ryan could see at least four armed men inside the chain-link fence, all toting AK-47 assault rifles.

"Let's lock and load before we go in," he said, taking out his H&K .45 caliber pistol and racking the slide. He slid the gun back in his waistband and covered it with his windbreaker. Rachel racked the slide on her Glock and put it back in her jacket pocket.

"I'll do the talking," she said.

"Be my guest," he replied with a grin. "My Mandarin is a little rusty."

"From what I can tell, it sucks," she said, no humor in her voice.

They strode toward the warehouse and when they reached the gate they stopped and waited.

A tall Asian man with a buzz-cut and an AK approached the entrance on the other side of the fence. "What do you want?" he said in Chinese.

"We're here to see Guowang," Rachel said in the same language. "We're friends of Shao Shan. My name is West."

The Asian man spoke into a walkie-talkie.

After a minute he unlocked the gate and let them inside the compound, which Ryan now realized housed three large buildings. Forklifts shuttled between the structures, moving loaded boxes stacked on pallets. He noticed the boxes were labeled with familiar names and logos: Ralph Lauren, Louis Vuitton, Sony, Canon, and many others. He was sure the items inside were counterfeit goods. The PI now understood that Guowang's criminal enterprise was extensive.

The guard escorted them into one of the warehouses. Once inside they were approached by another two men, also carrying AK-47's.

"No one sees Guowang without being searched first," one of the guards said. "If you are armed, we will take your weapons until you leave."

This is not going well, thought Ryan.

He was about to object when Rachel placed a hand on his shoulder and said under her breath, "We have no choice."

He shrugged and the guards frisked both of them, found their pistols and pocketed them. Luckily they missed the knife Ryan had taped to the small of his back.

After they were frisked they were led down a long corridor and into a large room, a part of the warehouse that had been converted into a living area. Leather couches were in the center of the space. Lounging on the sofas were three teenage Asian girls, who looked no older than thirteen or fourteen. The girls wore skimpy bikini tops and short-shorts. Garish make-up covered their young, doll-like faces. They were passing around a long pipe and from the scent in the room, Ryan figured they were smoking opium. Shao Shan had told them Guowang was involved with all types of criminal activity, including drug-running, racketeering, and prostitution. Obviously the teenage girls were underage whores.

Also in the room was a very large, powerfully-built Asian man sitting in a leather recliner, talking on a cell phone.

When Ryan and Rachel approached him, he put down his phone and clapped his hands loudly. The teenage girls immediately got off the couches and, after blowing kisses at the large man, hustled out of the room.

The Asian man stood. "I am Guowang. Shao Shan called and told me you would come to see me." He pointed to the couch. "Sit." The mobster spoke in a booming Chinese voice. And although Ryan could not speak much Mandarin, he could understand quite a bit of the language.

Guowang sat back down and the CIA operative and the PI sat across from him.

Ryan eyed the Chinese gang leader closely. He had a shaved head, hooded black eyes, and a crooked nose, as if it had been broken long ago. An angry, wide scar ran the whole length of his cheek down past his jaw line onto his neck, giving him a menacing look. He was extremely tall, probably close to seven feet, with broad, very muscular shoulders. For some reason that the PI couldn't figure out, the man was wearing a garish Hawaiian shirt, which seemed totally out of place in the middle of China.

Nearby Guowang stood the two guards who had brought them in, and Ryan noticed two other men in the room, all of them armed with AKs.

"I'm Rachel West," she said in Chinese, "and this is my associate Ryan."

Guowang nodded. "Yes. Shao told me about you. You are looking for information."

"That's right," she said. "We're trying to find a red-haired woman who lives in China. She runs an outfit called Veritas, which is engaged in criminal activity."

Guowang gave her a cold smile, which revealed stained and crooked teeth. "I am a simple businessman. I do not know any criminals."

"I'm sure you don't," Rachel said. "Let me rephrase. This woman I'm looking for runs a charity named the Veritas Foundation. They do relief work for poor and homeless people."

"Ah, in that case, I may be able to help you."

"You know her?"

"I may. Depending on how much you are willing to pay."

Rachel patted her jacket. "I brought money."

"Good. Chinese Yuans or U.S. dollars? I prefer American currency."

"I have dollars."

"Excellent."

"How much, Guowang?"

He gave her an icy grin, flashing his brown, crooked teeth again. "All of it."

"How do we know the information is good?"

His coal-black eyes burned with intensity. "I make it my business to know everything that happens in China. That is how I got my name, Guowang. It means King." He rubbed the wide scar on his face. "King of the Underworld."

Rachel nodded. "Okay." She removed a thick envelope from her jacket and handed it to the Chinese gang leader.

The man counted the cash and tucked it into his waistband. "The woman you are looking for deals in stolen military secrets. She sells to the highest bidder. The name she goes by is Amber. I do not know her last name."

"Amber doesn't sound like a Chinese name," Rachel replied.

"It is not. Although I have never met her, I know she is American."

"Does she live here in Chongqing?"

"This is a sewer," said Guowang. "No, she lives in Beijing."

"Can you tell me anything else about her?"

"No. She is very secretive."

Rachel nodded. "All right. In that case, I think our business is concluded. We'll be on our way."

Guowang showed his stained teeth again, the cold grin returning. "Actually, that is not true. Our business is not done. Not yet. You only paid me half of what the information was worth. I want the rest."

"That wasn't our deal," Rachel said forcefully.

The gang leader laughed. "I break deals every day. How do you think I got to be King?"

He chortled again and his four guards joined in the laughter.

Rachel shook her head. "I don't have any more money and Ryan doesn't either."

Guowang rubbed his scar. "I do not want more dollars. I want payment another way. You are a beautiful American woman. I have not had that in a long time." He leered. "Strip off your clothes, West. I want to inspect the merchandise before I taste it."

"Fuck you!" Rachel growled as she rose from the couch.

Guowang, a wicked grin on his face, stood also and reached out with his beefy hands. He grabbed and squeezed Rachel's breasts. "I like a woman with spirit."

She tried to pull away but she was no match for the giant brute.

Ryan saw red, enraged by the gangster's actions. He bolted off the couch and punched the man with a fierce right cross and followed it with a solid uppercut. Then he kicked him in the groin and the gang leader howled in pain.

Guowang, his nose and lips gushing blood, staggered back and dropped to the floor.

The PI sensed someone close behind him, spun around and saw a rifle stock flying toward his face. He felt a searing pain as the wooden stock hit him and then everything went black.

Chapter 56

Chongqing, China

J.T. Ryan woke up sometime later, his head pounding with pain.

He peered around the dim room, which looked like an empty metal shed. Sitting up on the concrete floor, he realized his hands were tied behind his back. Ignoring the ache in his head, he rose to his knees, then slowly stood.

Where the hell is Rachel? he thought suddenly.

He recalled what the gangster had tried to do to her and once again was blinded with rage. *I'll kill that bastard. So help me God.*

But first he had to escape this makeshift prison. He approached the metal door, turned around and twisted the knob. As he expected, it was locked. And he figured there was probably a deadbolt too.

With his back to the wall of the shed, he paced the room, his fingers searching for a ragged edge of metal, something for him to cut the bindings on his hands. After searching three of the walls he found it, a torn steel piece. For the next five minutes he rubbed the rope against the jagged metal until it cut through the hemp. Luckily he only suffered minor cuts to his wrists.

With his hands now free, he went back to the door and inspected it. Like the walls of the shed, it was made of heavy-gauge steel. Without power tools or explosives he'd never be able to break it down.

How the hell am I going to escape? After sorting through his options, he settled on one. Reaching behind his back, he untucked his shirt and located the knife he'd taped to his skin. He peeled off the dagger and slipped it in a pocket.

Going to the center of the room, he lay on the floor and put his hands behind his back, as if they were still bound. Then he started moaning loudly and yelling for help.

"Bangbang wo! Bangbang wo!" he screamed in Chinese. *Help me! Help me!*

He kept this up for the next five minutes, yelling at the top of his lungs. Eventually he heard locks being turned and the door opened. The buzz-cut guard stood there, cradling his assault rifle.

"I'm sick!" Ryan said in Chinese with a loud groan. "I'm dying!"

"Shut up!" the guard groused.

"I'm dying! Help me!"

The guard advanced into the shed looking angry. "Shut up, you filthy American scum or I'll beat you to death myself! I am tired of your yelling."

Ryan kept it up, groaning loudly as he lay on the floor, watching closely as the other man approached. When he got close enough, Ryan kicked him with his booted foot, tripping the guard. As the man stumbled, he kicked him again, this time in the kidney and the man howled in pain, his AK clattering to the ground.

Instantly pulling the knife from his pocket, the PI shoved the blade into the man's side and then his gut and the guard fell, sprawling face up on the floor. The PI was about to stab him a third time when the man's eyes rolled white and his body went still.

Putting the knife back in his pocket, Ryan picked up the rifle and carefully approached the open door of the shed. He peered outside and saw several forklifts moving around outside, shuttling crates among the buildings. Further away he noticed semis being loaded. It was nighttime and the area inside the compound was illuminated by flood lights. Although the scene was fairly well-lit, there were some dead-spots that were in shadow, which would help conceal his movements.

The activity outside had masked the commotion inside the shed and no one seemed to have noticed. He scanned the area and saw several more storage sheds grouped nearby.

Could Rachel be in one of those? He desperately hoped so. Knowing the other sheds were probably locked, he went back to the dead guard and searched his pockets. Finding a loop of keys, he grabbed it and after slinging the rifle on his shoulder, gazed out of the shed again.

He'd have to be careful and time his moves to when the forklifts were busy and turned away from him. It would be slow going but he had no choice. There were way too many guards in the compound for him to take on all at once.

Stepping outside, he hid behind the metal shed and waited for the next few minutes. Seeing no one close by, he sprinted to the next structure. Quickly unlocking the large padlock, he pulled out his knife and slipped inside. The dim room was full of boxes, but no one was inside. After peering out the door again, he waited several more minutes until he raced over to the third shed and searched it. That one was empty as well, as was the next one. There was only one left he hadn't searched.

He waited anxiously for the next five minutes, saw a break in the activity, and sprinted to the last shed. Quickly unlocking it, he slipped inside and closed the door behind him.

Peering into the dim room, he saw boxes stacked to the ceiling. But off to one side was a body lying on the floor. *Was it Rachel?* It was so dark it was hard to tell. He crept over slowly, the knife in his hand.

Bending over, he recognized her by her long blonde hair – she wasn't moving and he noticed blood seeping from her lips. With a sudden dread he thought, *Is she dead?*

Kneeling by her side, he felt for a pulse on her neck. *She's alive, thank God! Just unconscious.* Putting away the knife, he patted her face softly, trying to revive her.

After a minute of this she woke with a start, pushing him roughly away with her hands.

"Bu shi! Bu shi! Bu shi!" she yelled repeatedly in Chinese. *No! No! No!*

Closing her fists she punched him.

"It's me, Rachel," he said, keeping his voice low as he blocked her blows. "It's Ryan."

Her eyes focused and seemed to recognize him because she stopped punching. "J.T. It's you."

"Yeah. Are you okay?"

She felt her face gingerly with a hand, dabbed away the blood trickling from her lip. "I'm bruised, but I'm all right."

He noticed both of her eyes were swollen and turning black-and-blue. Part of her clothing was torn. He became enraged again as he imagined what that animal Guowang could have done to her.

"Did he ...." he said.

"Rape me?"

He nodded.

"No. I fought the bastard off. Finally he gave up and went back to playing with his teenage whores. Then they put me in here."

Ryan grinned, relieved she'd been spared. "That's my girl."

She glared. "I'm nobody's girl."

"You know what I meant."

She stared icily at him, then the anger vanished. "I know what you meant. By the way, that was sweet of you back there. What you did."

"What's that, Rachel?"

"You fought for my honor. You punched Guowang and put him down. You should have seen him when he woke up. He went into a rage. I'm sure he would have killed you right then and there. Lucky for you he got an urgent business call."

Ryan caressed her face softly. "I'm just glad you're okay." He grinned. "But with those black eyes and bruised lip you don't look so pretty right now."

She returned the smile, but it must have hurt because she winced. "You're such a smartass, J.T."

"I've been called a lot worse." He turned serious. "Can you walk? We need to get the hell out of here."

"I think so. Help me up."

He put an arm around her waist and pulled her to her feet.

"I'm good," she said. "What's the situation outside?"

"Mostly forklifts moving pallets and trucks being loaded. It's nighttime, so I'm hoping the activity dies down soon so we can get the hell out of here."

Rachel nodded. "How many guards are there?"

"I counted at least fifteen armed men."

"That's a lot, J.T. I see you got an AK. Any other weapons?"

He pulled out his knife and showed it to her. The blade had dried blood on it and she said, "Looks like you've already put it to good use."

"Yeah. But we need to get another firearm."

"I agree. Got a plan?"

Ryan told her and she nodded.

He un-slung the rifle and handed her the weapon. Then, still holding the knife in his hand, he headed toward the door.

Chapter 57

Chongqing, China

Ryan opened the shed door partway and peered outside. He watched as the back doors of a semi were closed and moments later the truck started up and rumbled toward the main gate of the compound. Soon after a second semi headed in the same direction.

He looked on as the forklift drivers steered their rigs toward one of the warehouses. Using one of the bay doors they drove inside the building.

Within minutes, the lights inside the warehouse flicked off and Ryan observed a group of workers file out of the building and walk toward the gate. It appeared the day's work was finally done.

The only men remaining in the compound were the guards. A few of them had gone home, since he counted only twelve left, all carrying assault rifles. They took positions around the perimeter inside the fence, while some made the rounds of the buildings.

Ryan waited patiently until one of the guards who was near the shed stopped and lit up a cigarette. The PI sprinted behind him, pulled his head back with a hand, and slashed the blade across his throat. Blood spurted as the guard fought back momentarily. Then his body sagged and he slumped to the ground.

Ryan took the man's rifle and slung it over his shoulder. Grabbing the dead guard by the ankles, he dragged the body behind the shed.

Going around to the front, he motioned to Rachel and she exited the small building. Although the floodlights lit up most of the area, there were enough dim spots for them to use as cover.

She followed him as he made his way to the row of large fuel storage tanks that were located next to one of the warehouses. They crouched by the tanks and Rachel whispered, "How do you want to play this?"

"We need to shoot the tanks to make the fuel explode. That'll be a good distraction. We should be able to escape then. But we can't be too close when the tanks explode."

He peered to an area about a hundred feet away from their current position. That side of the compound bordered the Yangtze River. That area was also fenced, but no guards were nearby.

"I got an idea," he said in a low voice. "But you're not going to like it."

She frowned. "What is it?"

"Most of the men are guarding the front gate, which you would expect. What if we went that way?" He pointed toward the river.

"You can't be serious, Ryan. You want to swim away from here? Are you crazy? That water is so polluted I don't see how fish survive."

"I know. But there's only two of us. And twelve, check that, eleven of them. The odds aren't in our favor." In spite of the tension he felt, he grinned. "I know you'd hate to get your pretty hair dirty, but ...."

"Jerk. I should slap that grin off your face."

Impulsively he kissed her on the lips and surprisingly, she kissed him back.

When they pulled apart, her vivid blue eyes sparkled. "Let's do this, J.T."

"That's more like it. I'll take lead."

"Right behind you."

After checking to make sure there were no guards nearby, they crouched and slowly made their way from the warehouse, stopping by the fence. Ryan went to one knee, and started to aim his AK-47 toward the fuel tanks.

Rachel placed a hand on his arm. "I'll do it. I'm a better shot."

He nodded, knowing it was probably true. CIA operatives were some of the best trained agents in the world.

She kneeled, flicked her AK to full auto and carefully aimed the assault rifle. She fired off a ten-round burst, the shots finding the target instantly.

One of the tanks exploded, then a second and a third. In seconds the warehouse was engulfed in flames. The echoes from the massive explosion rang out throughout the area.

Ryan and Rachel turned toward the river and trained their rifles on the gate part of the fence. It was obvious this entrance was used to bring in cargo from boats.

They both fired, the rounds shattering the heavy-duty locks on the gate.

Slinging their rifles across their backs, they rushed forward, pushing aside the now-damaged gate and sprinted over the dock.

Without hesitating, they dove into the filthy, slimy river and swam away.

Chapter 58

Atlanta, Georgia

"What are you doing here?" Erin Welch said when she opened her apartment door.

Lisa Booth stood there looking excited. "I've got a lead!"

Erin shook her head slowly. "I don't like people showing up at my home. You know I have an office."

Lisa smiled brightly. "I know. Thought it'd be better if we didn't meet there."

Erin waved the young woman inside. "You're probably right. All right, come in. But this better be good."

"It is."

They went into the living room and sat across each other on the suede leather couches. "How'd you know where I lived?" Erin asked. "The Bureau keeps that confidential."

Lisa grinned. "I'm a good detective."

In spite of being aggravated by Lisa's unplanned visit, Erin found the girl's eagerness infectious. It reminded the FBI agent of herself, ten years earlier, when she'd first joined the Bureau. "I'll be the judge of that, Lisa. What's your new lead?"

"Is our deal still good?"

"What deal?"

"Where we share information, ma'am, to clear J.T.'s name."

"Persistent, aren't you?"

"I'm learning."

Erin studied the other woman as she picked up the tumbler of scotch from a side table and took a sip. "I guess you are. Yes, our deal is still on. We both want the same thing."

"Okay. I was able to break into the Veritas Foundation's email server."

Erin set the glass down. "I'm a law-enforcement officer. I suggest you don't tell me about any illegal acts you've committed."

Lisa's face turned a bright pink. "Oh. I guess I forgot about that ... am I in trouble?"

The FBI woman suppressed a smile and then shook her head. "I'll let it slide this time. Just tell me what you found out, not how you got the information."

"Yes, Ms. Welch. The president of Veritas, Steve Nichols, travels frequently to Washington, D.C. He meets with a man, but I couldn't learn his identity. Although most of the emails were encrypted or used code words, it was clear the meetings were about the foundation's business."

"That's interesting." Erin mulled that over a moment. A D.C. connection might shed some light on why Director Tucker had stopped her investigation.

"All right, Lisa. That's good work."

"Thank you, ma'am. What do you have for me?"

"What do you mean?"

"This is a two-way street. You promised to share information, remember?" Lisa gave her an expectant look.

Erin drank some of her scotch. "I've been trying to track down the redhead who lives in China. But so far I've had no luck. We have so little to go on that I haven't been able to narrow the search."

"That's too bad. I think she could be the key to solving this case."

Erin nodded. "Have you heard from J.T? And don't lie to me."

"No. I haven't. Last time you and I talked, you told me he'd almost been arrested several times. Has he been spotted since?"

The FBI Assistant Director shook her head. "He's completely dropped off the radar. He's vanished without a trace."

"Do you think he's ...."

"Dead? I don't know, Lisa. I just don't know."

Chapter 59

Washington, D.C.

Gray Man took off his suit jacket, loosened his silk tie, and undid the top button of his dress shirt. Then he opened his office refrigerator and took out the bottle of Dom Perignon he'd purchased a day earlier in preparation for today's meeting.

After uncorking the bottle of champagne, he placed it in a bucket of ice and pulled out two glass flutes from a cabinet.

He checked his watch anxiously, knowing Amber's jet had landed at Dulles an hour earlier and she would be arriving momentarily.

He was giddy with nervous excitement and had been all day, so much so that he'd had a problem focusing on his work. In fact, ever since Amber had called him 'dear' on the phone a week earlier and implied the prospect of an intimate relationship, he'd felt like a teenager again, eager for his first taste of sex.

Just then there was a knock at his office door and his assistant showed Amber Holt into the room. His assistant left and closed the door behind him as Amber swept into the room, her long auburn hair cascading past her shoulders. She was wearing a royal blue dress and royal blue heels and was carrying a blue leather satchel. To Gray Man the good-looking redhead resembled Aphrodite herself, and he stood there transfixed at the sight of her, motionless and actually speechless as he gazed at the vision of beauty, soon to be all his.

Seemingly oblivious to his presence, she settled on one of the sofas in the office and slipped off her high heels.

"Damn, that was a long trip," she muttered, then looked up and seeing him said, "Get me some wine, will you?"

"Amber, it's great to see you."

She stared at him, looking a bit confused. "Yes, of course. Good to see you too." She snapped her fingers. "About that wine."

"I have something special for you. Dom Perignon."

She nodded. "Much better than the swill you usually give me."

Gray Man, taken aback by her attitude, turned and filled two of the flutes with champagne and after handing one to her, sat across from her.

"Tell me," she said, after drinking some of the wine.

"Tell you what, Amber?"

"The operation. What else do you think I meant? Where are we on the operation."

"Oh, that."

She eyed him over the rim of the glass. "You're acting odd today, Gray Man."

"I ... when we talked last ... you seemed so different ... you implied .... " He gulped down the champagne. "You know ... you and I."

Amber appeared puzzled then suddenly must have remembered what he was referring to because she said, "Of course. How silly of me."

She rose, strode over, and sat right next to him. Fixing her gaze on him, she placed her hand on his thigh as she pulled his tie down a bit with her other hand. A surge of sexual excitement coursed through him.

"You know I want that too," she whispered seductively. She ran a palm through his hair as her other hand inched closer to his hardness. "I want it very badly," she purred. "But we need to wait ...."

"Wait? Wait for what?"

"Until the operation is complete, dear. I don't want our business to interfere with our personal life … you *do* see that, don't you?"

Gray Man was breathing heavy now and he desperately wanted to embrace the woman and tear off her clothes. But there was an iciness in her eyes that betrayed her sweet words, stopping him cold.

She cupped the bulge in his pants with her hand and he gasped.

"After our project is done," she purred, "I promise you, I'm all yours."

"You're right," he replied. "We need to finish the operation." He wasn't sure if she was being honest with him or simply teasing him, but at that moment he didn't care. All he wanted was to please her and do her bidding.

She smiled. "That's the spirit."

Rising from the couch, she refilled her glass with more champagne and sat down across from him. "Now," she said, matter-of-factly, "Where are we on the operation?"

Jarred by her sudden change in tone and attitude, Gray Man took a moment to regroup his thoughts.

After a minute he said, "I took care of several problems. The mine company president in Las Vegas and the congressman in San Francisco."

Amber gave him a cold grin. "Excellent. I knew you could do it." She downed her glass of champagne in one gulp. "And the senator?"

"I've dealt with him also. It took more money than I initially anticipated, but he's come around to our way of thinking."

She tucked her long legs underneath her on the sofa and in the process, the slit skirt of her dress opened wider, giving him a glimpse of her royal blue panties. While locking her eyes with his, she rearranged the dress so it covered her upper thighs fully.

"You're so efficient," she whispered, her voice dripping with honey. "At the rate you're solving our problems, I'm sure our operation will be complete in no time."

His heart began thudding again.

"I was thinking," Amber said. "After we're all done with this, we should go someplace warm. Someplace in the Caribbean. Just the two of us ... how does that sound, dear?"

Chapter 60

Beijing, China

The J.W. Marriott was situated in the Xiching district of the city, its central location facilitating access to the rest of the area. The hotel was on Xuanwai Street, within walking distance of Tiananmen Square and the Forbidden City.

Rachel West had stayed at the Marriott on several previous visits, its convenient location the reason she'd picked it again now.

Rachel was in the marble-walled bathroom of the luxury hotel suite, toweling herself off after taking several very long, very hot showers. It was the first time in days she'd felt clean after their swim in the filthy waters of the Yangtze River.

They'd been able to evade Guowang's men, catch a train to Beijing, and after accessing one of her CIA covert bank accounts, checked into the hotel.

After combing her damp hair, she checked her appearance in the bathroom mirror. The areas under both her eyes were still black-and-blue, but her swollen lip was mostly healed. She had bruise marks on her neck, hip, and legs, and those areas were still sore to the touch. Not too bad, she thought, considering the beating she'd taken fighting off the Chinese gangster. She'd suffered worse on other assignments.

Her only regret was that she hadn't killed Guowang, although the explosions she and Ryan had set off in the man's compound were undoubtedly very costly to him.

Slipping on a terry-cloth robe, she stepped out of the bathroom and found J.T. Ryan sitting on a wingback chair next to the king-size bed.

He glanced at her and grinned. "Thought you were going to drown in there. I was about to break down the door and rescue you."

"You've rescued me enough this week." She pointed to the bathroom. "It's your turn. You need to wash the stink off."

Ryan gave her a casual salute, stood up, stripped off his dirty clothes, and headed to the bathroom. She heard the shower running, and after mixing herself a vodka-and-tonic in the kitchen, she picked up her cell phone and tapped in a Beijing number. It was one of her Central Intelligence contacts in the city. He was an agent she'd known for several years and hoped she could trust.

After three rings the call was picked up.

"It's Rachel," she said, "I need your help."

"Good to hear from you. It's been awhile."

"It has, Thomas. Listen, I'm doing some off-the-books work here in Beijing."

"I understand. I'm guessing the 6th floor doesn't know about this," the man said, referring to the floor of the CIA headquarters building in Langley where the Agency's top executives were located.

"You're right about that. In fact my boss doesn't even know."

He let out a low whistle. "You're keeping Miller in the dark? You're skating on thin ice."

"I know. But I need your help. It's important, Thomas."

The man didn't reply for a long moment, then sighed. "All right. I hope this doesn't get me fired. What do you need?"

"I'm looking for an American woman living in Beijing. Very secretive, deals in military espionage. Her first name is Amber – I don't have her last name."

"Any other details you have on her?"

"She runs a shady organization called the Veritas Foundation." Then she filled him in on the sparse info she knew about the woman.

"Okay, Rachel. I'm assuming you've already tried tracking her down on Nexus and the Internet."

"Yeah, I have. I found nothing. I didn't use the Central Intelligence database – it could be traced back to me too easily. Don't use it either. Check with your CIs in the city."

"All right," he said. "This may take a few days."

"I figured. Thanks, Thomas."

"Next time I see you back at Langley, you owe me a steak dinner at the Capital Grille."

"You got it."

She hung up and rested the phone on the suite's marble-top dining table. Picking up her vodka-and-tonic, she drained the glass, then went to the kitchen and mixed herself another. She drank it down, the alcohol dulling the pain from her bruises.

Minutes later Ryan stepped out of the bathroom wearing a white terry-cloth robe, his hair still wet from his shower.

He approached her and said, "It's only noon. Kind of early to be drinking, isn't it?"

She grinned. "I'm in pain. It's for medicinal purposes only."

"I bet."

"I'll get you one, J.T."

"No thanks, I'm good."

She walked to the kitchen, mixed two vodka-and-tonics and returned, handing him a tumbler.

"I insist," she said, clinking her glass to his. She took a sip and watched the handsome man as he drank down part of his vodka.

She moved closer to him. "That's better. You smell nice and clean now. Yummy even." She drained her glass. "Drink up, J.T."

"Are you trying to get me drunk?"

"Drunk? No, not drunk." She gave him a sly grin. "I'm just trying to even the odds. You're 6'4" and built like a weightlifter."

Ryan finished his drink. "So?"

"When we make love, it's always a wrestling match. And you always end up on top. This time I want to be on top."

"It's not a contest," he said, smiling.

She reached out with a hand, grabbed the lapel of his robe and pulled him close so they were pressed against each other. "But it is."

She kissed him hard on the lips, her tongue greedily exploring his mouth and he kissed her back, embracing her tightly with his powerful arms.

When they separated moments later they were both breathing heavy and she could tell he wanted her as much as she wanted him. Taking him by the hand, she led him to the king-size bed in the bedroom.

Then she pulled off the bedcovers, and while holding his gaze, very slowly removed her robe, letting it drop to the floor. Reaching out, she unfastened the sash of his robe and slipped the garment off his shoulders.

Gazing at his groin, she said, "Looks like you're ready."

"Oh yeah. I'm more than ready."

"Get in bed," she said with a chuckle. "Let the contest begin."

Chapter 61

Beijing, China

Amber Holt was in the study of her palatial estate when there was a tap at the door and a petite Asian woman dressed in an ornate ankle-length kimono dress stepped inside.

The young Asian woman bowed and said in Mandarin, "Sorry to bother you, but something important has come up."

Amber put down her iPad. "What is it, Liling?"

"The security people just told me that questions are being asked about you."

"Someone is looking for me?"

"That is correct, Miss Amber."

"Who's asking?"

Liling bowed again. "We do not know who they are. But they are from here, in Beijing."

Alarmed by this, Amber rose from the leather recliner and began pacing the large study. "How's this possible," she muttered to herself. "Not many people know I exist."

"There is more, Miss Amber."

"More?" she demanded, glaring at the young woman.

Liling lowered her gaze and her cheeks flushed. She was a good assistant, but a person who didn't like confrontation. Amber knew she was a hard taskmaster and had already gone through a very long list of assistants. She didn't relish the prospect of having to train a new one.

"Yes, Miss Amber, there is more. The security people suspect the questions are being asked by someone associated with the American CIA."

Amber almost cursed at the young woman, but held herself back. It would be counterproductive, only making Liling more frightened. Instead she gritted her teeth as she processed the bad news. "Anything else?"

"Yes, ma'am. Some of the questions are also about the Veritas Foundation."

Amber's heart began to pound and her throat went dry. *How in the hell? What's going on?*

Rubbing her temple with a hand, she began pacing the study again for several minutes. Finally she stopped and glared at Liling. "Leave. I have to make a call."

The young Asian woman bowed, turned, and left the room, closing the door behind her.

The redhead went to the desk in the study and picked up the handset of the console phone. After activating the encryption setting, she tapped in a number.

Her call was routed through the Chinese Defense Ministry's labyrinth of offices until she reached Captain Zhou.

"Captain," she said, "it's important that I meet with General Chang as soon as possible."

"The general is very busy. His schedule is quite full."

"It's urgent." She lowered her voice and sweetened her tone. "I would consider it a personal favor if you could arrange it."

"In that case, Amber, I will make it happen."

"You're so kind," she said, knowing she'd have pay him in cash or in other ways. In either case it wouldn't be an imposition, since she rather fancied the dashing officer. "Now tell me where and when."

"The general is conducting another dedication service tomorrow, similar to the one you attended in Xian."

"Yes, of course, I remember. Where is this one?"

Captain Zhou gave her the details and she hung up. Then she pressed the intercom and said, "Liling, inform my pilot. I'll need the helicopter fueled and ready to go tomorrow morning. I want to leave at seven a.m."

"Yes, Miss Amber."

Chapter 62

Great Wall of China
Ming Section
Badaling, China

Amber Holt stood inside the stone watchtower and from her vantage point had a panoramic view of the Great Wall, as its tall ramparts wound their way over the mountainous terrain northwest of Beijing.

She watched as General Chang addressed a large group of reporters nearby, dedicating this newly renovated section of the Wall. Originated in 550 AD by the Qi Dynasty, the Great Wall ran a total of 3,000 miles, although over time half of it had crumbled into ruins. Its deterioration had been accelerated, Amber knew, by the invading Mongols in the 13th century and by the Manchu in the 17th.

But the Wall had become such a popular tourist attraction that the Chinese government was always restoring parts of it, like the Ming Section she was at now, and opening it up to visitors.

General Chang's amplified voice echoed over the valley below and as he droned on, she pulled her long hair into a ponytail to keep it from blowing around. It was a blustery day, and since they were at one of the highest points along the Wall, gusts of wind buffeted the area.

Finally Chang ceased talking, the reporters clapped dutifully, and after packing up their TV cameras and lights, they began to walk down the steps toward the exit below.

After the newsmen had all left, Captain Zhou motioned to her. She stepped out of the watchtower and carefully made her way down the irregular stone steps toward the general, using the metal handrail to steady herself from the gusts of wind. Luckily she had anticipated walking on the uneven steps and instead of her usual heels had worn flats today.

Chang stood close to one of the rampart walls and was attempting to light a cigarette, but the breeze was so strong that he gave up and threw the unlit cig to the ground.

"General," she said, plastering on a fake smile. "It's so good to see you."

He scowled, obviously in no mood for small talk. "Let's make this quick. I have two more of these infernal events to do today."

"Of course, General."

A blast of wind buffeted them and she smiled inwardly with relief. One positive side effect of the gusts was that they blew away Chang's offensive and ever-present body odor.

"General, I heard some alarming news yesterday and I need your help."

His eyebrows shot up. "Alarming? That sounds ominous."

"Yes. People, possibly American government agents, are asking questions about me and my foundation."

"How is that possible? You are a ghost. Only a handful of people know you exist. It is one of the reasons I like dealing with you."

"That's true, General. I am a ghost – but somehow I've been tracked down. That's why I need your help."

Chang nodded. "We are very close to completing our project. I have notified the Politburo of our progress and they are excited. More than excited. With this, China is on the threshold of crippling the American military and their country's energy infrastructure for decades. China will become the dominant superpower in the world. This will make my career. Everything I have ever dreamed of ... yes, of course I will help you. Anything you need. Just inform Captain Zhou. He will arrange it."

Chapter 63

Beijing, China

"You wore me out," Ryan said, gazing at her over the rim of his glass of orange juice.

"Is that a complaint?" Rachel replied, as she sat across from him at the restaurant of the Marriott Hotel. They were finishing breakfast.

He drained his glass. "Hell, no. Just making an observation."

Rachel smiled, her vivid blue eyes flashing. "Told you it was a contest. You didn't believe me. Do you now?"

Ryan studied the stunning-looking woman, who today was dressed in her usual polo shirt, black jeans, and a windbreaker. Her blonde hair was not pulled back – instead her long tresses flowed past her shoulders.

"Oh, yeah. I believe you now."

Her grin widened. "And this time I won."

Ryan returned the smile. "You won't next time."

"We'll see about that," she said. Then she spoke in Chinese. "Wo ai ni, J.T. Ryan."

He grinned. "I looked that up. I know what it means now."

She reached over and placed her palm on his hand. "Does that scare you?"

"I'm still here."

She rubbed his hand. "Yes, you are."

Just then her phone rang and she pulled it out of a pocket. "Hello," she said.

The CIA operative listened for the next several minutes, answering the caller cryptically, without mentioning their name. When she hung up the call, she said, "That was Thomas, my Agency contact here in Beijing. He was able to track down the secretive redhead. Her full name is Amber Holt and she lives in an estate outside the city."

"That's good news. Get an address?"

"Yeah." She checked her watch. "We should get going. It's not too far, but traffic is hell this time of day – it'll take us at least an hour to get there."

***

As Rachel had thought, traffic was a mess, but not unusual considering twenty-two million residents lived in the Beijing metro area.

Rachel, who was familiar with the city, was behind the wheel, while Ryan rode shotgun in their rented Chery sedan, a Chinese auto brand. They drove west on the Fuxing Men highway past the sprawling Yuyuantan Park until they reached an exclusive residential area consisting of mansions sitting on large properties of at least five acres.

When they reached the right address, they slowed and drove past the ornate gated entrance and parked a block away.

"How do you want to do this?" Rachel said, turning toward him.

Ryan gazed toward the seven-foot-high walls that encircled the property. "I say we lock-and-load, climb over the wall, kick ass and take names."

She gave him an amused look. "Not very subtle."

"I'm not a subtle kind of guy."

The CIA woman eyed the estate and after a few moments said, "I've got a better idea. I say we knock on the door and ask to see her. Thomas told me Holt is still a U.S. citizen. Besides my CIA ID, I also have one that identifies me as a State Department employee. I'll show her that one. She may want to at least appear like she's willing to cooperate with us."

"I doubt that will work, Rachel. She'll never go for it. We're strangers and she's super-secretive. I say we go in hard and fast, guns drawn."

She shook her head. "Let's try my way first. If that doesn't work, we'll go to Plan B and force our way in."

"You're a stubborn woman, Rachel West. All right, we'll try it your way first."

They took out their pistols, racked the slides, and after re-holstering them under their jackets, climbed out of the car. After approaching the impressive, Oriental-design gated entrance, they pressed the buzzer on the wall panel. Through the wrought-iron gate they could see into the large, lushly landscaped property.

One of the wall-mounted security cameras pointed toward them. From the intercom, a woman's voice asked in Chinese, "May I help you?"

Rachel held up her ID badge. "I'm Rachel West from the U.S. State Department. I'd like to speak with Amber Holt. We're conducting a survey of Americans living in China."

After a long moment there was a response. "Miss Holt will see you. Wait there. I will come meet you at the gate."

Rachel put away her ID and gave Ryan a suppressed smile. "Told you it would work."

He shook his head slowly and sighed.

"Kills you when I'm right, doesn't it," she said, her smile widening.

Several minutes later they watched as a golf cart drove towards them from inside the property. It stopped ten feet from the entrance and the massive wrought-iron gates automatically creaked open.

A young Asian woman dressed in a blue ankle-length kimono climbed out of the golf cart, and after giving them a bow, said, "I am Liling. I will take you to see Miss Holt. Please get on."

After the three people got on the large golf cart, the uniformed and armed driver turned around and drove through the extremely large and beautifully landscaped property. Ryan noticed four uniformed men patrolling the grounds, all of them wearing sidearms. Not bad odds if he and Rachel had to shoot their way out.

Eventually they reached a large circular driveway which fronted a massive, three-story mansion. Although the architecture was of a historic Chinese design with ornate columns and arches, it was clear the house had been built recently. Ryan saw an Olympic-size pool to the left of the mansion and on the right was a helicopter parked on a heli-pad.

The woman in the kimono escorted them inside and after ushering them into a room with floor-to-ceiling bookcases on several walls, gave them a small bow. "Please wait here," she said. "Miss Holt will join you momentarily."

She left the library and as they waited Ryan approached an antique roll-up desk at the side of the room. He quickly scanned through the stacks of documents on top of the desk.

A few minutes later a striking redhead entered the room, wearing a stylish burgundy dress which complemented her long auburn hair.

"I am Amber Holt," the woman said in a regal tone. "Since you are American I assume you'd rather speak in English."

"Yes, we would prefer that," Rachel replied. "As I told your assistant, I'm Rachel West and I'm from the State Department. This is my associate."

"Please have a seat," Amber said, waving them to the couches nearby. After they were seated she turned her gaze on Rachel. "You're doing a survey?"

"Yes. We're surveying U.S. citizens who have lived in China for some time."

Ryan studied the attractive redhead, still amazed she had agreed to meet with them. Although the woman appeared gracious on the surface, he sensed an underlying wariness under the pleasant veneer. He kept his hand close to his gun, ready to pull it if things went sour.

"Before we begin," Amber said, "I'll have some refreshments brought in." She pressed an intercom on a side table. "Liling, bring us tea and wine." Then she smiled at them, but to the PI it seemed forced.

After glancing at her watch, Amber said pleasantly, "What part of the States are you from?"

That seemed an odd question to Ryan. She was obviously a secretive and very wealthy woman. *Why would she care? Was the woman stalling for time?*

"I've lived all over," Rachel replied. "But in my current job I live in D.C. While we wait for the tea, I'll proceed since I know your time is valuable. Our survey is designed to get background information on the people associated with American charities. We understand you're involved with one such organization. The Veritas Foundation."

Amber tensed, then appeared to force herself to relax. "What makes you say that?"

At that moment the woman in the kimono came back into the room, pushing a serving cart laden with an ornate tea service, several bottles of wine, and hand-cut glassware. After asking everyone what they would like, she began serving them.

When she was done, Amber said, "Thank you, Liling. Is the other item we talked about on schedule?"

Liling bowed. "Yes. Exactly on schedule."

"Very good. You may leave us now."

Amber's smile vanished, replaced by a menacing look. "You can drop the act now, Ms. West. What's this really about?"

Rachel glanced at Ryan, then back at the redhead. "Act?"

"You're CIA, aren't you?" Amber said, her tone harsh. "I was expecting you."

Ryan stood abruptly and pulled his pistol from underneath his jacket.

"It's too late for that," Amber stated, glaring at them.

Just then the PI heard loud rumbling noises coming from outside the home. Sprinting toward one of the windows, he peered out. His heart pounded as he watched three Chinese military trucks pull up to the front of the mansion.

He turned to Rachel. "We got set up. This is a trap!"

The CIA operative pulled her gun and raced to the window as Chinese soldiers armed with assault rifles poured out of the three trucks.

Amber placed her hands on her hips and cackled. "You have two options. Die or go to prison. I've heard Chinese prisons are hell holes, so option one may be better." She laughed again.

Ryan's mind raced as the soldiers took positions around the home, their guns trained forward.

"What now?" Rachel asked, her voice strained.

Making a split-second decision, he said, "Grab her and follow me!"

"What's the plan?"

"Just do it, Rachel! It's the only chance we've got."

The CIA agent nodded, grabbed Amber's arm roughly and pulled it behind her back. The redhead struggled and tried to get free, as Rachel pulled her arm up. "By God, I'll break it if you don't cooperate!" She pressed the muzzle of her gun to the woman's head.

Amber howled in pain, her eyes watered, and she stopped resisting. "Okay, okay," she whimpered.

"Follow me!" Ryan shouted as he raced out of the room, his gun leading the way. With Rachel and Amber trailing behind, they went down a long corridor past several other rooms.

He spotted a French door and sprinted toward it. Glancing out the window, he saw what he was looking for: the helicopter parked on the heli-pad. He turned to Rachel. "That's our escape route. Stay close behind and keep a gun to her head."

"Got it," Rachel said. "You know how to fly one of those?"

"Kind of."

"Kind of? That's not reassuring."

"Got a better plan, Rachel?"

"Hell, no."

"Okay, then. Keep Amber close to you and keep the gun to her head. The soldiers won't fire then."

Rachel nodded and put an arm around the woman's neck and pressed her pistol against her temple. Amber's eyes went wide and she showed no resistance.

Ryan turned the knob and stepped outside with Rachel and Amber right behind.

As they slowly walked toward the helicopter, he counted at least forty soldiers surrounding them, their rifles pointed in their direction. With his pulse racing, he knew that all it would take would be one itchy finger to stray and they would be dead instantly.

When they reached the chopper, he opened the door and waited as Rachel pushed Amber inside. The CIA agent then got in, followed by Ryan.

"Keep the gun on her," Ryan said, as he inspected the aircraft's controls. It was a Bell 206 commercial helicopter. He'd never flown one of these, had only piloted an Army Blackhawk in Afghanistan a few times, but that had been under the watchful eye of a full-time pilot giving him precise instructions the whole way.

Quickly studying the controls, he was relieved to find that the cyclic joystick, throttle, and anti-torque pedals were similar to the Blackhawk. He pressed the ignition button but nothing happened.

"Shit," he groused.

Rachel turned toward him. "What?"

"I forgot. I need a key."

"Damn, Ryan! Now you think of that?"

He glanced out the windows, saw that the Chinese soldiers had surrounded the chopper and were edging closer to the aircraft. With his heart pounding, he pulled out his Swiss Army knife and pried off the metal cover under the dash. Bending over, he searched furiously trying to find the ignition cables. After a long moment he located them, cut the wires, and re-spliced them.

Sitting back up on the cockpit seat, he pushed the ignition button again and this time he heard the familiar whine of the jet engines as they began to spool. The rotor blade on top of the helicopter spun slowly, and after he adjusted the controls, the blade began to spin at high speed.

The roar of the twin-turbines was deafening as he increased the throttle while pulling back on the cyclic joystick. The chopper lifted off and hovered wobbly ten feet off the ground as he desperately tried to remember how to fly the complex machine.

Suddenly he noticed movement out of the corner of his eye and saw Amber struggle away from Rachel. The redhead pulled the door lever and jumped out of the helicopter. After Amber crash-landed on the ground, she began screaming at the soldiers and pointing to the chopper.

"Go!" Rachel yelled. "Go! Go!"

Ryan pulled the cyclic joystick while pushing the throttle to full power and the craft spun around crazily, rotating 360 degrees several times as it lifted higher in the air.

He heard the roar of gunfire from below, the rounds ricocheting and cutting into the chopper's undercarriage. Pulling hard on the cyclic while pressing the anti-torque pedals, he fought for control, his stomach queasy from the wild spins.

Seconds later he finally gained control and the helicopter rose fast and straight.

Ryan swallowed hard as the gunfire continued, some of the rounds cracking the windshield while others ripped into the metal hull.

He desperately hoped none of the bullets would hit the rotor or penetrate the fuel tank. Having seen military choppers shot down in combat, Ryan said a silent prayer.

Chapter 64

Beijing, China

Amber Holt limped painfully into her mansion's study and carefully lowered herself onto the deeply-upholstered sofa. It had been two days since the CIA people had almost abducted her, but the throbbing in her left leg from the fall was still severe.

She cursed, not from the pain because she knew that would ease soon, but from knowing that her home, her safe haven, had been invaded. Despite her penchant for secrecy, American agents had somehow found her.

Amber was secure for now. A platoon of Chinese army soldiers were permanently   stationed outside her house, giving her 24/7 protection. That was reassuring. And she was thankful that General Chang had followed through on his promise. But she also found the blanket of security stifling. The ever-present guards made her feel like she was a prisoner in her own home.

She lifted her aching leg and rested it on the ottoman in front of her as she mulled over the situation. She needed to get away, at least for a few days. To rest, relax, and recharge. And she knew there was only one place she could do that now.

Amber pressed the intercom on the nearby table.

A moment later Liling entered the room. The young Asian woman, who today was wearing a black kimono, bowed slightly. "Yes, Miss Amber?"

"I want my jet fueled and ready to leave tomorrow morning."

"Of course. To what destination shall I tell the pilot?"

"Paradise," Amber said.

"I will inform him."

"And this time, Liling, I'm taking you with me."

Liling appeared surprised, then looked apprehensive. She bowed again. "As you wish."

Chapter 65

Tianjin, China

Rachel West peered past the drawn curtains of the motel room window. It was a quiet nighttime scene outside, with few people about. The cars in the parking lot were old, worn vehicles. Dented mopeds, motorcycles, and even a few rickshaws were also parked on the lot.

But no signs of Chinese military, which was now her chief concern.

Luckily their helicopter hadn't crashed or been shot down, although one of the rounds had nicked the fuel tank, and when they ran out of gas seventy miles later they had been forced to land in Tianjin, an industrialized city southeast of Beijing.

Rachel turned away from the window of the squalid second-story motel room and sat at the rickety wooden table. Although it was two a.m., she was too wired to sleep. J.T. Ryan was sleeping soundly on the nearby bed, his light snoring the only sound in the room.

She pulled out her Glock and once again began disassembling it and then putting it back together again. For some reason she found the repetitive action reassuring.

Just then her cell phone buzzed and she removed it from her pocket. Her heart sank when she read the screen. She had dreaded this call, but knew it would be just a matter of time.

"This is West," she said.

"What the *fuck* were you thinking?" Alex Miller said angrily.

"I can explain."

"Too late for that."

"But, sir —"

"Shut up and listen."

Miller had been her boss at Langley for years. He was a quiet, reserved man most of the time and she'd never heard him so angry before. "Yes, sir."

"I got a call from the 6th floor today. My boss, the Director of Central Intelligence, was contacted by the Chinese Defense Ministry. They filed a formal complaint. You were harassing a Chinese resident who must be very high up the food chain in China. You were not conducting a sanctioned operation, Rachel. Otherwise I would have known about it."

He paused, and the vehemence in his voice rose another notch when he said, "You told me you were on vacation. You lied to me!"

"But, sir —"

"I told you to shut up and listen. You lied to me, Rachel. I'm sure all this is tied to Ryan. A criminal. In fact, you were seen with a man who fits his description. It was Ryan, correct?"

"Yes."

"I expressly ordered you to stay away from him."

"That's right, Alex."

"You disobeyed a direct order!" he shouted, and she held the phone away from her ear.

"I'm sorry, sir."

"The question I have is, why? You've never done anything like that before."

"Ryan's not guilty, sir."

"Then, damn it, he should turn himself in and let Erin Welch at the FBI help him."

"Alex, Ryan thinks the Bureau has been compromised."

There was silence on the other end and Rachel continued. "There's another reason I helped him."

"And what's that?"

"Sir, I have personal feelings for Ryan."

"I should have guessed," Miller replied, his voice still seething with anger.

"What happens now?"

"The DCI told me to fire you for conspiring with a wanted felon. Luckily for you, I still have a lot of pull at the Agency and I managed to talk him out of that."

Rachel breathed a sigh of relief. "Thank you."

"Don't thank me yet, young lady. I'm docking you a month's pay and putting a written reprimand in your file. And I'm reassigning you to India. There's a case in Mumbai I want you to work. You're to leave China immediately. And one more thing. If you ever, and I mean ever, go off the reservation again, you are permanently gone from the CIA. Am I making myself clear, Rachel?"

"Yes, sir. Crystal clear." She paused a moment, then said, "What about Ryan?"

"He's on his own."

She gritted her teeth to control her emotions. "But –"

"I'm not going to repeat myself. Leave China now! Consider yourself lucky you still have a job!"

Then he hung up.

Chapter 66

Tianjin, China

Ryan and Rachel sat next to each other on the lumpy bed, their gaze fixed on the floor. She'd woken him a short while ago and filled him in on Miller's call.

"I'm sorry," she said for the third time, sadness in her voice.

He turned towards her and the bed coils creaked. "It's not your fault. You did everything you could to help me."

She stared at him, her eyes misting. "Maybe I should just quit."

"The CIA?"

"Yeah."

He placed a palm on her cheek. "It's who you are. You can't quit."

Rachel shrugged. "I could always become a PI like you."

Trying to lighten the moment, he said, "The pay's lousy compared to what you make and you wouldn't be able to stay at the Four Seasons."

She smiled, but it was a sad smile. Her eyes glistened and he knew she was fighting back tears. And although he hated to admit it, so was he.

"All right, I won't quit," she said quietly. "I love the Agency. I'd make a lousy PI anyway. I hate donuts and bad coffee."

"If you hate those things you would make a terrible PI. That's part of the code, you know."

He studied her beautiful features, her vivid blue eyes, glistening blonde hair, and sculpted face, marred only by the black eyes. "So what's next, Rachel?"

"India. My flight leaves in two hours."

He nodded.

"And you?"

"When we were in Amber's home," he said, "I was able to read a printed-out email from a Russian man. It was a discussion he and Amber were having about a business deal they were involved in a few years ago. From what I could tell, the Russian guy felt Amber had screwed him out of the deal."

"Did you find out who the guy was?"

He nodded. "I got his name and where he lived."

"Where is that?"

"St. Petersburg, Russia."

"What are you going to do now, J.T.?"

"I can't stay here. The Chinese military will find me eventually. I have no intention of spending the next forty years locked up in prison in China."

Rachel wiped a tear from her cheek. "I'm going to miss you, John Taylor Ryan."

He caressed her face gently. "And I you."

"Please hold me," she whispered, her voice cracking. "Just hold me."

He put his arms around her and held her tight.

Chapter 67

Atlanta, Georgia

Lisa Booth followed the man as he made his way down the Terminal South concourse of Hartsfield Airport.

She'd been tailing Steve Nichols since he'd left his home early that morning, hoping to learn more about the Veritas Foundation president. She'd been unsuccessful in her recent attempts to break into the foundation's email servers and had to resort to what she considered old-fashioned gumshoe tactics.

Nichols stopped suddenly and approached the Delta counter along the concourse. Lisa, who fifteen feet behind, followed him and stood off to one side of the airline desk, pretending to read the newspaper she's brought along. She listened as Nichols changed his flight from Oklahoma City to a ten a.m. departure to Washington, D.C.

As Nichols left the Delta counter and strode toward the gate area, Lisa stayed behind and thought through what she'd witnessed. The man had booked a flight to Oklahoma with no intention of going there and at the last minute changed his ticket to D.C. It was obvious he was covering his tracks, fully expecting someone to be monitoring his whereabouts.

Next time she'd have to be better prepared. She needed to follow him to D.C., shadow him there, and find out who he was meeting.

It was clear to her now that there was still a lot about the PI business she needed to learn.

Chapter 68

Washington, D.C.

Gray Man unlocked his office door and stepped inside the room, disappointed with the outcome of his morning meeting. After locking the door behind him, he went to his safe and stored the briefcase full of cash he'd been carrying.

Pulling out his cell phone, he tapped in a number.

When the call was answered, he said, "The person at the Energy Department isn't cooperating. Even though my offer was very generous."

"I see. How do you want me to handle it?"

"That's your area of expertise," Gray Man replied. "Just make it look like an accident."

"Understood. When do you want this done?"

"Immediately. We're on a tight schedule."

"I'll take care of it. My usual fee?"

Gray Man mulled this over, then said, "If you do it within 48 hours, I'll give you a 20% bonus."

"I like the sound of that. Consider it done."

Gray Man hung up and put the phone away. He checked his watch, realizing Steve Nichols's flight from Atlanta would be arriving soon. As he focused on his upcoming meeting, he forgot all about the troublesome official at the Department of Energy.

Chapter 69

Paradise
South China Sea

Its original name was T'ang Shu Island, but after Amber Holt bought it years ago she'd christened it Paradise. Although it was just a spit of land in the middle of the South China Sea, to her it was a sanctuary, the place she went to when she wanted to recharge. Besides herself, her pilot, and her assistant Liling, no one knew about this place. Not even General Chang.

On the twenty acre island there was a long runway for her Dessault Falcon 7X jet, a dock for ship deliveries, and six buildings. Five of the buildings were for services, storage, and to house the island's staff, while the main structure served as the residence.

The residence was an ultra-modern, three-story building constructed of steel, glass, and stone, its extensive windows offering 360 degree views of the surrounding ocean.

Amber was in her massive master bedroom suite now, which took up the entire third floor. She was sitting in a deeply-upholstered leather sofa, her left leg propped up on a leather ottoman.

As she sipped merlot, she gazed out the floor-to-ceiling windows at the panoramic view of the water, finally feeling relaxed. Her left leg had mostly healed, the pain and bruising almost gone.

Just then Liling entered the room carrying a large wine carafe. After lowering her head slightly, the young Asian woman refilled Amber's glass. "Would you like something to eat, Miss Amber?"

The redhead eyed Liling, who today was dressed in a green-and-gold, ankle-length kimono. "No. I'm not hungry."

Liling bowed. "In that case, I'll be in the other room if you need anything else." She turned to go.

"Please stay."

The young woman turned back to Amber, who waved her to the sofa across from her. "Please sit."

After she sat, Amber said, "How long have you worked for me?"

"Six months and five days."

Amber flashed an ironic grin. "You're counting the days – you make it sound like a prison sentence."

Liling's eyes went wide. "Oh, no, ma'am. I meant no disrespect."

"None taken. I know I can be a bitch to work for."

Liling lowered her gaze. "I would never say that."

"You're a sweet girl. I've had lot's of assistants, but you've been the best yet."

The young Asian woman raised her gaze. "That is very kind. Thank you."

The redhead drank more of her wine as she studied the Asian woman's delicate features, her doll-like face, milk-white skin, and striking raven hair which was pulled back in a bun.

"Do you know why I invited you to come with me on this trip, Liling?"

The other woman shook her head.

"I thought it was time for us to become better acquainted," Amber said.

"I do not understand."

Amber smiled. "I'm sure you don't. You're not very experienced, are you?"

Liling looked perplexed. "Experienced? In what way?"

The redhead placed her wine glass on the nearby table and said, "Have you ever had sex with a woman?"

Liling's face turned a bright pink.

"I thought not, Liling. But I had to ask." She eyed the other woman again, who had a terrified look on her face.

"Oh, I get it now," Amber said. "You've never been with a man, either."

Liling's face flushed into a dark shade of crimson.

"Don't worry," Amber said, "I'll be very gentle with you."

The young Asian woman lowered her gaze and stared at her hands, which were primly folded on her lap. "Miss Amber, please, no."

"Now, now. Don't be difficult. I know you want to keep your job and all the money you make. I always pay my assistants twice the going rate. And I expect to get a return on my investment."

Liling sat silently, shaking like a leaf, here eyes locked on the floor.

"Take off your dress, Liling."

"Miss Amber, please do not make me do this ...."

Amber drank more of her wine. "Take it off. Now."

The young woman rose slowly, and with her eyes still downcast, started removing her dress.

Amber smiled. "Welcome to Paradise, Liling. Welcome to Paradise."

Chapter 70

St. Petersburg, Russia

Using one of his fake IDs, Ryan had been successful in flying out of China. He'd taken a British Airways flight, which after two connections landed him in St. Petersburg's Pulkovo Airport. Luckily Ryan's command of the Russian language was better than his Chinese, which facilitated entry into the country.

Before they had parted ways, Rachel had accessed a covert database and had been able to track down the Russian man who was mentioned in Amber's email. His name was Dimitry Ivanovich, a retired businessman who had connections with Russian government officials.

Once Ryan had exited the customs area of Pulkovo Airport, he'd taken a cab and was being driven to Ivanovich's home, which was located not far from the city center.

It was a gray, drizzly day with temps in the mid-forties. Ryan zipped up his jacket, since the heater in the worn taxi was not functioning. The cab drove east on the Dvortsovaya Nab Avenue which bordered the Neva River. Along the way they passed the imposing gold, green, and white facade of the city's famed Hermitage Museum and the Winter Palace. Then they turned south and took Nevskiy Prospekt Road. After crossing through the historic, upscale areas, they went into a zone of shabby high-rises, crammed with gray and dull apartment buildings. Unlike most of St. Petersburg, which is dominated by beautiful and historic Russian baroque architecture of the 1800s, this part of the city reminded Ryan of Moscow, with its cookie-cutter industrialized buildings of the 1950s Soviet Union.

The cab pulled to the curb of one of the shabby high-rises, and after paying the fare, the PI got out and went into the apartment building. The elevators were broken so he used the well-worn stairs to reach the dimly-lit corridor on the fifth floor. From everything he'd seen so far, Ryan sensed Ivanovich was not a prosperous man.

He knocked on the flimsy wooden door and after a few moments heard the shuffling of feet from inside the apartment. The door opened partway and a gaunt, stooped man in his mid-seventies stood there, leaning on a cane. The man was wearing a shabby bathrobe over sleepwear.

"Are you Dimitry Ivanovich?" Ryan asked in Russian.

"Yes, I am." The old man squinted at him. "Who are you?"

Ryan smiled, trying to put the man at ease. "I'm Mike Harrison," he said, using his fake ID name. "I'm in the import-export business and I have a proposition for you." He patted his jacket. "I brought Rubles."

The mention of cash appeared to peak the old man's interest and he opened the door fully. "Come in then."

The PI followed Ivanovich as he shuffled into the tiny living room. With the help of his cane he slowly lowered himself onto a lumpy couch.

Ryan sat across from him and leaned forward in the seat.

"Your Russian is good," said Ivanovich. "By your accent I can tell you are American?"

"That's right. I'm from the States. I run an import-export business there."

The old man nodded. "Tell me about this deal."

Ryan reached into his jacket, removed a thick wad of Russian Rubles and placed the cash on the chipped coffee table between them. "This is for you, Mr. Ivanovich."

The man's eyes widened. "As you Americans would say, what is the catch? No one gives away money for free."

"True. I just have a few questions for you."

Ivanovich's eyes narrowed and he gazed at the PI with suspicion. "Are you KGB? Or FSB, as they are called now?"

Ryan shook his head. "Nothing of the sort. I'm just a businessman." With his hand he pushed the stack of Russian currency across the table. "Please take it."

The other man didn't hesitate. One of his frail hands reached across, grabbed the money and stuffed it in the pocket of his bathrobe.

"Ask me your questions, Mr. Harrison."

"I met a woman who at one time did business with you. She's American but lives in China. Her name is Amber Holt."

At the mention of Holt's name the Russian man's face scrunched into a mask of hate. With vehemence he spit on the floor. "That bitch!" he growled. "I wish to hell I had never met that evil woman!"

Ivanovich pointed an accusing finger at Ryan. "If you are a friend of hers, leave now! You are no longer welcome in my house!"

The PI shook his head forcefully. "Far from it. That woman tried to have me killed."

The Russian studied him for a long moment as if judging his veracity. Finally he nodded. "All right. I believe you. She almost got me killed as well."

"Sir, I found communication between the two of you from years ago — you were involved in a deal and she pulled out of it. You were furious."

"Still am. I used to be a prosperous, well-respected middle-man in Russia." He spit on the floor again. "It is because of that cursed woman that I am now destitute, forced to live in this pigsty." He waved a frail arm around the dilapidated room with its shabby furniture.

"What happened, sir?"

"I will tell you. Maybe you can use the info to hurt that evil bitch."

He coughed for a long moment and when he regained his composure, he said, "I used to buy secret information from her about the U.S. military. Information I would resell to the Russian government. It was very lucrative for me. I lived in a grand dacha with servants and a beautiful mistress ...." His eyes got a far-away look as if he was recalling those times.

His voice took on a harsh tone when he continued. "Then one day Amber Holt reneged on a deal and started selling exclusively to the Chinese. My contacts in the Russian government were not pleased. Not one bit. They blamed me and had me arrested. They confiscated my dacha and my bank accounts." He waved a hand in the air again. "And now I live like this ...."

Ryan felt sorry for the old man, even if he was a criminal.

"Can you tell me about her operation, Mr. Ivanovich? How does it work?"

"The money passes through that phony charity she owns."

"The Veritas Foundation."

"That is correct. Some charity. It is a slush-fund, a front for her illegal activity."

Ryan nodded. "That's what I was able to find out as well. Who runs it for her?"

"A man in Atlanta, Steve Nichols."

"Yes, I know about him. Can you tell me anything else?"

Ivanovich rubbed his forehead as if trying to remember. "I know Holt screwed other people when she made an exclusive deal with the Chinese. She used to do business with an arms dealer in France – his name is Louis Mitterrand."

"Okay. Was there anyone else in her organization that you know of? Anyone connected to her foundation?"

The old man coughed again. He pulled out a handkerchief and wiped his mouth. "Let me think ... yes, there was someone else. A mystery man who I never met. I know he lived in Washington."

"Washington, D.C.?"

The Russian nodded. "That is correct."

"Who was he?"

"I do not know his real name," Ivanovich said. "But Amber referred to him as Gray Man."

Chapter 71

Hoover Building, FBI Headquarters
Washington, D.C.

"What progress have you made on the Ryan case?" Director Tucker asked tersely.

"We're working on it, sir," Erin Welch replied.

Tucker leaned forward in his executive chair and placed his hands flat on his desk. "I want results. I want Ryan arrested."

"As I said, we're working on it."

"From what I hear, you're not working on it very hard."

Erin gritted her teeth. "What does that mean? Are you bugging my office?"

His eyes narrowed. "No. But I have my sources."

"Spies, you mean," she muttered under her breath.

"I'm the FBI Director, Erin. I know what's going on under the surface at each one of our 56 field offices."

Unable to control her anger, she blurted out, "That just means you have brown-nosing agents willing to kiss your ass. If I knew which one of my guys was the rat I'd make his life a living hell."

Tucker hands tightened into fists. "You work for me, damn it. And I want results!"

She almost told him to go fuck himself but instead took a long breath. After a moment she said, "In spite of what you may have heard, we have been trying to find J.T."

He glared at her, then his features softened. "All right. I didn't fly you up to D.C. to berate you. I just want to emphasize the urgency of catching him."

Erin nodded. "Sir, it's like he's vanished into thin air. We almost arrested him several weeks ago and then ... nothing."

The director drummed his fingers on the desk. "I've talked to the other assistant directors and they say the same thing. Ryan's gone off the grid. I thought since you've worked closely with him for a long time that you'd have a better chance of finding him."

Erin thought through Tucker's words. It was true she wanted to locate Ryan. But she also felt he was innocent. "Director, I learned new information about the Veritas Foundation."

The man's eyebrows shot up. "We're handling that investigation out of this office."

"I know that. But —"

"But what?"

"Sir, the president of Veritas, Steve Nichols, makes frequent trips to D.C. I believe there's a connection that leads back to here."

Tucker shrugged. "A lot of people come to Washington. That doesn't mean anything."

Erin had anticipated he'd say this. It was clear the director was slow-walking the investigation into Veritas. *Is he dirty? Or is he just a puppet for someone higher up pulling the strings?*

She debated telling him what else she'd learned, fearing he'd bury the information. Still, he was the head of the FBI, the top law-enforcement officer in the U.S.

"There's something else I found out," Erin said, "regarding this foundation. It confirms our earlier conclusion that there's an international connection."

"What is it?"

"Steve Nichols's boss appears to be an American woman who lives in China."

Tucker's eyes grew wary. "Who is she?"

"I don't know, but I intend to find out."

He shook his head forcefully. "No, you will not. I'll follow up on this from here. You are not to be involved with the investigation of Veritas in any way. Is that clear? Your job is to find Ryan and arrest him."

"But, sir —"

He stood abruptly. "This meeting is over, Erin."

Chapter 72

St. Petersburg, Russia

Standing on the balcony of his hotel room, J.T. Ryan knew he had a big decision to make. From this spot overlooking the Neva River, he watched as the cargo ships below plied their way over the gray, cold water. But he wasn't thinking about the river traffic. Instead he was focused on what to do next. He was running out of options.

He'd barely managed to escape China. And now there was nothing else for him to learn in Russia. *What do I do now? Keep running? But where?*

He also realized there was no place where he could hide out forever. He would just be a fugitive, trying to blend in, hoping to evade capture. And with an FBI Code Red attached to his name, he'd always be looking over his shoulder, fearful of arrest. *Can I live like that for the rest of my life?*

It started to rain, the large drops splattering on the surface of the Neva River below. He gazed up toward the gray, ominous-looking sky, and felt the cold rain as it pelted his face.

Finally coming to a decision, he turned and went inside.

It was time for him to leave Russia.

Chapter 73

Paris, France

Ryan followed the man as he went up the steps of the brownstone.

Once he opened the front door, Ryan rushed him, pushing him inside and slamming the door behind him.

Pulling his gun, the PI pointed the weapon at the man's head. "Are you Louis Mitterrand?"

The Frenchman's eyes bulged as he nodded.

"You know Amber Holt," Ryan said, his voice hard. "Tell me everything you know about her."

Mitterrand nodded again, a terrified look on his face.

Ryan pressed the muzzle of the gun to the man's forehead. "Start talking."

Chapter 74

Atlanta, Georgia

Lisa Booth was driving north on I-85 when she felt her cell phone vibrate. Removing it from a pocket, she clicked on the call and read the screen.

It was a text message that cryptically said, *Elephants. One hour.*

Perplexed by the message and by the unknown caller, she racked her brain trying to figure it out. Five minutes later she still didn't know who the call was from, but had a pretty good idea of the location. *Is this a trap? Is someone plotting to kill me?* she thought, recalling the attempt on her life a while back. She didn't know the answer. But she was armed and she knew being a PI was a dangerous profession.

Lisa got in the right hand lane, eased her Mustang to the off ramp, looped around the access road and went back on the Interstate, this time going south. She figured she'd make it in plenty of time.

Twenty minutes later she parked her car in a lot of the Atlanta Zoo, paid the entrance fee, and strode into the sprawling zoological park. It was a cool, drizzly day and there were few people there. She zipped up her windbreaker to ward off the chill, checked the sign for the exhibits, then headed into the interior of the park.

After passing the lion exhibit, she reached the natural-looking habitat where the elephants were kept. There were three of the mammals visible: a large elephant and two much smaller ones – the mother with two of her calves, she figured.

Seeing no people nearby, Lisa continued walking along the curving concrete path that bordered the exhibit.

Sensing movement behind her, she whirled around, and spotting a tall, bearded man nearby, pulled her gun and held it at her side.

"Put that away," the man said, "it's me."

Not recognizing him, she kept her gun out, her finger on the trigger guard as she eyed him suspiciously. He was well over six feet and muscular and had a bushy beard and mustache. He was wearing jeans, a dark jacket, and an Atlanta Braves baseball cap pulled low over his eyes.

He took off his cap. "It's me, Lisa."

Finally realizing who it was, she holstered her gun and ran towards him, giving him a big hug. "J.T.!" she said breathlessly. "It's really you! God, I missed you!"

She held on to him tight, then felt awkward with the long embrace. Pulling away from him, she saw he looked uncomfortable also.

"Sorry about that, boss," she said. "I got carried away. I thought you were ...."

Ryan put the baseball cap back on his head. "Dead?"

"Yeah."

He grinned. "Sorry to disappoint you."

"Always the comic."

His face turned serious. "Were you followed here?"

"No, J.T. I was on the lookout for that."

"Are you being watched by the FBI?"

Lisa shook her head. "I don't think so. Erin and I kind of have an understanding."

"Good." He gazed around a moment, obviously checking to see if there was anyone else nearby. It was raining harder now, and the area was deserted. He pointed to a nearby picnic table covered with a large umbrella. "Let's go over there and get out of the rain."

"Okay."

They sat across from each other and she said, "You look so different – I didn't recognize you."

He smoothed down his bushy mustache and beard. "That's the whole point. The facial hair is fake."

"I like the clean-shaven J.T. better."

"Me too. But for now, it's my new look. To go with my new name." He reached into a pocket, pulled out a U.S. passport, and flipped it open to the identification page.

Lisa noted the passport photo matched his current appearance. "It says you're Mike Harrison."

Ryan smiled. "The real Mike Harrison died in 1942 in a car accident. I don't think he'll mind that I borrowed his Social Security number and background."

"How did you get this passport?"

"I always have a backup plan, in case things go south. I've kept fake IDs and cash in a safety deposit box for years."

Lisa nodded. "I'm just glad you're back."

"Me too. It feels good to be back in the USA."

"Where were you? I never knew."

"China."

"Wow. What was it like, J.T.?"

"Big. Crowded. Beautiful. And ugly too. China is a dichotomy. In some ways it's more advanced than we are in the States, but also more backward in other ways."

"Was it dangerous?"

Ryan nodded. "Yeah."

"Do you speak Chinese?"

"I little. Luckily I was with someone who's fluent."

"Who?"

"A CIA agent."

"What's his name?"

"It's a she, actually. Her name is Rachel West."

Lisa eyed him closely. "Is she pretty?"

"What?"

"Is she pretty?"

"Why do you ask?"

"Just curious."

"Rachel is very good at her job. She helped me quite a bit over there. I was able to find out a lot about the case. And yes, to answer your question, she is pretty."

Lisa nodded. "Have you known her a long time?"

"We've worked on several cases before."

A gust of cold wind blew rain on them and she zipped her windbreaker to her neck. "Are you and Rachel together? Like a boyfriend and girlfriend thing?"

"You seem awfully curious about her, Lisa."

"You didn't answer my question."

Ryan seemed defensive. "How is this any of your business?"

"I'm your business partner, remember? The last time you were involved with a woman you almost turned into an alcoholic. I'm just trying to watch out for you."

"Fair enough, Lisa. Yes, my relationship with Rachel is romantic." He pointed an index finger at her. "And to correct you, we are not business partners. You're my employee."

Lisa leaned forward in the seat. "When you were gone, I ran the office all by myself."

He seemed about to protest, then shrugged. "Yes, you did. And I thank you for that."

"I want more than thanks, J.T. I'm expecting that raise you promised me when I started."

Ryan shook his head slowly and smiled. "You drive a hard bargain. All right, I'll give you a raise."

"Really?"

"Really. You deserve it."

Lisa grinned. "Can we be business partners, too?"

"Don't push it, young lady."

"Okay."

Ryan gazed around furtively. There were still no people around the area and he seemed to relax. "I hate being on the run. Always looking over my shoulder. And I hate being on the wrong side of the law. I spent my whole life in the military and as a PI helping law-enforcement – and now ...."

She reached out and placed a hand over his. "Don't worry, J.T. We'll clear your name."

"Thanks for being in my corner."

Lisa grinned. "Don't mention it. We make a good team."

He smiled back, but it was a sad smile. She could tell being a wanted felon dominated his thoughts.

"Where are you staying, J.T.? You can't go back to your apartment, that's for sure."

"I just got off the plane two hours ago. I haven't even thought about that."

Lisa mulled this over. "You can stay with me. At my apartment."

He looked at her for a long moment before answering. "That's not a good idea. I don't want to get you in trouble. Remember, there's still a Code Red on me."

"Like I told you before, Erin and I have an understanding."

Ryan still looked doubtful. "There's another reason it's not a good idea."

She understood his meaning right away. "Oh, that. The man and woman thing. Don't worry, I have two bedrooms. I'll be a proper young lady and you'll be a true gentleman. Nothing is going to happen between us."

"How can you be so sure?"

"John Taylor Ryan, I've known you for months and in all that time you've never even come close to making a pass at me. You're a true Boy Scout." She smiled. "And there's something else I know about you. You're a one-woman-at-a-time kind of guy. I think this super secret agent woman, Rachel West, has got your heart and you won't stray, no matter how much you're tempted."

Ryan grinned. "You're right. You're pretty smart for being a junior detective."

She slapped his arm playfully. "Call me junior detective again and I'll pull my Glock on you."

Chapter 75

Atlanta, Georgia

J.T. Ryan took a long hot shower and after toweling off and getting dressed, came out of the guest bedroom and went into Lisa's living room.

He found her there, sipping coffee and eating a donut. The young woman was wearing a conservative knee-length black skirt, a simple white blouse, and a black jacket.

"Hey," he said, picking up one of the donuts from the box and biting into it. "These are good. Haven't had one in weeks."

She drank some of her coffee. "You look better without the beard and mustache."

Ryan felt his face, now devoid of the faux facial hair. "Feel better too." He sat across from her, poured himself a cup of coffee and took a sip. "Thanks for letting me stay in your spare bedroom. I appreciate it."

"No problem, J.T."

"So, where are you on the case?"

Her face brightened. "I made a lot of progress since you were gone."

Ryan smiled. "You better have, since I already gave you that raise."

"I was able to break into the foundation's email server. Turns out Steve Nichols flies into D.C. often." She continued, telling him what else she'd learned about the man and the shady charity.

"Good work, Lisa. Now I'll tell you what I found out in China and a few other places I went." He spent the next hour filling her in on the results of his investigation. By the time he was done the box of a dozen donuts was empty as was the pot of coffee.

"It all tracks, then," Lisa said. "The foundation is run by Amber Holt and a few other people – mainly Steve Nichols and this mystery guy called Gray Man."

"That's right. And since this Gray Man is based in D.C. it's a safe bet that's who Nichols goes to meet."

"What are they up to, J.T.? It's obvious the foundation is money-laundering. But what's their objective? Are they buying and selling military secrets to the Chinese?"

"That part's unclear. As I told you earlier, before we could interrogate Amber Holt, the Chinese military showed up. One thing's for sure – she's very well protected in China, which means whatever she's acquiring for them is extremely valuable."

Lisa nodded. "What do we do now?"

"We have one option. We follow Steve Nichols on his next trip to D.C. He'll lead us to this Gray Man."

Chapter 76

Washington, D.C.

This *is the final hurdle,* Gray Man realized as he waited to be shown into the senator's office. *If this next meeting goes according to plan, the operation will be a success.* All of his hard work for the past year would be rewarded. Financially he would be so well-off he'd be able to retire immediately.

And there was more. Much more. Amber would finally be his. She'd hinted at an island vacation for the both of them when everything was complete. As he fantasized about the stunning redhead, a jolt of sexual excitement crowded his thoughts.

Just then the senator's assistant approached him and he quickly silenced his carnal thoughts.

"The senator will see you now," the assistant said.

Gray Man rose and followed the young man into the very large, well-appointed office. The senator had been in Congress for over twenty years and was highly-influential. Because of this she rated one of the best offices in the Russell Senate Office Building.

The assistant left and closed the door behind him.

Senator Elizabeth Hawkins remained seated behind her desk and waved him to a wingback chair.

"Senator," Gray Man said cheerfully, a grin on his face. "It's good to see you again." He sat down and rested the large briefcase he was carrying on the floor.

Senator Hawkins didn't return the smile, her unattractive face impassive. In her sixties, she was a plump woman with short, frizzy hair. She favored dark colored, utilitarian-looking pantsuits, like the one she was wearing today. Her most prominent features were an exceptionally large nose and a shrill voice. Behind her back, Gray Man knew, she was derided in D.C. for her looks and her unpleasant personality. But she was such an influential person in the Washington power structure that those thoughts were never uttered publicly.

"I've been thinking about your offer," Hawkins said in her piercing voice.

Gray Man smiled again. "Of course. I'm sure you found it generous."

Her black eyes bore into his. "No. I did not."

Startled, he leaned back in the chair. "But last time we met, you seemed receptive ...."

"That was before I realized the full scope of what you're trying to do."

"I just need your vote, Senator."

Hawkins rubbed her bulbous nose. "I *know* what you need. You're not going to get my vote. Unless my demands are met."

"But, I'm offering you three million dollars. In fact, I brought some of the cash with me today." He patted the briefcase by his feet. "As a deposit."

She scowled. "Three million is chump change."

Although it was a cool 69 degrees in the office, moisture beaded on his forehead. "I see. I could revise my offer. To say ... four million."

Hawkins's scowl etched deeper on her face. "Don't insult me with petty cash. If I'm going to back your plan, you're going to do a lot better than that." She tented her hands on top of the desk. "I've been researching what you're up to and I put two and two together. I figured it out. It's an audacious scheme. Piece by piece, you've been buying up the assets of mining companies throughout the United States. And not just any mining companies, but those mining uranium." She paused a moment. "And you need my vote in the senate committee to complete the purchase. From my research I figure you're very close to having complete control."

Gray Man swallowed hard, then pulled down his gray silk tie and undid the top button of his dress shirt. No one before had come close to figuring out the objective of the operation. It was clear Hawkins was cunning, much more cunning than he had expected.

"How much, Senator?"

"How much what?"

"How much will it take to buy your vote. Five million?"

She bared her teeth in a cold, ugly grin. He noticed her teeth were uneven and stained.

"More than that. Much more."

The man shifted uneasily in the chair. Amber had only authorized him to spend five million on this transaction. "Name your figure, Senator, and I'll discuss it with my boss."

"I'll tell you what I want," she replied in her shrill, high-pitched voice. "I want a 50/50 split. I want to be equal partners on this deal."

Gray Man's eyes widened. "That's ... that's not acceptable ...."

"Those are my terms. Take it or leave it."

His thoughts raced, anticipating that Amber would never agree to that. He had one other solution, one he'd had to use several times before. But Hawkins was such a powerful, well-known lawmaker that he dreaded using that option.

The senator rose abruptly from her chair. "And if you're thinking of threatening me, forget it. I'm very well protected. In fact, I have my own security detail."

As if to prove her point, she pressed a button on her phone console and seconds later two burly, uniformed men entered the office, their hands resting on their holstered sidearms.

"If you would show my guest out," she said harshly to the guards, "he was just leaving."

Chapter 77

Buckhead
Atlanta, Georgia

J.T. Ryan and Lisa Booth had been tailing Steve Nichols for days. They had been taking turns, doing eight hour shifts, each of the PIs shadowing the man's every move.

It was seven a.m. and Ryan was watching Nichols's home now. Noticing the garage door roll up, he focused his binoculars to get a better look. He watched as the man put a carryon bag in the trunk of his Infinity sedan and moments later the car drove out of the garage and onto the street.

Ryan fired up his Tahoe and began following, staying a discreet distance behind. After driving through the exclusive neighborhood and making his way to the highway, Nichols headed south.

As he continued tailing him, Ryan pulled out his cell phone and pressed a preset number.

When Lisa Booth answered, he said, "Listen closely. Our target isn't going to his office today. I'm sure he's headed to the airport. Get us tickets on the next flight to D.C., but don't get us adjoining seats."

"You got it, boss."

"One more thing. Call Hertz and reserve us a rental in Washington."

"I'm on it, J.T. Which airport in D.C. do you think he'll fly into?"

Ryan thought about this. Nichols had a choice of three in the area: Dulles, Reagan National and BWI, Baltimore-Washington. "Reagan's the closest to the D.C. metro area," he replied. "I suspect he'll go there."

"Okay."

"Lisa, after you book this, head to the airport. I'll meet you there."

He clicked off the call and continued following Nichols. The man parked his Infinity in Hartsfield Airport's short-term lot and, staying a discreet distance behind, Ryan did as well.

He shadowed him into the terminal and then to the Delta ticket counter. It was obvious Nichols was changing his flight at the last minute, like he had when Lisa tailed him weeks ago.

Ryan gazed up at the electronic reader board. The next Delta flight into Reagan was leaving in an hour.

He turned back to the airline counter and saw the foundation president stride down the terminal corridor, pulling his wheeled carryon bag behind him.

The PI pulled out his phone and was about to call Lisa's number when he felt someone tapping his shoulder. Turning around, he saw the young woman, an eager look on her face.

"Hi, boss."

"Hey, Lisa." He pointed at the reader board. "Did you take care –"

"Already done. And I booked the rental car too."

He grinned.

"Told you I was good, J.T."

"Don't let it go to your head."

She snickered.

"Let's grab a quick cup of coffee before the flight," he said, "and we can go over our strategy."

They found a small cafe nearby and drank coffee at one of the tall tables without chairs. Ryan was in his current disguise: a fake beard and mustache, blue jeans, a dark blue coat, and an Atlanta Braves baseball cap pulled low over his eyes. He noticed Lisa had disguised her looks as well, putting her long blonde hair into a bun. She had also donned a floppy Panama hat. The rest of her outfit was her typical attire: a black, knee-length skirt, a white blouse buttoned to her neck, and a black jacket.

Lisa sipped some of her coffee. "I'm kind of new to this, J.T. How do we go about it?"

He smoothed down his bushy mustache. "My guess is Nichols won't rent a car in D.C. He'll probably cab it to the mysterious Gray Man. So I'll get a taxi also and follow him. In the meantime you get the rental. I'll call you when he gets to his destination."

"Got it. Then what?"

"Then," he said, "we do what PIs have been doing for ages. We watch and wait. And when the timing's right, we make our move."

They finished their coffees and headed down the concourse. By the time they got to the right gate, the Delta attendants were announcing initial boarding.

Ryan watched as Nichols got in the line for first class passengers and boarded. The PIs, who were booked in coach, got on a short time later.

The flight from Atlanta to D.C. is less than two hours and when they deplaned Ryan sprinted down the concourse toward the lower level and the cab stands. Being in first class meant Nichols not only boarded early but also deplaned first, giving the man a head start.

Luckily the foundation president seemed to be in no hurry and Ryan reached the taxi area at about the same time as the other man.

Nichols got a cab right away and the PI snagged the next one available.

After giving the taxi driver a generous tip, Ryan instructed him to follow the other cab. Traffic was heavy in D.C. and it took over forty minutes to travel the three miles from Reagan airport to downtown. Nichols's taxi passed the Capitol Building and Union Station and eventually pulled to the curb in front of an office building on K Street. Ryan was familiar with the area and knew that K Street was where many lobbyists had their offices.

The foundation president got out of the cab and went into the three-story building.

The PI quickly paid his fare, jumped out of the taxi and went inside, but by the time he got there he realized his target wasn't in the lobby.

"Damn," he muttered.

There was a directory in the lobby which listed the numerous office suites in the building. He scanned the list rapidly and finding nothing, reread it more slowly, assessing the types of businesses on the long list. Most appeared to be law firms with a few other companies sprinkled in. When he reread one of the names toward the end of the list he had a gut feeling it was the right one.

Turning away from the directory, he pulled out his phone and called Lisa's number. When she picked up he gave her the address, then went outside to wait for her to arrive.

He spotted a green Toyota Camry pull to the curb a while later, saw Lisa was driving, and climbed in the car.

"This is it?" she asked.

"It is. Nichols went inside a while ago."

"Were you able to follow him to the person he's meeting?"

"Didn't get here in time. But it turns out I didn't have to. I think I know who it is now."

She looked at him quizzically. "Who?"

"This mysterious guy, Gray Man, is the person Nichols is meeting. One of the businesses in this office building is listed as *David Grayson Enterprises, Inc.*"

Lisa smiled. "Gray Man. Grayson. It fits."

"And there's one other thing. Mitterrand, the French arms dealer I questioned in Paris told me Gray Man was a lobbyist. This whole area around K Street in D.C. is full of lobbyists."

"Okay. So what now, J.T.?"

Ryan pointed to the parking lot across the street. "Park in there. I need you to work your computer magic skills. Let's find out more about this David Grayson."

She drove to the lot, parked the Camry in a spot with good visibility of the building, and pulled out her iPad.

Ten minutes later she looked up from the computer tablet. "David Grayson is a registered lobbyist in Washington. He lives in D.C. and the address is not far from here. He's not married and lives alone. The business records show *David Grayson Enterprises* owns many other businesses."

"Any mention of the Veritas Foundation?"

"None than I can find, J.T. But it appears some of the businesses he owns are holding companies, shells with no employees."

"Makes sense. Having lots of companies means he could move large amounts of money around without arousing suspicion."

"That would be my guess too," she said, handing him her iPad. "This is the guy's website. It has a photo of him."

Ryan looked at the man's picture on the screen. He was totally non-descript. An average, bland-looking man with gray hair and a gray mustache. The most distinctive thing about him was what he was wearing: an obviously very expensive three-piece suit, gray in color. He also wore a starched white shirt, a gray tie, and gray pocket square.

"Now I see how he got his nickname," Ryan said.

"What should we do now?"

"We watch and wait. This is the boring part – we watch and wait."

And that's what they did for the next four hours. A little after five p.m. the building's employees began streaming out. A short time later they spotted Steve Nichols exit the structure, flag down a taxi, and leave the area.

Soon after David Grayson walked out of the office building, and like his photo, he was wearing a gray three-piece suit.

"That's our guy," Ryan said to Lisa. They watched as Grayson crossed the street and headed to the other side of the parking lot. The man climbed into a silver Lexus sedan and pulled out of the lot.

"Let's follow him," Ryan said, "but not too close. My guess is he's headed home."

Lisa fired up the Camry and merged into the heavy traffic. They tailed the Lexus for the next hour as the sedan made its way into Georgetown, a historic and exclusive neighborhood in D.C.

The Lexus pulled into the driveway of an expensive-looking, three-story colonial with columns supporting the wide portico. Grayson got out of the car and went inside the home.

Lisa drove past the house and pulled to the curb a short distance away.

"Did you bring the weapons?" asked Ryan.

"They're in the bag I checked in on the flight. It's in the trunk."

"I'll go get it," Ryan said as he climbed out. She popped the trunk, he retrieved the bag and got back in the Camry.

After they removed her Glock and his Smith & Wesson revolver and holstered them, she said, "How do you want to do this?"

"Quietly. I don't want to go in guns blazing. This is an upscale neighborhood. Any sign of trouble and the cops will get called. I'll be arrested immediately. Plus, I'm sure he's got a state-of-the-art alarm system – if we try to break in, that may trigger it. No, we have to do this a different way."

"Okay, J.T. And what way is that?"

"Let's go with the damsel-in-distress approach."

She looked puzzled. "What's that?"

"Pull up to the curb in front of his home. Then pretend the car won't start. I'll duck down in the seat so I'm not visible. Then you open the hood of this car. Give it a minute and then walk up to his front door and knock. You give him a sob story about your car won't start and your cell phone's dead. Ask to use his phone to call AAA. He'll let you in."

"Maybe he won't let me in. Maybe he's the suspicious type and tell me to take a hike."

"He won't, trust me."

"You seem pretty sure, J.T."

Ryan looked at her appearance. "Now comes part B of the damsel-in-distress plan."

"Huh?"

"Take off your hat, Lisa, and let your hair down."

She followed his instructions and her long hair flowed around her shoulders.

"Good." He eyed what she was wearing, the knee-length black skirt, white blouse buttoned to her neck, and a black jacket. "Do you have a low-cut blouse in your bag?"

She shook her head. "I don't own any low-cut blouses – I don't wear those kind of clothes."

"Okay. Then undo the top buttons of your blouse."

She blushed a little but went ahead and did as asked.

"Unbutton a few more," he said.

"I don't feel comfortable doing this."

"Don't worry, you'll only need to do this for a few minutes."

"All right," she replied grudgingly. She undid several more buttons of her blouse and Ryan could now see her bra and some of her cleavage.

Lisa looked down at her chest and her face turned a deep shade of crimson. "Oh my God! Don't look, J.T."

He stared out the window. "I'm not looking, okay? This isn't for my benefit."

"So what do I do now?"

"Listen closely. Get out of the car. Lift the hood. Then walk to his front door and knock. When he answers tell him your sob story. He'll let you in, you pull your gun and wait for me to come inside. Then I'll take over."

"What if he recognizes me? Remember, he's probably the guy who hired the hit man to kill us both. He may recognize my face."

"Trust me Lisa, he won't recognize your face."

"How can you be so sure?"

"He'll barely look at your face – he's going to be focused on your chest."

"How do you know?"

"He's a man isn't he?"

Lisa nodded. "Yeah. You're right."

Still averting his eyes, he said, "Are we clear on what you're going to do?"

"Yes."

"Okay. Let's do it." Ryan slid down in the seat and watched as the young woman started up the car and drove it to the front of Grayson's house. She climbed out of the sedan, raised the hood, and a moment later walked to the home's front entrance. He peeked over the Camry's window sill as the porch lights came on, Grayson opened the door, and Lisa went inside the house.

Ryan quickly got out of the car and strode to the front door, which was opened a moment later by Lisa. She was in the foyer, pointing her Glock at Grayson's head.

Ryan went inside, closed the door behind him, and pulled his revolver. Leveling the gun at the man's terrified face, he said, "Okay, Lisa. I got this."

"What happens now?" she replied.

"First, you button your blouse."

She looked down at her chest and quickly buttoned up. "Now what?"

"You get back in the rental and drive away. Come back in an hour."

"Why?" she asked.

"I need an hour alone with our friend here."

"Are you going to interrogate him, J.T.?"

"Yes."

"Then we should do it together."

"No." Ryan kept the gun trained on the panicked-looking Grayson.

"Why not?"

"Because."

"I need to learn all this PI stuff, J.T."

"I agree. But not today. You need plausible deniability. What I'm going to do isn't legal. I'm not going to get you into more trouble than I already have."

She glared. "I'm your partner! It's not fair."

Ryan stared at the young woman. "Lisa, please. Trust me on this. I'm just looking out for you. Okay?"

She let out a long breath and after a moment her angry expression dissipated. "All right. I'll leave."

"Thank you."

Grayson, who had been silent until now, said in a quivering voice, "What are you going to do to me?"

"Shut up," Ryan growled.

Lisa holstered her Glock. "I'll come back in an hour." She turned, went out the front door and closed it behind her.

Ryan locked the door and pointed his gun at the other man's head. "Which way is the kitchen?"

The man pointed. "That way."

"Go. I'll follow you. But one false move and you're dead."

The PI followed him into a large, expensively-decorated kitchen with marble countertops, marble floors, and built-in, custom-made appliances. He pushed Grayson onto one of the straight-back chairs in the room and slashed the revolver across the man's face.

Grayson's head snapped to one side, then it slumped forward, resting on his chest. His lip was bleeding, the bright red gore staining his impeccably tailored gray suit.

Ryan figured the man would remain unconscious for at least five minutes, giving him plenty of time to prepare. First, he found a roll of duck tape in the garage and with it he bound the man's hands to the chair's armrests. After that he used the tape to secure his legs to the chair. Lastly he slapped a piece of tape across his mouth.

Then he began searching the kitchen and garage for tools he could use. Finding a wheeled serving cart in the walk-in pantry, he loaded it with a wide assortment of kitchen utensils and other tools he'd located. Lastly he pulled out another chair and sat across from the unconscious man.

One of Ryan's duties in the Army's Green Berets had been as an interrogator. In his tours in Iraq and Afghanistan, he'd interrogated dozens of captured enemy. He'd learned that the fear of impending pain was more effective than experiencing the pain itself. Get a man to believe you'll torture him and nine out of ten times they talked. That was his hope today, since he hated to inflict pain unless absolutely necessary. Not that David Grayson deserved mercy. The PI was certain that he, along with Steve Nichols, had ordered the murder of the innocent woman who had worked for the Summit Company. And probably many more murders as well.

Tired of waiting for Grayson to regain consciousness, the PI slapped his face.

The man came to, his eyes blinking rapidly. Once his eyes focused, he got that terrified look again.

"I don't have a lot of time," Ryan stated, his voice harsh. "So I'll cut to the chase. I already know a lot about you, Steve Nichols, and Amber Holt. And how you all run the Veritas Foundation, that criminal organization that pretends to be a charity."

Grayson's eyes went wide hearing this.

"Nod your head," Ryan growled, "if you agree all this is true."

The man sat very still.

"Nod your head."

Grayson stared at him, blinked rapidly several times, but didn't move.

The PI ripped the duct tape off his mouth and in the process part of his lip tore off as well. Blood spurted, splattering onto Ryan.

Grayson yelped in pain and his eyes watered.

"We can do this the easy way or the hard way. It's really up to you, Grayson. You tell me what I want to know and I won't be forced to utilize the tools over there." Ryan pointed to the serving cart laden with knives, kitchen utensils, and several other tools he'd found in the garage.

The man's stare went bug-eyed when he looked at the cart. "Please, no ...."

Ryan was using the interrogation technique he called the 'laundry list'. With it he would describe the several forms of violent torture he threatened to use. He didn't intend to do it, just terrify the man into talking. And if his prisoner didn't break after hearing the list, the PI would drag him into the bathroom and waterboard him.

Ryan picked up a large kitchen knife and held it in the air, the titanium blade glinting from the overhead lights. He pressed the blade to the man's cheek.

"No! No!" Grayson screamed.

"I agree. I don't think the knife is a good idea either." He put down the blade and picked up one of those long lighters used to light a fireplace or a barbecue grill. "How about this? You like it better?" He flicked on the flame and held the lit end a quarter inch from the man's nose.

Grayson cowered in his chair, trying to move away from the flame.

"Not a fan of this?" Ryan asked. "I don't like it either." He edged the lighter even closer to the man's face. "The smell of burning human flesh is very unpleasant."

The PI turned off the utensil and put it back on the cart. Then he picked up a battery-operated drill and activated the on-switch. The drill's motor whined to a high pitch as the sharp drill bit rotated so fast it looked like a blur. Ryan pointed the tool at the other man's left eye and moved in close, the point of the drill bit only a half-inch from the eye's pupil. Grayson's face blanched and he started to hyperventilate.

That's when Ryan smelled a foul odor and realized Grayson had lost control of his bowels. The PI pulled away the drill and turned it off. "Yeah, I won't use the drill. It's too crude."

"Please, no, please stop ...." the man whimpered, as the stench of his excrement filled the room.

"Easy or hard, it's all up to you, my friend."

Ryan looked through the items on the serving cart again and found what he was looking for. "There it is! My favorite." He picked up the heavy-duty pruning shears and held it up for the man to see. "Now this is a very useful tool. It's great for cutting thick branches. Not surprisingly, it's great for cutting off other things. Like fingers and toes."

Sweat beaded off Grayson's terrified face. "No! Please no!"

Ryan opened the pruning shears, grabbed one the man's fingers and inserted it between the sharp blades. Grayson began crying uncontrollably as the PI tightened his grip on the shear's handle, the blades beginning to cut into the skin. Blood oozed from the finger.

"Stop!" Grayson screamed. "I'll talk!"

"You're sure?"

"Yes! Yes! Please stop," he begged.

"All right."

He let go of the man's finger and dropped the pruning shears on the cart.

Then he questioned Grayson for the next twenty minutes. The man confirmed much of what he knew, but also gave him very specific and very detailed information about the foundation, Amber Holt, and the incredible criminal conspiracy that was in the works.

Suddenly the PI heard the sound of a car pulling into the driveway. Checking his watch he realized it hadn't been an hour yet, so it was unlikely it was Lisa.

Sprinting to the foyer, he peered out one of the windows next to the front door.

There was a police cruiser in the driveway, it's rack lights flashing, the blue rays lighting up the night sky. *Did the neighbors hear Grayson screaming and call the cops?*

He watched for another second as two uniformed cops got out of the cruiser and cautiously made their way to the front door.

Ryan raced toward the back of the house, and finding the rear door, flung it open and fled into the darkness.

Chapter 78

National Peoples Congress Building
Tiananmen Square
Beijing, China

General Chang stepped up to the podium and looked at the twenty five men sitting in the large conference room. The group, known as the Central Politburo, represented the most powerful officials in the Chinese government. It included the General Secretary of the Communist Party, the President of the People's Republic of China, the Vice Premier, and every other high-ranking member of the country's provinces. Every major decision regarding all aspects of Chinese life had to be reviewed and approved by this group.

Chang unfolded a sheet of paper and placed it on the podium. These were his talking points for this morning's briefing, but in reality he didn't need the notes, since he'd memorized everything he wanted to say.

"Gentlemen," he began, "I wanted to brief you on the progress I've made on the American project. My operation has almost secured 100% ownership of the ore deposits in the United States. I expect that in a matter of weeks the balance will be acquired. Once that is complete the assets will be transferred from the Veritas Foundation to a shell corporation that we, the Chinese government, will control."

He paused and watched the expressions of the men in the room. Usually a dour group, the twenty five men smiled, gleeful at the news.

Then in unison the Politburo all stood and began clapping loudly while General Chang basked in the widespread approval of the group.

Chapter 79

Washington, D.C.

Ryan, his lungs ready to burst, collapsed behind a long row of bushes.

He'd been running at full speed for over thirty minutes and was now in a wooded, deserted park many miles from Grayson's home.

Lying on his back, he gasped for air as he stared up at the cloudy night sky. He stayed like that for several more minutes, then sat up and took out his cell phone.

When Lisa answered, he told her his location.

"Thank God," she said. "I drove by the house and saw a cop car in the driveway. I thought you'd been arrested."

"It was close."

"Where are you, exactly?"

Ryan gave her directions and hung up.

Ten minutes later he saw headlights through the trees and spotted the Camry stop about fifty feet from his location.

Standing, he peered around the park – there was still no one around so he jogged over and climbed in the car.

"Drive," he said.

She put the sedan in gear and sped out of the park.

"Keep it under the speed limit, Lisa. The last thing we need is to get pulled over."

She nodded, slowed the car, and continued driving, merging into a four-lane road soon after.

"Where to, J.T.?"

"It's late. No use heading to the airport now. We'll stay the night, go back to Atlanta in the morning."

"Okay, boss."

Fifteen minutes later they spotted a Holiday Inn Express right off the highway, stopped, and rented two rooms. When they reached the adjoining rooms, she said, "You want to tell me what happened back there before we crash for the night?"

Ryan nodded. "Sure. You need to know."

Lisa unlocked her door and they went inside the room.

The first thing Ryan did was to take off his fake beard and mustache. "No reason to wear this any longer. Grayson saw me with it. This cover's blown." Then he sat down on the bed. "Grab a chair and I'll tell you everything."

She grabbed the only chair in the room and placed it across from him. Sitting down, she glanced at the blood stains on his coat.

"Did you torture him, J.T.?"

He shook his head. "No."

The look on her face said she didn't believe him. "Tell me the truth."

"I only tortured him mentally. Luckily he broke before it became physical."

"Then where did the blood come from."

He grinned, in spite of the tenseness of the situation. "All right – I had to give him a few minor cuts and bruises."

"This is no time for jokes."

He turned serious. "You're right. The bottom line is, I scared him into talking."

"I'm glad you didn't have to torture him. The thought of you doing that ... makes me queasy."

"Trust me, I hate to do it. But sometimes there's no choice."

She shivered a bit and it was clear that the idea of torture frightened her.

"Listen to me," he said. "You'll never, ever, have to do that sort of thing." He touched her shoulder to calm her. "You're my computer expert, remember? Each of us have our own unique skills. That's why we work together well."

She nodded at this and her spirits seemed to lift. "You're right. Each of us has unique skills. I'm glad you see it that way."

Ryan leaned forward. "Now let me tell you what I learned from Grayson."

Chapter 80

Beijing, China

"You've really fucked up this time," Amber Holt spit out, gripping the phone handset with such force the plastic casing cracked a bit.

"I'm really sorry about this," Gray Man replied.

Amber briefly glanced out the window in her study, then eyed her desk to collect her thoughts. "Sorry doesn't *begin* to cut it. How could you let that guy Ryan find you? Are you totally incompetent?"

"I apologize. I won't let you down again."

She seethed with disgust. If she had been in the same room with him instead of 7,000 miles away, she would have slapped the hell out of him and kicked him in the balls.

Amber took a deep breath and willed herself to calm down. She still needed him. Without Gray Man the whole operation was in jeopardy.

"All right," she stated, her tone calmer now. "What's done is done. We need to focus on what's next."

"I'm glad you see it that way, Amber. I've added a security detail to protect me 24/7. Ryan won't be able to get to me now."

"Good. When Ryan questioned you, did you tell him anything about the operation?"

There was silence from the other end. Eventually he said, "No. Absolutely not. The police got here in time."

"You're sure you told him nothing?"

"Yes, Amber."

She couldn't tell if the man was telling the truth or if he was lying. But either way her plan was in jeopardy in light of what Senator Elizabeth Hawkins demanded.

"On a separate topic," she said, "I've been thinking about the senator."

"What have you decided?"

"I can't agree to her terms. No way will I accept a partnership with that bitch. This is mine! All mine!"

"I figured that would be your answer. What do you want me to do?"

"Take care of her, Gray Man. The same way you've taken care of the others who stood in our way."

"That's going to be difficult."

"Just fucking do it!" she screeched and slammed down the phone.

Chapter 81

Washington, D.C.

Senator Elizabeth Hawkins lived in an exclusive neighborhood of D.C., consisting of luxurious townhouses and high-rise brownstones.

The man drove past the senator's two-story townhouse and pulled to the curb. He'd been doing surveillance in the area for three days and had a good idea of her schedule. Hawkins was dropped off at her home by a limo at about seven in the evening and picked up at seven a.m. the following day.

Today had been no different.

It was midnight now and the home was dim inside, with only the portico lights on. During his surveillance, the assassin had spotted one bodyguard, a bulky man in an ill-fitting suit who was always with her, shadowing her every move. The assassin knew he had to eliminate that threat first, once he got inside the home.

But first things first – he had to quietly break in.

After checking the load on his suppressed Ruger semi-auto, he climbed out of the Dodge van and walked toward the townhouse. Using the elaborate landscaping for cover, he crept toward the back of the home and slowly approached the French door rear entrance.

Peering into the dim interior he spotted a blinking red light near the door. It was obvious the place was protected by an alarm system and the system was operational.

He had expected this.

Reaching into his backpack, he took out a device that looked like a micro-laptop computer and started typing on the keyboard. He spent the next several minutes keying in a variety of numbers until the red blinking light inside the home went dark. His jamming device had worked.

After putting away the computerized jammer, he took out his lock-pick tool, fiddled with the lock and slipped inside. Drawing his Ruger pistol, he crept through the dark interior past a den and a large kitchen, then into a wide corridor that led to a staircase.

He figured Senator Hawkins's bedroom was on the second floor. He also expected the woman's bodyguard to be located on that floor as well, in one of the spare bedrooms.

Silently he approached the stairway and was about to step on the first rung when the overhead lights blazed on in the corridor, blinding him momentarily.

He whirled around and found two men aiming pistols at him.

"Drop the gun!" one of the men shouted. "Do it now!"

Chapter 82

FBI Field Office
Atlanta, Georgia

Erin Welch's desk phone rang and she picked up the receiver. "Welch here."

"It's Special Agent Wilson."

"Good to hear from you. It's been awhile."

"I thought you'd want to know, Erin. Yesterday we arrested a man here in D.C. He'd broken into the home of Elizabeth Hawkins, the U.S. Senator. It was clear his intent was to murder her. She had beefed up her security detail recently and luckily her bodyguards got to him in time."

"I see."

"We think," he continued, "the guy we arrested is connected to the death of Congressman Rodriguez in San Francisco. You may have heard about that."

She had. Erin was always suspicious when elected public officials died, even from seemingly accidental causes. "Yeah. I heard about that. But why are you calling me?"

"I know about some of the crap you've been through with Director Tucker. He's a class A asshole in my book. He won't prosecute this case worth shit. Too political. I heard through the grapevine you were working on that foundation case and thought this might be tied to that."

"Thanks, Wilson. I appreciate you letting me know."

"No problem."

Erin checked her watch. It was ten a.m. She knew Delta had a noon flight every day to D.C. If she left her office now she'd be able to make it.

"I'll see you later today," she said and hung up.

Chapter 83

Hoover Building, FBI Headquarters
Washington, D.C.

Erin Welch stepped into the interrogation room and shut the door behind her.

A small, wiry man was sitting at the table, his hands shackled to the metal loop on the table's surface. Erin sat across from him and opened the file Special Agent Wilson had given her.

She quickly scanned the content of the report. Marco Alessi had a long rap sheet: multiple arrests for armed robbery, assault with a deadly weapon, extortion, and car jacking going back to his teenage years. He'd served time in several penitentiaries, his latest a five-year stretch at Georgia State Prison. GSP, located in Reidsville, Georgia, is the main maximum security facility in the state. The report went on to say that he was a suspect in several murder-for-hire killings, but nothing had been proven. Last month, however, San Francisco PD had issued an arrest warrant for Alessi in connection with the death of Congressman Rodriguez. Initially ruled an accidental explosion, the case had been reopened and reclassified as murder, with Alessi as the main suspect.

Erin closed the file and eyed the wiry man.

"You're in deep shit," she said harshly, as she slapped the file down on the table. "By your rap sheet I know you've done time – your longest stretch was the nickel you did at GSP." She shook her head slowly. "But this time you're going to get the needle. The death sentence. No two ways about it."

Alessi sneered. "Who the hell are you?"

She pulled out her cred pack and flicked it open. "Welch. Assistant Director, FBI."

The man glanced at the creds, then back at her, his sneer gone replaced by a stony expression. "I'm not saying anything to anybody without my lawyer present."

Erin rose from the table. "That's up to you. But I'll give you some advice. We have you for attempted murder of a U.S. Senator. And there's an arrest warrant for your involvement in the suspected murder of a U.S. Congressman. And the explosion you set off killed an additional ten other people. San Francisco PD has very incriminating evidence connecting you to that case. And all of this is on top of your lengthy arrest record."

She crossed her arms in front of her. "No attorney is going to get you out of this mess. You're a dead man, Alessi. You just don't know it yet."

The man blinked rapidly and fidgeted in the chair, the shackles on his legs clanging.

"The way I see it, Alessi, you've got one shot at getting a prison sentence instead of the needle." She picked up the file folder from the table. "But that shot goes away once I walk out."

Erin turned and strode toward the door.

"Wait," the man said, his manacled hands jerking up, the metal creaking.

She turned around and faced him.

"Wait. How can I beat this thing?"

"You can't, Alessi. Let's be clear about that. You're going to be doing life in prison no matter what. But if you talk to me and tell me what I want to know, I'll see you get a deal." She glanced at her watch. "But you have five seconds to decide. Once I'm out that door, the deal is off the table."

265

"But if I talk I'll incriminate myself!"

She grimaced. "You think I care? You're a low-life loser. A bottom-feeder. A piece of scum. But I think you've got valuable information on a case I'm working. You talk to me and I'll get you a deal. As an Assistant Director in the FBI I can make it happen." She checked her watch again. "Time's up."

She marched to the door and turned the knob.

"I'll talk!"

Erin faced him. "You're sure?"

"Yeah."

She studied his features, the slumped shoulders and resigned expression on his face. It was obvious he was ready to talk.

Erin went back to the table and sat down. "I've been conducting an investigation into an outfit called the Veritas Foundation. It's a phony charity based in Atlanta. I believe you're tied to their criminal activity. Is that correct?"

The man nodded.

"Is that a yes, Alessi?"

"Yes."

"Did Veritas hire you to kill Senator Hawkins?"

He nodded again. "Yeah."

"And Congressman Rodriguez?"

"Him too."

"Now we're getting somewhere. Did Steve Nichols, the president of Veritas hire you to do the hit?"

"Nah. It wasn't him. Somebody else."

"Who?"

Alessi seemed reluctant to talk. "He hired me to do the hit – he could hire someone else to take me out."

Erin pushed her chair back abruptly and stood. "Don't waste my time. Either you tell me *everything* or I'm out that door."

His eyebrows shot up. "All right ... all right ... Grayson hired me. David Grayson."

She sat back down. "Who's he?"

"A lobbyist. His office is in D.C. He's the main man behind Veritas."

"Okay. So this Grayson hired you to kill the senator and the congressman. Why?"

The man shook his head. "I don't know why. He just paid me to do it."

Angered by his response, she reached across and slapped him hard across his face.

He flinched and drew away from her, but the shackles prevented him from moving much.

"I swear!" he yelled. "I don't know why he wanted it done."

Erin considered this. It was probably true. Grayson had no need to tell him the reason. "Okay. I'll accept that for now. But I want more. Much more. What else did Grayson pay you to do?"

"Aren't two murders enough?"

She slapped him again to jar his memory. "Talk!"

He squirmed in the chair and after a long moment said, "There was one other thing. I planted evidence on a PI in Atlanta."

Erin leaned forward, startled by this. "You what?"

"Grayson had me plant phony evidence of a terrorist plot at this guy's apartment. I planted explosives and bomb making equipment, plus pictures of the U.S. President and other stuff."

"Was it John Ryan's apartment?"

Alessi nodded. "Yeah, that's right. He was the PI. He was investigating Veritas and Grayson wanted him out of the way. He figured if Ryan was suspected of terrorism he'd be locked up."

Erin breathed a sigh of relief.

This meant J.T. was innocent, as she had suspected.

But now she had proof.

Chapter 84

Hoover Building, FBI Headquarters
Washington, D.C.

"He's innocent," Erin Welch repeated.

Director Tucker shook his head. "You can't be sure of that."

"I have proof, sir." Erin reached into her briefcase and pulled out a file, which she slid across Tucker's desk. The two people were in the director's office.

Tucker opened the file and began reading.

She leaned forward in her chair. "It's all there, Director. Alessi's signed confession, plus corroborating evidence that he purchased the explosives and other material that he planted in Ryan's apartment in Atlanta. It all proves that J.T. Ryan was set up. He's not guilty of terrorism. In fact, he's not guilty of anything."

Tucker looked up from the file, a stony expression on his face. "It appears you're right."

"Sir, you need to take the Code Red off Ryan. Immediately."

He glared at her. "Don't tell me what to do! You work for me, remember?"

Erin gritted her teeth and was about to blast him for not agreeing to the obvious, correct option. Then she decided on a softer approach.

"Director," she stated in a calm, even tone, "it's the right thing to do. We both know that. This information clearly proves Ryan is innocent."

Tucker closed the file and let out a long breath. "All right. I'll remove the Code Red."

"Thank you, sir."

"Now that we've settled this, I've got other matters to attend." He checked his watch. "I have a staff meeting coming up."

"There is one other topic," Erin said, "that we need to discuss."

His eyebrows arched. "What?"

"Sir, the hit man, Alessi, clearly implicates the Veritas Foundation in a murder-for-hire scheme. Since Alessi and Veritas are both based in Atlanta, which is my jurisdiction, I feel I should be part of the investigation into the foundation's criminal activities."

Tucker's features hardened and his hands formed into fists. "I've told you before, we're handling that case from this office."

"I know, sir. But in light of this new evidence –"

The director thumped his fists on the desk. "I said no, damn it."

She ground her teeth and bile surged up her throat. It was obvious the man was protecting someone. *But who?* she thought. *And why? In any case, I'm sick of it and can't be silent any longer. Even if it costs me my job.*

"Sir, I insist I be part of this investigation."

Tucker rose abruptly. "I said no. And I mean no. This meeting is over."

Erin grimaced and stood. "Then you give me no choice, Director. I'll give you 24 hours to reconsider. If you don't let me participate in the Veritas case, I'll contact the press. I'll tell them you're part of a conspiracy to suppress evidence."

The man's face blanched.

Grabbing her briefcase, Erin turned and stormed out of the office.

Chapter 85

Department of Justice Building, DOJ Headquarters
Washington, D.C.

"**Thank** you for seeing me on such short notice," the FBI Director said as he and Attorney General Robert Donovan shook hands and sat down in Donovan's office.

The Attorney General gave Tucker a questioning look. "On the phone you said it was urgent?"

"Yes, it is. You remember the case you asked me to slow-walk a while back?"

"Which one?" asked Donovan.

"The Veritas Foundation."

Donovan picked up the Mont Blanc pen on his desk and twirled it with his fingers. "Ah, yes, that one. I remember. I asked you to take it away from that FBI woman in Atlanta."

"That woman, Erin Welch, just left my office. She threatened to tell the news media that I'm involved in a cover up if I don't bring her back into the investigation."

The AG dropped the pen on his desk as a shocked expression crossed his face. "The press? She'll get the press involved?"

"That's right, sir."

"You can't let her do that," Donovan demanded, his voice hostile. "Get rid of that bitch. Fire her!"

Tucker shook his head. "It's not that simple. First, she's an Assistant Director of the FBI. I can't fire someone at that level without cause. And beyond that, sir, the evidence against Veritas is overwhelming."

"Evidence? What evidence?"

"The person who runs Veritas, David Grayson, hired an assassin to murder Congressman Rodriguez. And in addition to his death, another ten innocent people were killed in the resulting explosion and fire. And there was an attempt to murder Senator Hawkins."

"Veritas did that?"

"Yes, sir."

Donovan grimaced. "This is getting ugly. I never expected murder to be part of this ... I figured it was about money-laundering –" He abruptly stopped talking in mid-sentence, as if realizing he'd said too much.

"I have no choice," the FBI Director stated. "I have to allow Welch back in the investigation. And with her on it ... she's good ... it's all going to come out. Whatever Veritas was up to will be exposed. I have no doubt of that."

Chapter 86

Beijing, China

Amber Holt was in her home's office poring over financial statements when her desk phone rang. She read the info screen and picked up the handset immediately.

"Robert," she said sweetly, "I'm glad you called. Ever since we met last, I've been thinking about you ... about us ...." Her mind wandered a bit as the image of the tall, good-looking man filled her thoughts. Over the years, she had teased him mercilessly, hinting they could become lovers in the near future. It was a tactic she often used to get her way, but in Robert Donovan's case, it had ceased being a tactic. She wanted to have sex with the handsome Attorney General as much as he wanted her.

"We have a crisis," Donovan stated, his voice harsh.

His cold tone brought her back to reality. "Crisis?"

"That's right, Amber. I can't protect Veritas anymore."

"What are you saying?"

"Just that. I can't impede the investigation."

She gripped the handset tightly. "We have a deal, remember? I pay you very well to do exactly that."

"That deal is off. It's too risky for me. The Director of the FBI won't play ball anymore. There's murder involved. There's evidence."

"Listen to me," she screeched, "you sorry son-of-a-bitch. I don't *fucking* care what there is. I want you to put a lid on it. That's what I pay you to do!"

"I'm sorry, Amber. I really am. But there's nothing I can do at this point. I just hope I can save my own ass when this thing breaks open."

Amber, her thoughts a furious tangle of anger and fear, tried to process the implications of what the man was saying. She clutched the phone as if her life depended on the call. Which in many respects it did.

"Please, Robert, please fix this ...."

"I wish I could," he replied despondently. "You know I do. You know how I feel about you. It's not just the money you pay me. I always hoped we could ... well, that's all over now." He paused a moment, then said, "One other thing you should know. Your man Grayson – his name came up. His cover's blown. The FBI believe he hired a hit man to kill a U.S. congressman and a senator."

Damn it all to hell, she thought. *It's all falling apart. All my plans. My future.*

"Robert ... please," she pleaded, her voice cracking, "help me ...."

But the Attorney General had already hung up.

Chapter 87

Atlanta, Georgia

J.T. Ryan entered the diner and sat at the counter. A pudgy waitress with curly hair handed him a menu, and after filling a mug of coffee and placing it in front of him, she moved on to another customer.

Ryan scanned the menu and a minute later heard the jingle of a bell announcing other patrons had entered the restaurant. He glanced their way, and seeing who they were, tensed immediately. The two uniformed cops sat at a nearby booth.

The PI pulled his baseball cap lower over his eyes and hoped his current disguise, a bushy mustache and fake scar on his cheek would hold up.

The cops were obviously regulars because the pudgy waitress walked over, and after joking around with them, filled their coffee cups, took their orders, and headed toward the kitchen.

Sitting on the counter stool, Ryan tried to be as inconspicuous as possible. But that was difficult for someone who was 6'4" and built like a weightlifter. He buried his face in the menu and pretended to read it.

In his peripheral vision he noticed that the cops, being cops, seemed to study all of the patrons as they glanced around. One of them pointed toward Ryan and the two spoke in hushed voices. One of the police officers had brought a laptop with him, and opening the lid, clicked on the keyboard.

This can't be good, thought Ryan.

He set down the menu, pulled out a five dollar bill and dropped it on the counter. Then he rose slowly, and as if in no hurry, casually strode toward the door.

"Stop! Police!" a voice yelled out from behind him.

He turned back.

The two cops, their guns drawn, stood five feet away.

"You're under arrest," one of the cops said.

Chapter 88

Fulton County Jail
Atlanta, Georgia

"This is your lucky day," Erin Welch said as she reached the jail cell door. Through the steel bars she saw J.T. Ryan slouched on the metal bunk.

Ryan sat up on the cot. "Doesn't look so lucky from my perspective."

Erin showed her FBI cred pack to the corrections officer standing in the corridor and handed him Ryan's release papers. The man read the document, selected a key from a loop at his waistband, and unlocked the door.

"C'mon, J.T.," Erin said, "let's go."

A bewildered-looking Ryan stood and walked out of the cell. "Where we going?"

"That's up to you," she replied. "You're free to go anywhere you want."

"I am?"

Erin grinned. "You are."

"But the Code Red?"

She shook her head. "It was lifted two days ago. You've been cleared of all charges."

He still looked confused. "Then why was I arrested yesterday?"

"The wheels of justice turn slowly. It takes time for the word to filter down. Blame it on government bureaucracy. The beat cops who arrested you didn't realize you'd been removed from the FBI Code Red list."

Instantly Ryan's face changed from confusion to elation. He beamed. "Well, I'll be damned! You were right. This is my lucky day."

She returned the smile. "I'll give you a ride. My car's outside. Where do you want me to drop you off?"

"Let's go to your office. I've got lots to tell you."

She pointed to his unshaven face and unkempt hair. "First things first. You've been in lockup a while. You've got a pungent aroma. You need a shower and a shave. I'll drop you off at your apartment – get cleaned up and then we'll meet."

He rubbed the stubble on his cheeks. "Sounds like a plan, Erin." He grinned again. "By the way, thanks for getting me out of here."

"You're welcome." She cocked her head. "How many times does this make?"

"Does what make?"

She crossed her arms in front of her. "You know what I mean. How many times have I sprung you from jail?"

He suppressed a smile. "This time I was completely innocent."

She shook her head slowly. "The operative word is *this* time. The other times I've pulled your ass out of the fire was because of your Rambo tactics."

"Well ...."

"C'mon, J.T. Let's get out of here."

***

Three hours later Ryan and Erin were in her FBI office in downtown Atlanta. Freshly showered and shaved, the PI was wearing a white buttoned-down shirt, jeans, and a navy blazer. Erin was impeccably dressed in a light gray silk blouse, a blue Versace jacket and skirt.

"I'm curious," he said, "how'd you get the FBI to drop the Code Red?"

"Because I'm a hell of an Assistant Director," she replied with a straight face.

"I already knew that," he deadpanned. "But really."

Erin reached into a desk drawer, took out a file, and slid it across her desk. He picked it up and began reading.

"It's all there, J.T. An FBI agent I know in D.C. called me and told me they'd arrested a man attempting to murder a U.S. Senator. The guy was also suspected of killing a congressman in California. I questioned the perp and it turns out he's from Atlanta and was hired by the Veritas Foundation to commit the murders. Apparently the main person behind Veritas is someone named Grayson. He hired the killer. And it turns out the killer also planted the terrorist evidence in your apartment."

"David Grayson?"

"You know who he is, J.T.?"

"I do. I interrogated him last week and got him to talk. He told me everything we need to know about the criminal activities of Veritas. Since the contract killer implicated Grayson – did you arrest him?"

She shook her head. "No. Grayson's vanished. He must have gotten word that we have an APB out for him and took off. We've got every FBI field office in the country looking for him."

"I hope you find him. He's the main guy behind the foundation. He and Amber Holt, an American woman who lives in China. When I was there I talked to her as well."

Erin frowned. "You were in China?"

"It's a long story. But, yeah, I was there for quite a while."

She gave him a long look then snapped her fingers. "That's how you did it. That's how you were able to evade arrest."

"I had no choice. I had to get out of the U.S. in order to get totally off the grid."

"You certainly did do that. You can fill me in on your China trip some other time." She leaned forward. "Tell me about Grayson and the foundation's criminal conspiracy. You said you got him to talk?"

"Yeah. He sang like a jaybird."

Her eyebrows arched. "How'd you get him to cooperate?"

"Don't ask."

"More of your Dirty Harry tactics, J.T.?"

"Like I said, don't ask."

She placed her hands flat on the desk. "Fair enough."

Ryan rose and began pacing her office. He'd been cooped up in jail and was enjoying the freedom to stretch his legs. "It turns out," he began, "that Grayson works for Amber Holt. She's the real head of Veritas. Grayson is her operations manager in the U.S. He handles the money-laundering, the payoffs, the bribery, everything."

"So Veritas is mostly about money-laundering?"

"It's a hell of a lot more than that," he replied as he sat down again and faced her. "It's a criminal conspiracy much bigger than we ever suspected."

Erin picked up a pen and began jotting notes on a legal pad. "Tell me."

"Amber Holt makes money stealing U.S. military secrets and selling them to the highest bidder. They're mostly foreign governments like Russia, China, Iran, and North Korea. She uses the Veritas charity as a front for her criminal activities – the money flows in there and gets washed in with the contributions from suckers who believe the foundation is doing real charity work."

"Okay. I'm with you so far."

"Well, according to Grayson, Holt hatched a new plan several years ago. Something that would make her incredibly wealthy – a billionaire. This new plan of hers entailed selling U.S. military secrets to the Chinese government exclusively, cutting out the other countries. Then she came up with the mother lode – something the Chinese desperately wanted."

She put down her pen. "What is it?"

"The Veritas Foundation, through subsidiaries and shell companies, is buying the uranium mine deposits in the United States. From what Grayson told me, they're very close to owning 100% of the uranium deposits in the U.S. Once they have that, they'll transfer the assets to a shell company named UraniumNow, which for all intents and purposes will be owned by the Chinese. This transfer will be done in secret, and UraniumNow will have a figurehead president who is an American, but the real owners will be the Chinese government. On the surface it will be run by respectable people, but the Chinese will be pulling the strings."

Erin's jaw dropped. "Uranium? That's the metal ore that fuels U.S. military nuclear reactors. And the civilian nuclear power plants across our whole country."

"That's right, Erin. If Veritas is successful, China will control all of the uranium needed to fuel those nuclear reactors."

She shook her head slowly. "That's frightening. Think of all the influence the Chinese would wield if that were to happen. But how is it even possible? There are government committees in congress and officials at the Department of State and the Department of Energy to prevent any one group from buying all of these metal deposits in the first place."

"True. That's where the bribery comes in. Grayson told me he was bribing members of congress and officials in government agencies with millions of dollars."

Erin nodded. "Maybe some people couldn't be bribed. That may be why Congressman Rodriguez was murdered and why there was the attempted murder of Senator Hawkins."

"I agree," he said. "If the bribes didn't work, Veritas resorted to murder."

Chapter 89

Beijing, China

Amber Holt was in the study of her mansion when she heard a light knock at the door. She glanced up from her iPad and saw Liling in the doorway.

The young woman gave her slight bow. "Miss Amber, I thought you should know. The military troops guarding the house appear to be leaving."

Alarmed by the news, Amber bolted from the couch and raced to the window. The Chinese soldiers who had been posted there weeks earlier were packing up their gear and climbing into military trucks.

Her heart thudded as four trucks and several other military vehicles started their engines and rumbled out of her property, their exhaust pipes spewing columns of black smoke.

Turning from the window, she sprinted out of the study and into her nearby office, where she picked up the phone's handset and clicked a number she had on speed-dial. Her call was routed through the labyrinth of the Chinese military's headquarters building until it reached General Chang's office.

"General," she said when she finally reached him, "the soldiers you sent to protect me have left my home."

"I am aware of that," he replied in an aloof tone.

"But why?"

"Amber, my sources tell me the project is going very badly for you."

Her adrenaline pumping, she said, "It's true we've had some setbacks. I just need to regroup."

"You have put me in a very precarious situation. I had already informed the Politburo that success was at hand. Now I find out from my Chinese Embassy sources in the U.S. that the uranium deal has fallen apart."

Her thoughts raced as she tried to come up with a reply that would placate the man. "Two weeks, that's all I need," she lied, knowing that was an impossible timetable given all that was happening.

"I do not believe you anymore, Amber. The key senator you needed has rebuffed your offer, there have been murders, and attempted murders. The FBI will unravel this in no time."

Her heart sank – General Chang was more clued-in than she had previously thought. "General, please, give me more time."

"I will not!" he shouted. "I have to think of myself. You have put me in a very dangerous position. I do not know how the Politburo will react."

"Can you at least send back the soldiers? The CIA may come for me again."

"You are on your own, Amber."

Then the general hung up.

Chapter 90

Beijing, China

Amber's stomach churned and bile came up her throat.

She felt queasy and disoriented from the phone call. Everything she had worked for was falling apart. Even her own personal safety was in question, now that the Chinese government wouldn't protect her. Her well-planned, idyllic future was in shambles.

Amber sat at her desk for the next hour, agonizing over her options. Finally, after her tortured thoughts resulted in a pounding migraine, she realized she only had one option left.

I have to cut my losses.

Chapter 91

Richmond, Virginia

David Grayson had been on the run for days, fleeing Washington D.C. with literally the clothes on his back and a suitcase full of cash.

He was holed up in a dilapidated motel in the outskirts of Richmond, desperately trying to figure out what to do next. Now that the FBI was after him, he knew it was only a question of time before he was arrested.

Grayson sat on the room's lumpy bed, staring at his cell phone. He realized there was only one way out. But he also knew he had let her down miserably. She would be furious with him and for good cause. The uranium deal was history. Now that the FBI was *really* investigating it, the conspiracy and his part in it would be revealed. UraniumNow, the shell company he had created, would be worthless soon. Its assets, the uranium ore mines it owned, would be seized by U.S. authorities. And the Veritas Foundation's assets would also be impounded. The only thing of value Grayson had left was the suitcase full of cash and the cell phone he was holding.

Finally, after another long moment of tormented indecision, he turned on the phone and tapped in a number he'd memorized long ago.

"It's me," he said, his voice guarded.

"Gray Man!" Amber replied. "I'm so glad you called! I've been so worried about you."

"Things are not going well. The FBI ... they're after me ... I'm on the run ...."

"When I called you last week, I told you there was a possibility the FBI would be looking for you. But then I didn't hear from you and I thought the worst. That you'd been arrested, or worse, that you were ... dead. I was sick with worry about you ...."

"I'm sorry, Amber ... it's all ... falling apart. And it's all my fault ...."

"Don't beat yourself up," she replied, her tone soothing. "We'll sort this thing out. You'll see."

"You're not angry?" he asked, incredulous. "I thought you'd be furious."

"We just need to regroup, Gray Man. With both of us working as a team, I know we can do it."

His spirits soared, realizing she didn't blame him. "What should I do now? I'm on the run. The FBI is sure to find me."

"I have a solution," she said. "You have to leave the States. Where are you now?"

"Outside of Richmond, Virginia."

"What's the closest airport to there?"

He told her and she said, "Okay. I'll send my jet to pick you up there. They'll bring you to me."

"Where's that, Amber?"

"The only safe place I have left. Paradise."

Chapter 92

Midtown
Atlanta, Georgia

Lisa Booth parked her Mustang in the underground lot and made her way up to their PI office on the seventh floor. She unlocked the door and stepped inside and was startled to find J.T. sitting at his desk, his feet propped on its surface.

"You shouldn't be here," she whispered. "You should lay low, stay hiding."

Ryan grinned. "Not anymore."

She frowned. "What do you mean?"

He filled her in on his arrest and his subsequent release by Erin Welch.

"They've cleared your name? You're no longer on the Code Red list?"

He set his coffee cup down on the desk. "That's right. I'm not on the terrorist watch-list anymore."

Lisa beamed, ran up to him and gave him a big hug. It felt awkward after a moment and she pulled away, blushing slightly.

"That's great news," she said, a little embarrassed by the extended embrace.

Ryan seemed oblivious to her embarrassment and continued drinking his coffee.

Sitting behind her own desk, she turned to face him. "So what happens now?"

"There's an APB out for David Grayson – according to Erin he fled D.C. But I'm sure they'll find him soon."

Lisa nodded. "And Amber Holt? What about her?"

"I filled Erin in on what I learned about her when I was in China. Erin's contacted the State Department and the FBI's overseas offices. They've put an APB on Holt. Now that we know she's involved in this uranium conspiracy and the murders for hire, the full weight of the U.S. government will locate her and make an arrest."

"I'm glad. This whole conspiracy makes me sick to my stomach. To think Americans like Grayson and Holt would sell out their country is ...."

"Treasonous," Ryan said, finishing her sentence.

She nodded. "Treasonous."

Ryan stood, went to the coffee maker on top of the file cabinet and refilled his cup. "Want some?" he asked.

"No, thanks. I already had plenty this morning."

She opened the lid on her laptop and booted up. "So what do we do now, J.T.?"

He pointed to the thick stack of case folders on her desk. "Are those new cases that came in since I went overseas?"

"Yep. I haven't had a chance to tackle them yet. There's some from the Department of Homeland Security and the U.S. Marshalls. There's also a couple from the Secret Service and from Atlanta PD."

"Then let's get to work, Lisa. I'll take half of them and you start on the rest."

"You got it, boss," she said, picking up half the folders and handing them to him. "What about the Veritas Foundation? What happens with that?"

"That's in Erin's hands now. She's got the ball – she'll run with it."

Chapter 93

Hoover Building, FBI Headquarters
Washington, D.C.

Erin Welch paced the empty conference room as she waited for Director Tucker to arrive.

She heard the door open and saw the director step inside, his face defiant.

"What is it this time?" he said, bristling. "I'm getting tired of you asking for these last minute meetings." His eyes flashed menacingly. "I've got the whole Bureau to run. That's 56 field offices across the country. You're just one cog among many. Remember that, Welch."

"You'll want to hear what I have to say, Director."

"I doubt that."

She pulled out a chair and sat at the conference table. "Please sit, sir."

He remained standing. "Don't tell me what to do."

"Suit yourself."

He scowled. "You wanted me to let you back in the Veritas case. Against my better judgment, I allowed you to do that. What do you want *this* time?"

Erin pulled out a file from her briefcase and flipped open the cover. "Sir, I wanted to share with you the results of my investigation into the foundation."

For the first time this morning, a hint of uncertainty crossed the man's face.

"Director," she began, "the evidence against Veritas and its corporate officers is damning. We've verified it with bank records, money-wire transfers, their company records, and we've questioned a multitude of witnesses. Steve Nichols, David Grayson, and Amber Holt, the three people at the top of the Veritas conspiracy were involved in murder, money- laundering, bribery, blackmail, and a few other felonies. And there's more. Something even more heinous."

Tucker, a worried look on his face, pulled out a chair and sat down across from her. "What could be more heinous than murder?"

"Treason, sir."

"Treason?"

"Yes, Director. Veritas was attempting to purchase 100% of the uranium ore of the United States and transfer control of that to the Chinese government."

Tucker's face turned white and his jaw dropped. After a long moment, he said, "That's an incredulous accusation. You have no proof."

She closed the folder and pushed it across the conference table. "It's all there. In black and white."

He gingerly picked up the file and scanned the pages, his face growing paler by the second. "I had ... no idea."

Tucker closed the folder and looked up at her. "I don't know what to say."

He checked his watch nervously. "I have another meeting to attend. We'll have to conclude this conversation another time."

"There is no other time," she fumed. "We'll finish it now."

He rose abruptly and attempted to pick up the file folder, but Erin snatched it away.

"I'll keep that," she said. "Sit down, Director."

He looked hesitant, glanced at the door, then back at her. Finally he shrugged and sat back down.

"I found out something else," she continued, "something that's even more damning than all the evidence I've shown you."

Tucker frowned. "What?"

"Sir, you never even started an investigation into Veritas. I've talked to all the key agents in the D.C. office. No one here knows anything about the foundation's case. You took my case files months ago and locked them away. You did nothing with them."

Perspiration beaded on his forehead and he undid the top button of his dress shirt and pulled down his paisley tie.

"Whether you knew it or not, Director, you covered up a whole host of crimes, including murder and treason."

His shoulders slumped.

"Erin," he said in a faltering voice, "you've got to believe me ... I had no idea ...."

"Why did you do it? Why? Were you bribed? Is that it?"

He shook his head forcefully. "No! Absolutely not! I took no bribes."

"Why then? Why risk your career?"

"I was ordered to do it."

"Ordered? By who?"

Fear showed in his eyes. "I can't say."

"It's too late for that now. Who was it?"

He took out a handkerchief and wiped the perspiration from his forehead. "The AJ."

"The Attorney General of the United States?"

"Yes," he said. "Robert Donovan."

"But why would he want to cover this up?"

Tucker shook his head again. "I don't know why. I just followed his orders. Was that so wrong?"

Erin ground her teeth and clenched her hands into fists. "Hell, yes, it was wrong! People died because you did nothing. One of our country's vital energy supplies was compromised because you did nothing."

"What can I do to fix this?" he whimpered, his eyes welling up.

She shook her head slowly. "You disgust me, Director. To think I held you in such high regard for years. Now ... now you're pathetic."

The man brushed tears from his cheeks with a hand.

Erin leaned forward. "You have one option. Resign immediately as FBI Director."

"And what then, Erin. What'll happen to me?"

"That'll be up to a judge and jury to decide. Your resignation is the first step."

Chapter 94

Washington, D.C.

Scott Tucker sat at his kitchen table, staring at the two objects in front of him.

It was well past midnight and he had been sitting in his home's kitchen for over four hours. On the table were two items. One was a bottle of Chivas scotch, now empty. Next to the empty bottle was a loaded Colt .44 Magnum revolver. A gun he usually kept in his bedroom nightstand for protection.

But tonight he wasn't thinking about possible burglars.

He was replaying in his mind the fateful meeting he'd had earlier in the day with Erin Welch.

His resignation as FBI Director, he now realized, had been the easy part.

What would come next would surely be much, much harder.

As the nation's top cop, Tucker knew the drill well. Charges would be filed against him, he would be arrested, and considering the seriousness of the charges, no sane judge would grant him bail.

He would be incarcerated until his trial date. He would be convicted. A lengthy prison sentence would follow.

And the public humiliation would be constant, from the time of his arrest until his release from prison many, many years from now.

Can I face that? he wondered. *Do I want to?*

His eyes welled up and he let the tears flow freely.

Seeing no other option, he picked up the revolver and pressed the muzzle of the gun to his right temple.

Tucker closed his eyes and pulled the trigger.

Chapter 95

Washington, D.C.

The sniper peered through his rifle's scope and adjusted the crosshairs. He was using a Barrett M107 sniper rifle. The M107 is a high-precision, long-range weapon that is the standard for military snipers in dozens of countries around the world.

Although his target was in an office building a mile away, the custom-made Schmidt & Bender scope allowed him to see clearly into the man's office. The target, a tall, handsome man, was at his desk, clicking away at a laptop.

Using his laser range finder and a small computer, the sniper made a few final adjustments to account for wind speed and several other factors. Then he slowed his breathing and slid his finger past the trigger guard until it rested lightly on the trigger itself.

He took another moment to zero in on the target and squeezed off the shot.

A split-second later the armor-piercing .50 caliber round cracked the bullet-resistant window a mile away. The target slumped forward on his desk and blood began to pool under his lifeless head.

The sniper quickly picked up his spent shell casing. Then he stored the rifle, bipod, laser range finder, and computer into a case. That done, he made his way down from the roof of the building. Five minutes later he reached his SUV, which was in a nearby parking garage.

He climbed inside the vehicle, stripped off his latex gloves, and pulled out a burner cell phone. He tapped in an international number and waited for the other side to pick up.

***

Amber Holt was in her home office in Paradise, in the South China Sea. Her encrypted cell phone was on her desk and it began to vibrate. She had been expecting this call.

She picked up the phone. "Yes?"

"It's done," the man on other end said. "The Washington target has been eliminated."

"Excellent. And the one in Atlanta?"

"I took care of that two days ago."

Amber breathed a sigh of relief. "Very good."

"When will you make the wire transfer to my account?"

"As soon as the news reports confirm what you've told me," she replied. "Then I'll transfer the money immediately."

"Good doing business with you."

"If I have any other work," she said, "I'll be in touch."

She hung up the phone and rested it on the desk. Then she gazed out the floor-to-ceiling windows of her home office. It was a cloudless, sunny day and she could clearly see the whole of her island and beyond that, the vast open waters of the South China Sea.

Things are looking up, she mused. The Washington target, Attorney General Robert Donovan had been dealt with. Along with the Atlanta target, Steve Nichols.

Dead men tell no tales.

Yes, things are definitely looking up.

Chapter 96

Paradise
South China Sea

Amber Holt caressed Liling's cheek a moment and then her fingers slid across her lips. Next she gently traced the young woman's neck, her hand finally coming to rest on her soft breast.

"You've given me a lot of pleasure," Amber said as she looked into the other woman's eyes. Liling, who lay naked next to her on the bed, stared back, her eyes showing a trace of fear.

Amber smiled. "It still scares you a bit, doesn't it."

The young woman lowered her gaze and said nothing.

"Don't worry, Liling, the more we do it, the easier it gets." She laughed. "You'll eventually get to the point you'll like it. That was true for all of my previous girls and I'm sure that'll be true for you."

Liling glanced up, the nervous look still there.

"Get dressed," Amber ordered. "Go make my lunch. This workout's made me hungry."

"Yes, Miss Amber."

Liling put on her pink and gold kimono, pinned the loose strands of her hair into her bun, and turned to go.

Just then the loud whine of jet engines filled the bedroom and Liling walked to the windows.

Amber pulled a sheet over her naked torso. "Who is it?"

"Your plane, Miss Amber. It has returned."

"Excellent. My guest has arrived. Show him into the living room while I dress."

Once the young woman left the bedroom, Amber went into her walk-in closet to pick out her clothes. She wanted to make her guest feel extremely welcome and knew exactly what to wear.

First she picked out her underwear, the skimpy royal blue panties and bra, over which she wore a clingy, low-cut royal blue dress with the thigh-high-cut slit skirt. After carefully combing her long, auburn tresses, she gazed at her reflection in the floor-to-ceiling mirror.

Perfect, she thought. *Absolutely perfect.*

Dabbing on her favorite perfume, she strode out of the bedroom on the mansion's third floor and went down to the living room on the second.

"Gray Man!" she exclaimed excitedly. "I'm so glad you're here!"

David Grayson, who had been staring out the massive windows, turned around. "Amber! It's so good to see you."

She rushed up to him and gave him a big hug. He returned her embrace and when she broke it off she led him by the hand to a nearby leather couch.

"Let's sit, Gray Man. You must be exhausted from the long flight."

He nodded. "I am."

She sat across from him and studied his haggard features. "It must have been so horrible for you – running from the police ...."

"It was. I'm a finance guy, not an outlaw."

"You poor man," she cooed in a sympathetic voice. "But that's over with now. You're here. And here you're safe."

He gazed around the vast, beautifully furnished room. "What is this place? I never knew about it."

She gave him a sly smile. "Nobody does. It's my little secret. I bought this island years ago. I christened it Paradise. It's hundreds of miles from land, so it's extremely private." She waved a hand in the air. "I have everything I need here. All the creature comforts."

He nodded, and then his eyes grew wary. "I'm sorry about what happened. About Veritas and our operation. It was ...."

Amber shrugged. "That's the past. We have to look toward the future."

"But the foundation's money – the U.S. authorities will seize it – in fact, they may already have."

She waved a dismissive hand. "I have other bank accounts. Accounts you know nothing about. I'll be fine. I'll be less rich. But still rich enough."

"You're not mad at me?"

"Like I told you on the phone, Gray Man. It wasn't your fault."

He seemed incredibly relieved by this and let out a long breath. "I'm glad. I was really worried about that."

She smiled suggestively and tucked her long legs underneath her on the couch, the slit in her skirt giving him a glimpse of her skimpy panties.

His eyes focused on her body like a laser beam and she could tell he was becoming aroused.

"The important thing is," she whispered seductively, "we're safe and we're finally together."

"Yes, yes, that's right," he replied, his eyes still glued to her split skirt.

She adjusted the cloth of her dress so it covered her panties. "Why don't we have lunch. Then I'll give you a tour of Paradise. After that we can relax ... you and me ... get to know each other. Intimately. How does that sound?"

"Sounds perfect, Amber. It's what I've wanted for a long, long time."

She ran her tongue seductively over her lips. "You're such a dear man. I can't wait to get you into bed."

Amber pressed the intercom device on the nearby coffee table. "Liling, bring us lunch in here."

After a long, leisurely meal which included rare merlot wines from Amber's extensive collection, she led him through the mansion's many opulent rooms, which included a vast entertainment and media room, a library, a space-age kitchen, a dining area, a solarium, a gym, a wine cellar, and other areas. During the tour they encountered the home's many servants, all dutifully at work. As soon as any of them saw Amber they stopped what they were doing and cast their gazes to the floor. Amber had imported the island's servants from very poor Asian countries and paid them extremely well, demanding total obedience in return.

Amber and Grayson took the elevator to the third floor, which consisted solely of a huge master bedroom. The walls were all made of floor-to-ceiling glass, giving the room a panoramic view of the surrounding sea.

When they entered the bedroom, Amber said, "This is my favorite room in the whole house. This is where I sleep and do other much more enjoyable things. After we finish our tour, we'll come back here. How does that sound?"

Grayson swallowed hard as he took in the bedroom's massive bed, large Jacuzzi tub, well-stocked bar, and extensive sitting areas. His eyes fixed on her, the anticipation evident on his face. "I'd like that very much."

Amber reached out with her hand and caressed his cheek. "You will be rewarded, Gray Man. For all you've done for me."

He swallowed again, his eyes burning with desire.

"Now let's go finish our tour of Paradise."

"We could skip that," he said, his voice slightly hoarse.

"No, you silly man. You need to see it all. I *love* showing it off. You don't want to deprive me of *that*, do you?"

Amber's hand slid off his face, traced his chest and came to rest on the bulge in his pants. She cupped his hardness and stroked it lightly. "Don't worry, Gray Man. I'll take care of you."

He moaned and his eyes closed for an instant, the pleasure of her touch evident on his face.

Then she took him by the hand and led him out of the room.

Once outside the mansion, she pointed out the various service buildings, the servants dormitory, and the other structures on the small island. After that they walked past the greenhouse, the tennis courts, an Olympic size outdoor pool, and an elaborate garden area. As inside the home, the outside servants, groundskeepers, and armed guards stopped what they were doing when they saw Amber and gazed at the ground.

"I saved the best for last," she said, pointing to a building at the end of the gravel path they were on. "I have a small zoo here on the island."

"A zoo?"

"Yes. I keep all my favorite pets there." She smiled. "I told you I have everything I want here in Paradise."

They continued walking along the path and entered the high-ceiling building. Inside the structure were dozens of very large cages which housed a variety of wild animals, including lions, tigers, monkeys, snakes, exotic birds, and several other species. It was warm and humid in the building to replicate the animals's African weather. At one end of the structure was a natural habitat where a small elephant and a giraffe roamed.

Once she had shown Grayson all of the cages and described each of the animals, she clapped her hands loudly and said, "Go. Leave us."

There were several people in the building, animal trainers and feeders, and when they heard this they stopped what they were doing and exited the structure.

After they had left, Amber took Grayson's hand and led him into an adjoining room, which contained a large indoor pool at the far end.

"I thought we'd go for a swim, to cool off," she said.

"I didn't bring a swimsuit," Grayson replied.

She grinned. "You won't need it." She slowly unzipped her dress and it dropped to the floor. His eyes got big seeing Amber's voluptuous body, barely contained in the skimpy underwear.

"Get down to your skivvies," she said alluringly. "That'll do."

Grayson quickly removed his suit jacket, shirt, pants, and shoes, revealing his skinny, un-athletic body. The only thing he was wearing now was his boxer shorts and she noted with satisfaction that the bulge in his groin was even more pronounced.

"Eager, aren't we," she said, running her tongue over her lips.

The man, his breathing labored, didn't reply. His eyes were locked on Amber's barely clothed body.

She took him by the hand again and led him to the edge of the pool.

"Let's go in the water to cool off. You first," she said with a grin.

His concentration was so focused on her voluptuous curves that he barely noticed the thrashing of the pool water. He finally tore his eyes away from her and gazed at the pool.

He jumped back, his face showing fear. "What the hell! Are those ..." he stammered, " ... are those sharks in there?"

Amber's grin widened. "It is. I enjoy all the animals in my zoo. But I like my sharks best. They're my favorite pets."

Grayson stared at her in horror as he moved back several feet from the water's edge. "You want to swim in there? Are you crazy?"

Her smile vanished. "No, Gray Man. I want *you* to swim in there." She knelt down, and lifting the lid on a storage bin, removed a Sig Sauer pistol and pointed it at Grayson.

His eyes went wide when he saw the gun. "Is this a joke? This isn't funny."

"It's no joke." She motioned to the pool, where three large sharks and several more smaller ones swam, their exposed fins causing water to splash over onto the pool apron. "Remember what I told you when we were inside my house?"

He gazed at her, his eyes as big as saucers. "What? What are you talking about?"

"I told you I was going to reward you, Gray Man. For all you've done for me. Now you're going to be rewarded." She flashed an icy grin. "I keep my promises."

"But you said," he croaked, "that you ... that you didn't blame me ... for what happened ...."

"You were a fool for believing that. But then again, you wanted to believe it, didn't you? You wanted forgiveness. And you let your lust cloud your judgment. You wanted me so badly, you'd believe anything to get me into bed. Men are such fools." She cackled. "I want to see you die. But first I want to see you suffer. You *fucked up* my operation. Now you're going to pay for it."

He held his palms in front of him. "Please, don't do this ... we can ... still make it work ... we'll start again ...."

"It's too late for that," she replied, seething. "Get in the fucking pool!"

"No! Please ... I beg you ...."

"Be a man about it. Don't beg." She leveled the gun at his head. "Jump in! Now!"

"I'm afraid, Amber ... please ... I can't ...."

"It'll be quick. I promise. The sharks haven't been fed yet today. It'll be over in a matter of minutes."

His face was as white as a sheet and his body trembled with fear.

"Get in!" she shouted. "Get in the *fucking* pool! I'm tired of this game."

"No ... I won't do it ...." he managed to say weakly, his voice cracking.

"You will do it. One way or the other. You will get in that damn pool."

"Shoot me, then," he croaked. "Kill me ... that's better than ...."

She re-aimed the pistol and pulled the trigger, the round tearing into his leg. He screamed in pain and stumbled to his knees, blood spurting from his thigh.

Amber stepped around him and began pushing him forward toward the pool. Still howling, he tried to resist, but he was growing weaker from his gaping wound.

Although he was a thin man, she had trouble pushing him in, so she got on her knees to get better leverage. She began shoving his body forward again, inching closer to the pool's edge.

He was still struggling as she gave him one final push and Grayson splashed into the water.

The sharks circled him and instantly began to tear into his flesh, the clear pool water turning blood red. His piercing screams were muffled as his body was dragged under the surface. The thrashing in the pool continued for five more minutes as Amber gazed on.

"You got your reward," she spit out, her voice ice cold. "Welcome to Paradise, you bastard."

Dead men tell no tales, she thought.

I finally cut all of my losses. Robert Donovan. Steve Nichols. And now Gray Man.

Amber rose, went to a cabinet and took out a towel. She wiped off Grayson's blood from her hands and legs and put on her royal blue dress. Unfortunately, the hem of the expensive dress got stained by the leftover blood. She cursed Grayson one last time for being so difficult in the end.

Then she walked out of the pool area and exited the zoo building. She strode along the gravel path toward her mansion. It was a sunny, cloudless day, which lifted her spirits.

In fact, by the time she reached the house she felt better than she had in weeks.

Chapter 97

Paradise
South China Sea

Amber Holt heard it long before she saw it, a low rumble coming from far away.

She was walking through the island's garden on her way back to the mansion. She had spent the last two days mulling over what to do next. Now that the Veritas Foundation had been exposed as a fraud and the uranium deal had collapsed, she had been debating her next scheme. Her finances had been badly damaged, there was no doubt of that. But she still had plenty of money to sustain her lavish lifestyle.

Amber had planned well, stashing away hundreds of millions of dollars in Swiss numbered accounts. Some of the funds had come from her criminal activities, while other funds were from donations to her phony charity.

As she neared the massive home she heard it again, a deep rumble growing louder. She gazed up at the overcast sky and saw only the ominous-looking clouds. It would rain later today, she knew.

Then she saw it.

A large cargo plane breaking through the dark clouds.

She stopped in her tracks as the jet circled the island, obviously lining up its approach to land on the long runway. The aircraft was still too far away to identify. But there were no deliveries planned for today, nor was she expecting any guests.

Puzzled, she studied the jet as it lowered its landing gear and flaps and went into final approach. As the cargo plane bled altitude she was able to make out its tail markings.

Her heart sank, seeing the logo. A yellow star superimposed on a red flag.

It meant only one thing. A Chinese military aircraft.

But why? What does it mean?

And how did they find me?

After her last conversation with General Chang a week ago, she had quickly packed up her key belongings and left mainland China, fleeing to Paradise. The general's harsh tone had been clear: she was on her own – he would no longer protect her from the American authorities.

The cargo plane landed and rumbled down the runway, the loud whine of its jet engines tapering off as they powered down. It rolled to a stop a minute later and the cargo doors at the rear of the plane lowered down.

Amber's security force, which was composed of fifteen armed guards, had gathered close to the runway, their weapons still holstered. They had obviously recognized the Chinese military markings and knew better than to impede whatever the visitors intended.

She watched as a platoon of armed soldiers, over forty men she estimated, emerged from the cargo doors. They were followed immediately by a black SUV. The vehicle exited the runway and, using a side road, reached the mansion's circular driveway moments later.

This can't be good, thought Amber, as she strode toward the black SUV. Still, she needed to face whatever was in store. She had never run from a fight in her life and wasn't about to start now.

The passenger door of the vehicle opened and a handsome officer stepped out of the SUV. Recognizing him immediately, she breathed a sigh of relief.

She approached the man and said, "Captain Zhou, it's good to see you again." She smiled broadly.

His expression was somber. "It is Colonel Zhou now."

She eyed his shoulder epaulets and noticed his new elevated rank. "Congratulations, then." She waved toward her mansion, which was behind her. "Let's go inside and we can celebrate your promotion."

Zhou shook his head. "We have no time for that. You need to come with us."

Bewildered by his hostile tone, she nevertheless tried to maintain a brave front and forced another smile. "Please, Colonel. Let's go inside. I'd like to welcome you to my home. By the way, how did you find me? I never told the general about this place."

Zhou scowled. "We have had it under surveillance for quite some time."

Her smile faded. "I see. No matter. Let us go inside. We can have a drink and relax."

By this time the platoon of Chinese soldiers had surrounded her house and one squad approached them, their AK-47 rifles at the ready. Out of the corner of her eye she noticed her security people were nowhere to be found. They had melted into the wooded parts of the island, not intending to resist the army's superior numbers.

Zhou shook his head, the scowl still on his face. "We have no time for that, Miss Holt. Come with us. Do not make this more difficult than it has to be."

Not wanting to be overheard, she moved forward so she was only inches from Zhou and whispered, "What's going on? Whatever it is, I know we can resolve it."

"I doubt that."

She placed a hand on his arm. "Please. Let's have a drink inside." She smiled suggestively. "I'll take care of all your needs."

He pushed her hand away roughly. "Your whorish ways will not work with me. Not anymore."

"But –"

"You are under arrest, Miss Holt."

Amber's heart hammered in her chest. "Arrest? Who ordered this? General Chang?"

Zhou grimaced. "No. General Xi Chang has been stripped of his rank. In fact, the Politburo has held his trial and sentenced him to life in prison. He is at Qincheng."

Amber had heard of Qincheng. Located near Beijing, the maximum-security facility was China's most notorious prison. It had the worst conditions imaginable and housed the most dangerous prisoners. The filthy, dirty penitentiary was the Chinese equivalent of a U.S. Supermax prison, where escape was impossible.

"Qincheng?"

Zhou nodded. "That is correct."

"And me? What about me?"

"Your fate is the same, Miss Holt. The Politburo has already held your trial and found you guilty. Your sentence is life in prison."

"At Qincheng?"

"That is correct." Zhou motioned to his soldiers and two of them grabbed her forcefully and handcuffed her hands behind her back. The metal cuffs felt cold and tight against her smooth skin.

"Please, Colonel," she pleaded, "don't do this."

"Take her away," the officer ordered.

The soldiers dragged her toward the waiting plane.

Chapter 98

Atlanta, Georgia

J.T. Ryan was in his Tahoe, driving south on the Georgia 400 highway when his cell phone vibrated. Taking out the phone, he clicked on the call.

"Congrats, J.T.," a familiar woman's voice said.

"Rachel West," he replied, "my favorite CIA agent. So you heard about the Code Red being lifted."

"I did. And I'm glad. You weren't cut out to be on the wrong side of the law."

"That's the truth. Where you calling from, Rachel?"

"That's classified."

"Okay. You coming back to the States anytime soon?"

"Possibly. Why?"

"Thought we'd get together for coffee, or dinner, or whatever ...."

She laughed. "I like the whatever best."

He visualized the sexy, stunning-looking blonde in his mind. "Me too."

"On a serious note, J.T., I have some news for you."

"Yeah?"

"My CIA sources told me something interesting about the woman we were after in China."

"The redhead, Amber Holt?"

"That's her, J.T. The Chinese government arrested her recently and she's been sentenced to life in prison."

"That's good *and* bad news. I'm glad she's been locked up but I wish we could have done it."

"Don't worry," she replied, "they put her in Qincheng, China's most notorious prison. Her life there will be a living hell."

"In that case, I'm glad it worked out the way it did."

"I'll call you when I get back to Langley," Rachel said with a chuckle, "so we can whatever." Then she clicked off.

Ryan put away his phone and continued driving south on the highway. He got on I-85 soon after, exited the interstate at the downtown exit, and made his way to the FBI building.

Fifteen minutes later he was in Erin Welch's office, sitting opposite her desk.

Erin reached into a drawer, took out an envelope and handed it to him.

"What's this for?" he asked, opening the envelope and looking at the enclosed check.

"It's a bonus. For all the hard work you and Lisa Booth did on the Veritas case."

He nodded. "Thanks. It's a generous amount."

Erin, who appeared happier than he remembered in a long time, was wearing a classic black Dolce and Gabbana business suit with a stylish white blouse. She smiled. "One of the perks of being in charge of this office. I have a discretionary account to reward exceptional effort."

Ryan slipped the envelope into his navy blazer. "I just got some good news about that case – my source told me Amber Holt was imprisoned by the Chinese government."

"I hadn't heard that." She cocked her head. "You surprise me sometimes – you know things an FBI Assistant Director doesn't know."

"One of the reasons you hire me."

"True enough, J.T. I wanted to talk to you about a couple of things. First, the Bureau has seized all of the financial assets of the Veritas Foundation. Their bank accounts have been frozen and all of the foundation's offices in the U.S. and elsewhere have been shut down. In time, any legitimate monies donated to the 'charity' will be returned to the donors. All of the criminal money will go to the U.S. Treasury."

"That's great," he replied.

"I'm sure you heard that U.S. Attorney General Robert Donovan and Steve Nichols, the Veritas president, were murdered."

"I saw it on the news."

Erin nodded. "We're still looking for the assassin, the sniper who killed them."

"What about David Grayson?" he asked.

"Still missing. We lost track of him after he fled D.C. We hope to arrest him eventually."

"I saw that FBI Director Scott Tucker committed suicide recently. Is that connected with Veritas also, Erin?"

"I'm afraid so. I confronted Tucker with all the evidence against the foundation, and the fact he had impeded the investigation into the criminal conspiracy. I forced him to resign, then ...." She shook her head slowly, a sad look on her face. "I expected him to be tried and go to prison, not to commit suicide ... if I had known ...."

"You can't blame yourself for his suicide, Erin. You had a job to do. And so did he. And he failed to do that job."

She nodded, but he could tell she felt guilt over the man's death. "I know."

"What about Attorney General Donovan? What role did he play in all this?"

"From what I can piece together," she said, "Donovan was taking bribes from Veritas. He led a lavish lifestyle, one well beyond his government pay as AJ. We found several of his off-shore bank accounts."

"So it was all about money," Ryan said.

"Yes. It was all about the money."

"And Tucker? Was he taking bribes also?"

"No," she replied. "Not that I could find. He was just following orders from the AJ."

Ryan thought about all this for a moment. "And the uranium deal?"

Erin's face showed elation. "That's the good part. The uranium deal is completely dead. The Chinese didn't get control of anything. The uranium mines are being returned to the original U.S. owners."

He shook his head. "We came so close to a very bad outcome. Too damn close. How can we prevent something like this from happening again?"

"The FBI has arrested a long list of government employees who accepted bribes. And there's several ongoing investigations into congressmen and senators who may have been complicit. A lot of people are going to jail. But ...."

"But what, Erin?"

"It was all about greed. It was all about people wanting more, much more money than they have. And the willingness to commit any crime, including treason, to get it." She paused a moment. "And no matter how many laws we have on the books, greed will always be a huge problem."

Ryan grinned. "That's why we have good cops like you. To put away the bad guys."

Erin returned the smile. "And that's also why we hire guys like you to help us."

There was a file folder on her desk and she flipped it open. "This is the second thing I wanted to talk to you about today. I received a new case and I'm going to need your help on it."

"What's it about?"

Erin removed a sheet of paper from the file and handed it to him.

As Ryan quickly read through the document, he realized this new case was big. Bigger than any other FBI investigation he'd worked on previously.

Erin looked at him expectantly. "Are you in?"

He gazed back at her, knowing that if he became involved, it had the potential of changing his professional and private life forever.

"Yes, I'm in," Ryan replied.

But deep down he wasn't sure he was making the right decision.

END

***

About the author

Lee Gimenez is the award-winning author of 13 novels, including his highly-acclaimed J.T. Ryan series. Several of his books were Featured Novels of the International Thriller Writers Association, among them THE MEDIA MURDERS, SKYFLASH, KILLING WEST, and THE WASHINGTON ULTIMATUM. Lee was nominated for the Georgia Author of the Year Award, and he was a Finalist in the prestigious Terry Kay Prize for Fiction. Lee's books are available at Amazon and many other bookstores in the U.S. and Internationally.

For more information about him, please visit his website at: www.LeeGimenez.com. There you can sign up for his free newsletter. You can contact Lee at his email address: LG727@MSN.com. You can also join him on Twitter, Facebook, Google Plus, LinkedIn, and Goodreads. Lee lives with his wife in the Atlanta, Georgia area.

***

Other Novels by Lee Gimenez

The Media Murders
Skyflash
Killing West
The Washington Ultimatum
Blacksnow Zero
The Sigma Conspiracy
The Nanotech Murders
Death on Zanath
Virtual Thoughtstream
Azul 7
Terralus 4
The Tomorrow Solution

THE MEDIA MURDERS, a **J.T.** Ryan Thriller
is available at Amazon and many other bookstores in the
U.S. and Internationally.
In paperback, Kindle, and all other ebook versions.

SKYFLASH, a J.T. Ryan Thriller
is available at Amazon and many other bookstores in the
U.S. and Internationally.
In paperback, Kindle, and all other ebook versions.

KILLING WEST, a Rachel West Thriller
is available at Amazon and many other bookstores in the
U.S. and Internationally.
In paperback, Kindle, and all other ebook versions.

THE WASHINGTON ULTIMATUM,
a J.T. Ryan Thriller
is available at Amazon and many other bookstores in the
U.S. and Internationally. In paperback, Kindle, and all other
ebook versions.

Lee Gimenez's other novels, including
- Blacksnow Zero
- The Sigma Conspiracy
- The Nanotech Murders
- Death on Zanath
- Virtual Thoughtstream
- Azul 7
- Terralus 4
- The Tomorrow Solution

are all available at Amazon and many other bookstores in the U.S. and Internationally.

In paperback, Kindle, and all other ebook versions.